THE INGÉNUE

An Alex Halee Thriller

TERRY TOLER

The Ingénue
Published by: BeHoldings, LLC.

Cover and interior designs: BeHoldings, LLC.
Editor: Jeanne Leach

For information send inquiries to support@terrytoler.com.

Our books can be purchased in bulk for promotional, educational, and business use. Please contact your bookseller or the BeHoldings Publishing Sales department at: sales@terrytoler.com

For booking information email: booking@terrytoler.com

First U.S. Edition: October, 2020
Printed in the United States of America
ISBN 978-1-7352243-6-7

BOOKS BY TERRY TOLER

Fiction

The Longest Day
The Reformation of Mars
The Great Wall of Ven-Us
Saturn: The Eden Experiment
The Late, Great Planet Jupiter
Save The Girls
The Ingenue
The Blue Rose
Saving Sara
Save The Queen
No Girl Left Behind
The Launch
Body Count

Non-Fiction

How to Make More Than a Million Dollars
The Heart Attacked
Seven Years of Promise
Mission Possible
Marriage Made in Heaven
21 Days to Physical Healing
21 Days to Spiritual Fitness
21 Days to Divine Health
21 Days to a Great Marriage
21 Days to Financial Freedom
21 Days to Sharing Your Faith
21 Days to Mission Possible
7 Days to Emotional Freedom
Uncommon Finances
Uncommon Marriage
Uncommon Health
Suddenly Free
Feeling Free

For more information on these books and other resources visit TerryToler.com.

PRAISE FOR THE TERRY TOLER NOVELS

"Terry Toler books are so riveting!"

"When you think you've got the plot worked out, he puts a twist on it and surprises you."

"I couldn't put them down and kept reading one after another."

"Never a dull moment in a Terry Toler novel."

"I love them. Every book has plenty of action and conflict."

"Terry Toler is my new favorite author."

"I love the new style of writing he has invented."

"Not everyone can write an ending like Terry Toler."

"Great writing style! Every novel captures me in the first chapter and then I can't put them down."

"I love all the twists and turns."

"I don't even like fiction, but I love your books."

"You really know how to draw an audience into your story, and I am a perfect example of that."

"I have to force myself to quit reading, so I can get some work done."

"Every time I finish a chapter, I say it's going to be my last, and the intrigue doesn't let me. I have to keep reading one more chapter!"

"Your cliffhangers are epic."

"I recognize a Terry Toler book from the first page."

"Your books have it all. Romance. Intrigue. Mystery. Suspense. And endings that make you come back for more."

"I'm hooked on Terry Toler books."

"The Eden Stories are revolutionary. You've created your own new genre of fiction."

"Wow! That's all I can say."

"When I finish a book, I think about it for days which is the characteristic of a great author."

"I can't wait to see what you come up with next."

"I love the characters. They draw me in, and I find myself rooting for them."

"Blessed be the Lord my strength, which teacheth my hands to war, and my fingers to fight."
Psalm 144:1

Ingénue: a young and naïve girl.

I

"With some degree of confidence, I can say that the wars of the future will not be fought as much with bombs, guns, missiles, and tanks. It will be fought with code. Cyber war is the greatest threat our country faces."

Jack Winters, Secretary of Defense, United States of America.

It seemed like a good idea at the time.

Now, sitting in a dark, dank basement—essentially a makeshift North Korean interrogation room—with my arms and legs strapped to a chair, I wasn't so sure. Blood oozed from the wounds from my last beating. I was rethinking the strategy that got me into this predicament.

A waste of time.

Thinking about how to get out of the situation instead of second guessing what got me into it was a better use of my energy.

"What is your name, and who do you work for?" the North Korean asked roughly.

"I told you. My name is Joe Hardy, and I want to work for you." My real name was Alex Halee. I was a senior officer of the CIA, specializing in cyber espionage.

"I don't believe you," he said, swatting away a fly that had annoyed me only seconds ago.

The inside of the room was hot and humid. Sweat poured off my head, arms, and bare chest. The Korean had unbuttoned my shirt. I still had no idea why. One lone bright light was shining in my face, an obvious flimsy attempt to duplicate an interrogation they had no doubt seen in an American movie.

The Korean was short, not muscular, small build, thin like a bird, clear glasses with jet black hair. Totally unsophisticated in interrogation and torture techniques. That didn't mean his strikes didn't hurt. They did. It's just that I had an advantage the man wasn't aware of.

The bindings on my legs and hands were already loosened enough to where I could easily escape and kill him any time I wanted. But that wasn't my plan. If I kept the ruse up long enough, I might salvage the mission.

Is it still considered a mission when I did this without the CIA's approval?

A debate raged in my head.

What difference does it make, Alex?

The strangest thoughts came in my head at the most unusual times. A child psychiatrist called it ADHD. My CIA handler said I was a genius. My girlfriend said it was my lame excuse for not listening to her when she was talking to me.

Anyway, I saw it as a gift that had gotten me out of a lot of jams over my three years of doing extremely risky things for my country. The ADHD made me not want to do anything for long. Like right now. I didn't want to sit in that hot room, strapped to that chair, and let the lowlife hit me over and over again. At some point, my hyperactivity was going to propel me to abandon my mission, or whatever it was, and kill him.

But giving up didn't come easily to me. Killing the man would mean I failed. Suffered needlessly. I'd give him one last chance.

I was stubborn that way.

"Get me a computer. Let me show you what I can do," I implored.

Jethro, the name I gave my interrogator, couldn't bring me a computer that would do what I wanted it to. The computers were in a room somewhere. Probably hundreds of them with thousands of wires and connections and broadband speed I'd need to execute my plan. That's what I wanted. To get in that room. Into the room where North Korea had launched a cyber war against the United States.

Jethro seemed to be growing impatient. Maybe he had ADHD as well. A man burst into the room, interrupting my thoughts which I was thankful for. I didn't want to start another senseless debate in my head.

Jethro jumped like he was startled, and I did the same. The new guy made me sit up and focus because he was holding a Type 88-2 assault rifle. The equivalent to the Soviet AK-74, except it held thirty times the number of rounds if modified which this one was. The man had thin combover hair.

Once again, I noticed the strangest things at the strangest times.

Focus.

Combover guy clearly had no idea how to use the gun, which once I did focus, was the only good thing I could think of at that moment. The way he carried and handled it made that conclusion obvious. However, that changed the calculus. A gun could kill me. It could go off accidentally. Or on purpose. ADHD or not, I wasn't going to sit around doing nothing for much longer.

I quickly assessed the situation. Even though he wasn't skilled, the man knew enough to aim and fire and probably shoot a bullet through my heart if the rifle didn't jam which that particular rifle wasn't known to do. I calculated that would take him at least seven seconds. Maybe longer with the modification, which added almost five pounds to the overall weight. That made a difference for a man who barely weighed a hundred and fifty pounds. Seven seconds was a long time for him to react, aim, and fire. The element of surprise would work in my favor.

Freeing my bonds, crossing the room, and disarming him would take half that time.

Probably.

If I didn't hesitate.

Or trip.

If my bindings were sufficiently loose.

Fifty-fifty. He might kill me before I could kill him.

Avoid that scenario, Alex. Not a good plan.

Pretending to be scared of the man seemed like a better strategy. Let him think he was in control. If he didn't feel threatened, then he wouldn't feel a need to deal with the threat. Maybe he'd relax a little.

Probably.

"Let's kill the American and get back to work," the gunman said, and I realized my thinking was flawed. So much for my analysis of the situation.

With that statement, an argument ensued between the two men. Jethro wanted to get more information and find out why I showed up on their doorstep. One of them mentioned the CIA in the argument. He wanted to know how I even knew what the building was.

Combover guy was more impatient than Jethro. Naming my enemy combatants had become a game for me. The name Jethro came from the idiot son on Beverly Hillbillies. Combover wanted to shoot me and go home for dinner. Probably not ADHD. He was just being a jerk. The unskilled and undisciplined often were, I knew from experience. The argument raged on for nearly two minutes. Jethro was clearly the leader, but not asserting himself enough, in my opinion.

Shouldn't I have a say?

The need to interject myself into their argument rather than let it play out was overwhelming. I didn't want them deciding my fate.

"I can help you," I said. "I'm American. I know things you don't. I'm good at getting around firewalls. Give me a chance."

Jethro was thinking. Combover guy seemed as if he'd already made up his mind. Unfortunately, he was the one with the weapon. But Jethro had authority over him. Hopefully, the chain of command would win the day. Superior rank would in America. I wasn't sure how that worked in North Korea.

"Why would you betray your country?" Jethro asked me, leaning close into my face. I could smell his last meal. It was all I could do to keep from gagging. Throwing up on him wasn't a good strategy at the moment, so I swallowed hard to keep from it.

"Why does anybody do what we do?" I retorted. "For money. I expect to be paid."

"We don't need your help," Jethro shouted.

"You don't know what you're doing!" I said, matching his tone in a threatening voice.

The Korean man hit me with his fist. A glancing blow, grazing my chin and lower lip. I could taste blood. Jethro winced in pain as his knuckles cracked, obviously bruised by the contact with my strong jaw. The idiot didn't know that an open slap with the palm of his hand would do more damage and not hurt his hand. Not that the man could muster enough power to do permanent damage.

I'd been slapped harder by Jamie, my girlfriend back in the states, who was also a CIA officer. Making her mad wasn't a good idea. This guy was a pansy compared to her. She also didn't have as much patience as I had. These two yahoos would already be laying on the floor, writhing in pain or worse.

Tension was rising in the room. Combover guy fidgeted with the trigger on the gun.

I was losing patience as well. Getting hit in the jaw wasn't fun, even if it was by a geeky nerd posing as a tough guy. Anger was building inside of me. Not so much from the hit but from the frustration of going to all this trouble.

This wasn't the mission.

The mission called for me to fly to South Korea and find the location of the North Korean cyber facility, known as The Judas Group, while working out of a South Korean computer lab. Finding the facility was easy enough even though others had been working on it for several months. That was all I was supposed to do. That's when I got the not-so-brilliant idea to sneak across the border, walk right up to the facility, knock on the door, and offer them my services.

My plan had worked. Sort of. I was inside a building, but not in the right building and not in the room. Somehow, I needed to talk my way into the computer room housed in the other facility.

"You Americans are so arrogant," Jethro said smugly. "You think you're the only ones who know how to use a computer. We have men just as smart. Smarter!"

"That's where you're wrong," I continued to implore. "You can do things like phishing and emails. You can create viruses and malware. But you can't hack into the most secure systems in the world. I can do that. I can hack into a bank and transfer a million dollars into your account. Right now."

"That's impossible!" Jethro said with just as much intensity. Spit was flying through the air and into my face.

The worst form of torture.

"The bank's systems are encrypted," he continued. "How can you do that when the rest of us in the world can't?"

"I just can. You have to let me show you. Get me a computer."

The wheels were turning in his mind as he looked up to the ceiling, clearly thinking. He was probably figuring that he had nothing to lose. The thought of a lot of money in his account might be enough to persuade him. The man probably made twenty-five to thirty dollars a month. Twice the wage of the average North Korean since he was in the military but barely a living wage.

"Why would I come here if I couldn't do what I say?" I added. "I risked my life to work with you."

"Okay," Jethro said against Combover's objections. "How much time do you need?"

"One hour."

He barked instructions to the man with the gun. "Release his bindings but keep the gun on him at all times," he said.

I was going into the room. I hoped it wasn't a huge mistake.

2

Wonsan, North Korea

The Wonsan Kalma Tourist zone was a huge complex of hotels with a marina, a sports area, and several children's amenities including water slides, a theme park, and more. Although construction was ongoing and much of the resort area wasn't open yet, it was still a target-rich environment for Bae Hwa.

The thirteen-year old girl liked to steal backpacks. For no other reason than the thrill of it and the interesting things she found in them.

Tonight, Wonsan Resort was busier than usual. Along with tourists, foreign investors were allowed to conduct their business activities in the area. Which was exactly why it was built. To attract more international tourists and businessmen to North Korea. Min Yang, the "Divine Leader" as he preferred to be called by the people, was looking for more ways to promote economic development and line his pockets.

The heavy UN sanctions had taken a toll on North Korea's economy and the resort was supposed to be completed, but the construction had slowed almost to a complete stop, much to the displeasure of the "Leader Centre," Yang's official title.

Bae took a deep breath of the coastal air and smiled. She'd spent the entire day cooped up in a stale school building, listening to a boring teacher drone on and on, filling the student's heads with state propaganda. Today's lesson had focused on the socialist doctrine of self-reliance. That man was the master of his destiny and the

North Koreans were to become strong and self-reliant to create a great nation.

A contradiction in practice considering that everyone was dependent upon the state for their very existence. Something she could never express out loud.

Blah! Blah! Blah. She shook her head as if she could rattle the day's lesson out of her brain.

Out here by the sea near the beach, she felt free. From her vantage point, she had views in every direction. To the east was the Sea of Japan or the East Sea, as it was also known. To the south was the Kalma Peninsula and international airport where planes took off and landed every few minutes.

Looking back to the west and north, the mountains rose in sharp contrast from the city with scenic spots such as Mt. Kumgang, Lake Silung, Chongsokjong, Lagoon Samil and Masikryong Ski resort. She'd been to all of them. That came from being a girl born into privilege.

She scanned the area below her for a *babo*. A mark. Her next victim. Babo was the North Korean word for idiot. Bae felt that anyone stupid enough to have a backpack stolen by a thirteen-year old girl was a babo and deserved any ridicule she could heap upon them.

Several were within her line of sight. A fat man was trying to take a selfie and had set his backpack down on the concrete sidewalk. He stood with his back to the ocean, his hand high in the air holding a cell phone, struggling to get the camera at the right angle. Probably trying not to get too much of his bald head.

The thought and sight of the man made her laugh. He was too easy a prey. He might have money in the bag, but the rest was probably smelly tourist stuff. By looking at him, she figured the bag probably had more food than anything else.

A bunch of kids played in the playground. Parents left several backpacks unattended on the benches. She'd learned from experience that those weren't worth the effort. They were filled with diapers, children's wipes, bottles, and little bags of snacks. More stinky things. Not to mention the insides were full of germs.

A college student caught her eye. His backpack would be full of books, writing instruments, paper, and maybe a cell phone. Probably not. What did she need with all that? That's what hers was full of.

A cell phone would be interesting. Only a few of the elites were authorized to have one. More and more people were buying them on the black market. But the penalties of having an unauthorized cell phone were onerous. It wasn't worth the risk.

One of the foreign investors was carrying a briefcase. She really wished she could steal one of those. They were too hard to run with. She'd learned that the hard way. A businessman left his briefcase sitting on the ground next to him at a restaurant a few months before. Bae grabbed it and took off running, awkwardly. The case was heavier than she thought it would be.

Still, the cases were tempting. She'd lain awake at night thinking about what might be in them. Passports. Money. Checkbooks. Appointment calendars. Important business papers. These were the types of things that interested her. Maybe letters from secret lovers.

Wouldn't it be funny to send one of those notes to the man's home for his unsuspecting wife to read? Bae had a vivid imagination. That was only one of the sinister thoughts that came into her head in her late-night fantasies.

Mostly, she was just bored. Which was probably the reason why she stole things. She didn't need the money. Her parents had plenty. Though it wasn't her money, she had everything she needed. Her parents spoiled her, which was probably part of the problem as well. Because she had everything, she wanted things that weren't hers. Things she couldn't have because they didn't belong to her.

Bae was a thinker, not a feeler. School testing labeled her a genius. She analyzed everything. Including herself. Ad nauseam. That was working against her at the moment. She needed to force herself to decide and quit thinking.

So, she made one.

Tonight, nothing but a businessman would do. She wasn't going to waste her time on mothers with little kids, college students, disgusting bald tourists, or businesswomen. Women in business held no positions of importance in North Korea. Even though by law women were equal to men, the only women of influence were relatives or wives of leaders.

Women like her mother.

That decision to focus on a businessman narrowed her options considerably and raised the risks dramatically. Not just any businessman would do. It had to be one who was being careful with his bag. Why? It meant something of value to him was in the bag.

How did she know he was being careful? Telltale signs. He'd keep touching it, assuring himself it was still there. If it had a strap, it would be draped over the chair or on the table rather than hanging loose. The bag would be expensive and not well worn. A rich person would only carry a new briefcase to an important meeting.

How he was dressed was a clue. He had to be in a suit. Was his hair mussed, or perfectly groomed? Was it dyed or graying? Once she narrowed in on a target, she analyzed his every move. How did he use a napkin? Did he dab at his mouth, or clumsily wipe food off his face? These were all questions she considered.

She wanted someone who paid attention to detail almost as much as she did.

Almost.

A babo always made mistakes. If the man really wanted to protect the case, the strap would be around his shoulder not around the chair. Instead of on the floor on the outside of the chair, it would be on the inside, between his legs, with one foot against it at all times, so that he would feel any movement. Most people didn't think of these things.

She scanned her immediate view. One target stood out from among the rest.

An older gentleman, probably in his mid-fifties, was dining at the restaurant by the pier. Older was good. He couldn't run as fast.

At his feet, lay, not a briefcase or a backpack, but a satchel.

Interesting.

Bae had never stolen a satchel before.

The letter D was engraved on the metal lock. Probably his initial. Only a wealthy person could afford such an extravagant indulgence. The bag was on the left side of his chair, not the right. A big mistake. The right faced the inside of the restaurant. The left was close to the sidewalk facing out. If the man was smart, he would've asked for an inside table.

He obviously wanted a table with a view because he kept gazing out at it. But he kept looking down at the satchel, touching it, and he was fidgeting, like there was something important in it. Maybe something valuable. Perhaps something he didn't want anyone to know about.

The man was well dressed in a designer suit. His nails were manicured. He appeared to be middle eastern, although she couldn't be sure. She'd never personally met any middle eastern men. He was definitely not from any of the Asian countries. From what she knew of the middle east, they were wealthy. Perhaps an oilman or even a person of royalty. That excited her even more.

He didn't have his food yet. That was a good thing. It would give her time to formulate a plan. She'd wait until he had his food for obvious reasons. That would distract him and cause him to hesitate when she made her move. Who'd want to leave a hot meal they just started eating to chase after a bag no matter how important it was? Especially if he was hungry. The bag would ultimately win out, and the man would give chase but only after a brief moment of indecision.

He'd also stumble out of the gate. The napkin was already in his lap. Instinctively, he'd take it off his lap and put it on the table. He'd have a fork in his hand. If she timed it right, he'd have a knife and a fork so both hands would be occupied. She'd wait until he took a bite. It's harder to run with a mouth full of food.

A bolt of excitement went through her now that she was satisfied, she had the right target. Her thoughts turned to developing an escape route. The sidewalk was wide and extended all along the beach like a boardwalk. Good for running. A lot of people ran along on the boardwalk, so she wouldn't seem out of place.

She scanned the path she wanted to run. What she saw next made her pause. Two members of the NKAGF, North Korea Army Ground Force, were smoking a cigarette in the direction she preferred to go. The plan in her mind was to come up from behind the man, not from the front, so he wouldn't see her coming and then take off running in the direction she was heading. That would lead her right into the guards.

It would be awkward to turn and run the way in which she'd come. Bae was also right-handed. She preferred to grab the satchel with her right hand in one fluid motion. That wasn't an option. There was no way she could run that way. She'd have to come up from behind him, distract him because he'd feel her presence, then pivot, grab the satchel with her left hand and then take off running.

She'd have to get off of the boardwalk, then run onto the grass and then between the buildings because they could see her on the boardwalk for a great distance.

For a minute, she reconsidered and thought about choosing a different target. But she was intrigued. She wanted to find out what was in that satchel.

A decision had to be made soon. The man was just served his meal.

Without hesitation, she came out of the shadows from her hiding place and started walking toward him.

3

It occurred to me that this might be my last opportunity to get out of this alive.

The leader and his armed sidekick led me out of the makeshift interrogation basement—an abandoned office building, actually—and walked me toward what was a newer, and expansive, four-story, high-rise where the cyber lab was located. The buildings were several hundred feet apart and were connected by a dirt sidewalk. The walk would take about seven minutes. Enough time for me to make a quick assessment of my surroundings.

Disarming the one man and killing both would be as easy for me as beginner Sudoku. The sun was setting, and the woods were nearby. I could get away undetected, cross back over the border of South Korea, and spend the night in my luxury hotel room with room service, a jacuzzi tub, satin sheets, and a morning massage.

According to the calculation in my head, I had about six hundred feet to decide which was the distance between the two buildings.

Enough time to decide since my brain could process the debate quickly. A skill that came from my years of working with the fastest computers in the world. I could actually see the SPOD spinning in my mind, which caused me to almost laugh out loud. Officially, in the macOS lingo, the spinning icon on a computer was called the spinning wait cursor or the spinning beach ball. My CIA trainer, Curly, called it the SPOD, or the spinning pizza of death.

It was his way of saying that if you have to think about it and decide a life or death matter that quickly, then you were unprepared and were thinking your way to death. He was right. I hadn't sufficiently thought this through. Walking into a den of rattlesnakes made more sense.

I often heard his voice in my head in times like this.

Halee, I could hear him say in his gruff and always short tone.

Curly never called me by my first name, Alex, it was always Halee.

Don't rely on luck, Curly said. *Don't place yourself in a situation where you don't have the skill to get out of it. Eventually, your luck will run out.*

This felt like one of those times. Curly would say I was crazy to go inside that building. He emphasized preparation above all things. The risk should already be assessed before I was in the situation. A mission like this, required weeks of surveillance. He'd want me to know how many people were in the building. Were they armed? If so, with what kind of weapons. He'd encourage me to secure blueprints of the building layout if possible. Assessing entry and exit points were vital information. Did the building have an alarm system?

Video cameras?

Stairways?

Elevators?

Hiding places?

Escape routes?

Above all else, what was the probability of success? Curly always insisted that those things be thought through before entering a hostile environment. That didn't mean circumstances didn't change. There was always the unexpected. In our business, we often had to think on the fly on almost every mission. Curly insisted that if we had to think on the fly, make sure our fly isn't open. If it was then you probably forgot something. Something that could get you killed.

Curly was famous for his euphemisms.

"What are you grinning about?" Jethro asked me.

I just shrugged. No time to explain. We were halfway to our destination, and the debate was still raging.

The MSO doesn't have to be a hundred percent, but it should be damn close, Curly ingrained in us the concept. The MSO—mission success odds—was the most important calculus in any mission.

Don't take unnecessary risks, he said often. *If the MSO is too low, you have to abort.*

Curly's words were winning the argument. He had another saying, *Stupid will kill you faster than an opponent's weapon*. Going into the building alone with no advanced preparation, no weapon, and with no plan on how to escape seemed like a stupid thing to do.

The CIA had limited operations in North Korea for a reason. It was too dangerous. If I failed, I could spend years of torture and hard labor in a North Korean prison, and the CIA could and would do nothing to help me.

We were getting closer to the building.

With two hundred remaining feet left, the decision became obvious. The SPOD quit spinning in my head. Escape was the best plan. Cut my losses and live to fight another day.

I couldn't make myself do it.

I was stubborn that way.

The potential reward outweighed the risks. In a few moments, I could be inside the North Korean cyber facility. Something that sent a surge of excitement through me like a lightning bolt. The curiosity drew me to it like a magnet. If I succeeded against the odds, the cyber war would shift in our favor with one stroke of a keyboard.

When would I ever get another opportunity like this?

What's your plan, Halee? I heard Curly say.

I have a plan. I answered.

I'd seen the building when I first arrived. It looked to be about ten thousand square feet. *If you've seen one office building, you've seen them all.* Two elevators and two stairways would be standard. The main doors were in the center of the building. That's where one set of elevators would be. Service elevators were usually in the back where there was a loading dock.

Stairway exits were on the two ends of the building. I could see the exit door on one side and assumed the other emergency exit door was on the other. More than likely they were locked to outside access but would open from the inside. That was universal. What's the point of having an emergency exit if the door doesn't open from the inside?

That gave me four possible exit points.

A large dumpster full of trash stood in the back, and the lid was open. In a worst-case scenario, I could jump from the roof or a window into that dumpster, and it would likely catch my fall.

Avoid that option if at all possible.

I also had a weapon.

Remember, you're always armed, Curly said.

What he meant was that I was trained to kill a man a hundred different ways with my bare hands. My legs, feet, shoulders, head, elbows, and knees were weapons when used properly. Almost anything can be turned into a weapon if I was resourceful. The desks would have office supplies, scissors, letter openers, writing instruments, rulers, and staplers among other things that could be turned into a weapon. Even a computer monitor could kill a man if brought down on his head with the proper amount of force. It could also stop a bullet, as Curly displayed for us in one training session.

I felt emboldened as I talked myself into it.

Most of the people inside would be geeks. Small, thin, nerds with glasses. The average North Korean male was five foot five and a hundred fifty-four pounds. I was six foot four, two hundred and thirty pounds. Admittedly, a geek as well, but also the starting quarterback for the Stanford Cardinal football team that lost to Alabama in the National Championship game. I could bench press two of the geeks with my eyes closed.

An enigma was what my handler called me. A rare combination of star athlete and computer whiz. The best hacker the CIA had ever produced, my success proved. Although, I had most of the skills when they hired me. Along with my computer savvy, I felt confident I could handle the North Koreans if a fight broke out. Most of the nerds would run away or cower behind a desk.

I noticed security was minimal. Min Yang ruled North Korea with an iron fist. Dissent was met harshly and swiftly. The need for an armed presence was limited even at such a sensitive site. The dictator was smart enough to know that excess security would draw attention to the building. There were no armed guards out front. No fencing surrounding it. No gates monitoring vehicles in and out. American satellites would spot the unusual activity around the building and investigate further, so Yang kept it to a minimum. This building looked like any other office building in North Korea, by design.

We were close now.

What's the MSO? I heard Curly say with more urgency, demanding I put a percentage on the odds of success.

That almost stopped me in my tracks. I did slow my steps to give me more time to think. Not having an immediate answer, I stopped and bent down to tie my shoe, buying me more time.

"Let's go," the armed man said roughly as he pushed the back of my head with the muzzle of his gun. That was almost enough to make the decision for me. I would like to end his miserable existence. But I refrained. I had a bigger picture to consider.

I stood tense for a moment before I began walking.

What are the odds? Curly demanded.

The SPOD in my head began spinning again.

I'm sure the North Korean has a boss. He could say no.

I only have one hour.

Is there equipment fast enough and powerful enough to do what I want it to do?

Will the CIA let me transfer a million dollars into the man's account?

That was the biggest wildcard. When I logged into the system, I would have to make the CIA believe it was me. As far as they knew, I was in that hotel in South Korea. They would be skeptical. It would be a risk on their part. If they let me in, and I was a hacker, they could have real problems shutting down the system in time to prevent real damage.

If they did believe it was me... that didn't mean they'd automatically authorize the money. I wasn't on an official mission. They'd know I was in North Korea but wouldn't know why. It's possible I was being tortured and entering the system under duress.

The door was less than twenty-five feet away.

What are the odds of success? Curly shouted.

Fifty-fifty.

The interrogator used a passkey to open the front door to the building. He waited for me to walk through ahead of him.

Abort! Abort! Curly was insistent.

Too late. I walked in the door as the SPOD in my head ground to a halt.

4

"Myusshiyeyo?" Bae asked the businessman sitting at the restaurant table.

She asked him for the time. Her heartbeat was pounding so hard in her chest that she could feel it in her ears. The adrenaline pulsed through her veins as the excitement of stealing his satchel was heightening her senses.

Everything was coordinated and executed perfectly. She came up to him from behind so he couldn't see her clearly. The watch was on his right arm, meaning he had to turn away from her to look at it. As he did, she picked up the satchel with her right hand, pivoted so she was facing away from him, and let the satchel droop low almost to the ground, holding it only by the strap.

The man seemed annoyed by the question which was all the better. He didn't bother making friendly eye contact.

"Yeoseosshi," he said roughly. "Six o'clock."

Bae knew it was five after, but the satchel man didn't seem to want to be bothered with the task of giving her the exact information.

"Gam-sa-ham-ni-da," Bae said as she started to walk away. The appropriate formal and polite way for a young child to say thank you to an older man.

This is too easy, she thought to herself as she commanded her feet to walk away, slowly, deliberately, without calling attention to herself even though every fiber of her being wanted to run.

It was too easy.

She heard an expletive. Before she could react, the man reached out and grabbed her left arm. Still seated, he didn't have leverage, so she squirmed away and took off running daring not to look back.

Several people were walking toward her. A mother pushed a stroller. A jogger. Another businessman in a suit. The fat tourist who took the selfie earlier. The mother wouldn't try to stop her more than likely. Too dangerous for a mom with a baby. The jogger had headsets on so he couldn't hear what was happening. Maybe he'd see it and he looked to be in shape. But her experience was that joggers were focused on their running.

The fat man still had the camera in his hand, so he was oblivious to what was going on around him.

The man with the suit was her biggest worry. She slowed her pace to a fast walk, staying on the opposite side of the sidewalk from the man in the suit. Surprisingly, there was no reaction from anyone. Nothing in any of their faces gave away that there was any commotion behind her.

Bae took the opportunity to glance back. The satchel man was walking toward her. At a quick pace, but it appeared that he was trying to be as inconspicuous as her.

Why?

She considered dropping the satchel and running away. He probably wouldn't follow her as long as he had his bag back. But now she was even more curious. What was in the satchel that made the man not want to make a scene?

She'd figure that out later. He was gaining on her. Satchel man was tall with long strides and came toward her with a purpose. To the left was the sea. She could run faster than he could on the sandy beach, but it was out in the open for hundreds of yards. To her immediate right, was a hill, which was not conducive for running.

Just a few steps ahead, were some shops. She headed for those.

The man was so close that Bae could hear him breathing hard. She took off running. The man shouted and quickened his pace. A shop owner swept the sidewalk just up ahead. He looked that way and saw the chase unfolding. He tried to grab Bae, but she ducked under his arms and left him grasping at air.

She sprinted now. The excitement turned to panic. An alleyway just ahead on the right between two buildings was her lifeline, so she took it, immediately regretting her choice. A fence at the end blocked her escape.

Too late to go back to the boardwalk.

Bae ran straight ahead and leapt on to the chain link fence and bolted over it, tearing her shirt in the process, and scraping the side of her waist on the metal prong at the top. Fortunately, the satchel handle had not gotten caught on the fence, but she tumbled over it anyway, and landed hard on her shoulder.

Bae let out a scream from the pain. She reached back and touched the wound and found blood on her hand.

Another scream formed. This time because the man was at the fence. If the fence hadn't been there, he'd already been on her.

She took off running again. It took him longer to get over since he wore dress shoes and a suit. That gave her a slight head start. Another alleyway was ahead, but she was afraid to take it. The hill was her best option. She scurried up it like a cat. The grass was slightly wet, so it would be harder for the man to keep his footing.

At the top of the hill, was a dirt road. With only a slight hesitation, she went to the left. After a hundred feet or so down the road, the man had not yet emerged from the hill. Bae veered off the road and laid on the ground behind a bush, and tried to catch her breath. From her vantage point she could see the man finally reach the top of the hill and step into the middle of the road looking both ways, obviously not sure where she had gone.

She laid perfectly still, holding her breath, not wanting to move or do anything to give away her position. The man pulled out a gun from his suit.

What?

She let out a slight gasp.

Did he hear it?

He must have because he started to walk her way. It took every bit of self-control not to scream at the top of her lungs. All she did was steal a satchel. A petty crime for a thirteen-year-old girl. Why was he hunting her with a gun?

Getting off of the boardwalk had been a mistake. At least there were people around. He wouldn't dare pull a gun in a crowd. Here she was all alone. He could kill her if he wanted and no one would know. It might take days for them to find her body. Her imagination ran wild.

She thought about running again, but he could easily catch her on the road, or worse, just shoot her in the back. The thought suddenly made her angry. Who was this man and what in the satchel was so important that he would kill to get it back?

He must've known she was hiding in the bushes because he walked slowly down the road, deliberately, carefully checking both sides about every ten feet.

When he got close, Bae bolted out from behind the bush. With the element of surprise, she was able to lower a shoulder into him from behind and sent him into the bushes on the other side of the road.

He let out a yell and another expletive. This time Bae didn't look back. She just kept running. Down the road. Then up some steps. Through a backyard. Onto the pavement into an open area. She could hear the man's footsteps on the pavement below.

Why won't he give up?

He was close to her again.

Her lungs burned. Every muscle in her legs screamed for her to stop.

She kept climbing until she was on the cliffs overlooking the sea. Her light frame was an advantage. She bounded up the cliffs like a goat.

A little cry of pain gave away her position. The jagged rocks cut her hands.

The man laughed. He muttered something. Bae thought he said that he had her now. The cliffs were getting steeper.

He was probably right. Bae couldn't keep going much longer. Fatigue had set in and was overwhelming the adrenaline that pushed her forward.

For a moment, she wondered if this was how she was going to die.

The satchel man climbed faster than her. He was bigger and stronger and could take large bounding steps. Her only advantage was that she could scurry between the rocks. He had to stop to watch where she went.

He was tiring as well. She could hear the grunts of exhaustion as he stopped a couple of times to catch his breath. That gave her some confidence as she continued upward. Higher. Eventually, she'd get to the part where it was too steep to climb. At that point, she would run out of options.

The area was called Lover's Point. Couples often came to the lookout point, for some time alone and for the spectacular views. Bae barely noticed the sea in the distance. She was too focused on where the man was.

Satchel man made a mistake. He tried to take the most direct approach and reached a dead end in the steepest part. He'd have to backtrack. Bae stayed on the trails. This gave her a temporary advantage. She abruptly changed directions and started going down, taking him by surprise as he let out his own yelp.

He shouted more expletives. Bae was running fast now. Downhill. Too fast for such a steep incline. If she twisted an ankle or fell against a rock, it would be over for her.

Satchel man apparently didn't want to give chase. He took out his gun again.

A shot rang out. The bullet caromed off a rock only a few feet from her. The sound echoed off the side of the cliffs and caused a ringing in her ears.

"Help me," she cried out, but no one was around to hear her.

There were people far below them, on the street, but they were a good distance away. Running in the open was not an option. So, Bae hid behind a large rock. The satchel fit in a crevice in the rock, so she hid it there.

Satchel man was even with her now, but twenty or so yards away, to her left. He hadn't seen her go behind the rock. He struggled to maintain his footing. His left arm kept reaching to the ground to catch his fall. The gun was swinging wildly in his right hand.

He was below her before he saw her. A smile formed on his face. She didn't have the strength to go back up the hill. Going down wasn't an option.

What would he do to her?

Bae started to cry.

As he neared, he lost his footing again. Satchel man reached out with his right hand to catch his fall. The gun was still in that hand.

As his hand hit the ground, his body weight continued going down.

Gravity was stronger than the hand trying to hold up the weight. Bae could see his hand bend awkwardly with the gun still in it.

A muzzle flashed.

A loud popping sound echoed off the rocks.

The gun went off. The man fell on top of it.

Bae covered her ears.

Satchel man lay motionless on the ground. Facedown.

Bae tried to process what was going on. Was he shot?

After several minutes, she approached the man cautiously. He wasn't moving.

Was it a trap?

With as much strength as she could muster, she put both arms on his side and pulled him over. There was no blood. Just a hole in his shirt, right below his heart.

His breathing was labored.

He's still alive.

Bae grabbed the gun out of his hand. He made no effort to resist.

He kept going in and out of consciousness.

What do I do?

Before she could decide, he took a last gasp for air. His body convulsed, his eyes blinked several times, and then he slumped back to the ground.

"He's dead!" she mumbled to herself.

I think.

She wasn't sure. She'd never seen a dead person before.

Bae looked around. There was no one who saw what had happened. She held the gun out from her body, not sure exactly how to carry it.

I have to get out of here.

She started down the mountain, and then suddenly remembered the satchel. The reason all this had happened.

Racing back to the rock, she took the satchel out of the hiding place and considered leaving it by the body.

If she did that, then all of this would've been for nothing.

It was growing dark, now. No one would see her. The sun set

quickly over the mountains. It would be pitch dark in just a few minutes.

She stayed on the mountain, careful not to be seen. When it was completely dark, she walked down the hill and toward her house.

The gun was thrown into a nearby pond.

Once home, Bae ran up the stairs to her room, hid the satchel, and fell onto the bed thinking about what just happened.

I'm in big trouble! she concluded.

At least I'm alive.

5

The third floor of the North Korean cyber warfare lab was like what I expected. Sterile and uniform. Emotionless. Much like the rest of the country, only even more so. The roughly three thousand square feet consisted of rows of several hundred desks in a large open room. The desks weren't more than three feet wide and three feet high, all with the same blue top and tan-colored legs. Like something you might see in a six-grade classroom back in America.

On each desk sat a computer. Facing each computer was a young Korean, age ranging from seventeen to thirty. Every person in the room wore a green uniform. They all had the same blank, joyless look. No women were in the room. I assumed because they wanted the men to have no distractions.

A large picture of Emperor Min Yang was the only thing on the wall.

Two dozen or so supervisors walked up and down the aisles, looking over the worker's shoulders. The supervisors' gaits and mannerisms were robotic, synchronized almost. They held their hands behind them in the small of their backs. Their heads were up and chests out like they were General George Patton inspecting his troops. Several looked over at me with curiosity. An American had probably never been in that lab before.

The room was a stark contrast to Google, where I applied for a position right out of college.

Strange that my mind would go there.

The Googleplex workspace in Mountain View, California, featured more than three million square feet of space and sported two swimming pools, beach volleyball courts, a bowling alley, and several recreational facilities, including a gym, work out area, sauna, spa, pool, ping pong tables and a variety of lounges for social gatherings. A worker could get an afternoon massage or take a nap in the "sleep room."

They offered me a position on the spot. I turned them down on the spot after thinking about it for less than a minute. The salary package had given me pause. Six figures. Full benefits. Matching contributions in a retirement plan. Not bad for a twenty-two-year old fresh out of college.

I still turned them down. At the moment, I was wondering if I had made the right decision. Why exactly was I subjecting myself to this abuse for less than a third of the wages and benefits from the CIA?

I knew why. The idea of sitting at a cubicle, eight hours a day, entering code that someone else wrote, would be like torture to me. Now that I had experienced actual torture, I realized how foolish and naïve that thought was. The job at Google looked rather good at the moment as I raised my hand to my face to touch the tender lip that was swollen from my recent experience with real torture.

I wondered the same thing about the robots working on the computers in this place. How could they possibly spend all day every day sitting at their desks, sending thousands of spam emails, hoping to get one unsuspecting victim to give them access to his computer?

The thought of shutting them down and putting them out of work brought a smile to my face.

"What's so funny?" Combover guy said, bringing me back to present reality.

"Your face," I said to him in Spanish, assuming he didn't know the language.

I actually felt better about the whole situation which was why I was acting more brazen. He was the only gunman on the floor. The entrance had about a dozen armed guards, but they were downstairs. I'd avoid using that door to exit. Other than that, I didn't see any other threats.

I could tell the Combover guy wanted a confrontation. He kept shifting his weight and fidgeting with his gun. He seemed anxious for his buddy to get back, as was I. Jethro had gone into that office and was having an animated discussion with a man, I could only assume was the head honcho over the entire floor. A conclusion reached only because he was the only one with an office.

It didn't appear the conversation would be over anytime soon. That was expected. Getting access to their computers wouldn't be easy, so I was patient. It gave me time to survey the room to see what information I could glean from my vantage point.

What I saw almost knocked me over.

On the wall was a large computer screen. I hadn't noticed it before because it was behind us. The screen displayed numbers. Red. Like a ticker tape. Or a sports book at a casino. My guess was production numbers. It was updated almost by the second. Each line was a different category of cyber hacking.

I studied them carefully, to glean everything I could from them.

Crypto jacking. 1473. $179,265.

Crypto jacking was the term used for a scheme to attack a victim's computer with virus and malware for the purpose of stealing their information. Most were financial schemes, although some were to gather information such as social security numbers, addresses, dates of birth, passwords, and telephone numbers. The numbers meant they'd stolen almost two hundred thousand dollars from 1473 victims. I wondered if that was a day's worth of activities.

The fact that they kept a running total of the information in American dollars was telling. Most of their victims must be Americans. A rage was building inside of me.

I tried to make sure my mouth wasn't agape and had to consciously keep it closed. It took every bit of self-control to not grab Combover guy's gun and start shooting.

Anonymous. 73. $

Anonymous was a notorious hacking group. Decentralized. A loose group of hackers whose purposes was to take down websites. The dollar amount was blank. I knew North Korea wasn't Anonymous, but they were clearly working with them. Today, they had effectively hijacked and destroyed seventy-three websites.

I hate these people.

Don't hate the sinner. Hate the sin.

Someone once said that to me, and the words were ringing in my ears, reminding me of that truth. So, I tried, even though it was still hard to do. Truthfully, I didn't try too hard. Righteous anger was a good thing in my line of work. Jesus overturned tables and drove out the moneychangers in the temple. I wanted to run through the cyber lab and overturn all the computers and drive them all out with a whip.

It took every bit of my resolve to stop myself. I needed to see what the supervisor was going to do first.

Crymeariver. 249,756. $1,047,722.00.

Crying Shame. 1,465,226. $14,982,673.45.

I shook my head in disbelief.

Crymeariver was a ransomware attack that targeted computers running Microsoft windows operating system. They encrypted the data and held it ransom. Companies paid the ransom in bitcoins. We never knew the total number of computers affected, but it was estimated to be over two hundred thousand. I now knew the actual number. *249,756.* I also knew that North Korea was behind it, something we always suspected but were never able to prove.

Until now.

Crying Shame must be a new ransomware attack. I had to warn Brad. All that mischief was happening right here in front of my eyes. Just gathering this intelligence was worth the risk I had taken to get in the building. Although it wouldn't be worth anything if I didn't get out of this alive.

I looked back over to the office. The conversation between Jethro and the supervisor was still going. I was tempted to bolt out of the building and go back to South Korea to report all of this to Brad. The next lines on the screen gave me even more pause.

American Financial

The Bank of South Korea

Jingo.

Apparently, The Judas Group was targeting all of them and had an entire line devoted to each one. No numbers were next to them. So far, they hadn't succeeded, but it was only a matter of time. A few years before, American First Bank announced a massive data breach. More than a hundred million credit card applications were accessed by hackers.

Jingo, a mobile game producer, had 218 million user log-in credentials stolen. Apparently, The Judas Group was going after them again.

South Korea.

I knew they stole almost a billion dollars a year from Asian banking entities. Most of that happened in Pyongyang.

Pakistan came up on the screen.

Why were they targeting Pakistan?

I have to shut down this lab. It was one thing to sit in a computer lab in South Korea and talk about world-wide hacking. Another to be in the actual room. I had too many questions to bolt now. I had to get my hands on a computer.

My heart was flipping somersaults while my fingers were moving as if they were anxious to get a keyboard and start typing.

My CIA handler had cautioned me, saying, *The hackers you'll have with you always*. A reference to what Jesus said about the poor.

That may be true, but I could make a big dent in these operations if I could gain access to a computer, and my interrogator could convince the supervisor to let me.

Anger reached a boiling point inside me. I didn't know how long I could hold it back. These people were thieves. Plain and simple. Cyber bullies and thugs. I wanted to put a stop to them. People lost hard-earned money to them.

The thought of bringing it to its knees, was exhilarating. The CIA would give anything to have a man in this room.

And here I was. I somehow had to get my fingers on one of those keyboards.

Would I be able to?

That question was about to be answered.

The conversation was over.

Jethro and the supervisor left his office and were walking toward me. My whole body tensed. Combover guy must've sensed it as well as he turned his gun on me.

The main guy, the supervisor, had a smile on his face. Was that because he was about to have me killed or because he was happy to see me?

I'd soon learn my fate.

6

My interrogator and the Korean lab supervisor had finished their discussion, came out of his office, and were walking toward me. Combover stiffened and put his gun to my side. Fortunately, the safety was still on.

The nearest exit was on the other end of the room. I shifted my weight slightly to my right foot and rotated my body just enough for Combover man not to notice. With one motion, I could disable him, gain possession of his machine gun, and be out the exit door and into the woods before the downstairs guards could be notified.

I hope that's not necessary.

When the supervisor extended his hand toward me, I breathed an imperceptible sigh of relief.

Until he mentioned his name.

Then it was all I could do to keep my mouth from flying open in disbelief.

"Hello, sir," the man said. "My name is Soo Lee Tark. Most people call me Lee."

I now saw the resemblance. He'd had extensive cosmetic surgery to change his appearance or I would've recognized him earlier. Tark was an alias. The man's real name was Gi Man Pok, a fugitive on the FBI's ten most wanted list for cybercrimes against America and the world.

"Joe Hardy," I said almost instinctively, as I took his hand and shook it, surprised at the firmness. I tried to process all of the ramifications of coming face to face with Pok.

"I'm pleased to meet you," he said with a slight bow.

His eyes were dilated which were a sign of deception. He was clearly skeptical of me and my motives, which was understandable, but he was also trying to trick me into trusting him. I wondered if the dozen guards at the downstairs entrance were on their way as we spoke.

I decided to play along. With my hands together in front of me in the prayer position, I bowed slightly as well in an act of respect.

"Step into my office," Pok said. The interrogator was sent away and Combover man followed us with instructions to wait outside the door as Pok closed it.

Going into his office was a tactical mistake if the guards were on their way. I'd be trapped in the office. My sense was that Pok would let this play out. He was obviously curious as to why I was there.

I was more curious about him. If that was even possible.

Several years ago, Pok went into hiding. No one in the CIA knew where he was. This whole mission was worth it just to gain that intelligence information. My handler would be pleased. If I lived long enough to tell him. The office had large windows facing out into the bullpen. I kept warily looking out to see if the guards were coming. There wasn't much I could do if they were.

Pok was considered the best hacker in the world. He was the head of the Lazarus Group. A North Korean state-sponsored cyber hacking group that had wreaked havoc in financial markets. The group stole $571 million dollars from Asian financial markets last year alone.

The Judas Group must be operating out of another lab. That caused a change in my strategy. Offering him a million dollars would be meaningless. He could steal that in the time it took me to offer it to him.

I needed to play on his ego and his distinction as the best hacker in the world. A mantle I believed belonged to me.

Pok offered me a chair, which I took as I quickly surveyed the office. Not one paper was out of place. There were no personal items: family photos, mementos, books, or unnecessary clutter. One lone picture of the divine leader hung on the wall behind him. On his desk was an Apple desktop computer. A newer model but nothing fancy. Probably purchased in China by the government and issued to him. It would serve my purposes, if I were able to talk my way to the other side of the desk.

"Tell me about yourself, Mr. Hardy," Pok said in a friendly manner.

"Please call me Joe," I responded.

He nodded dutifully.

"Where did you go to school, Joe?" he asked.

I knew that Pok was trained at the Yang-so University in Pyongyang.

"Stanford," I replied, which was the truth. Curly always taught us to keep our cover stories as close to the truth as possible.

His hand fiddled with the computer mouse. A nervous habit. Pok probably had ADHD as well.

"I know of Stanford," Pok replied. "Is California where you grew up?"

"Why don't we skip the chit chat?" I said abruptly.

"I like to know who I'm working with," Pok retorted.

"All you need to know is that I'm the best hacker in the world."

He let out a skeptical chuckle.

That was my new strategy. Create a competitive challenge. I was banking on him wanting to keep me alive long enough to prove he was better.

"How do I know you don't work for the CIA?" Pok asked.

My turn to laugh.

"I did work for the CIA," I said. "Now I'm a freelancer. I sell my services to the highest bidder."

"Why would I need your services?"

That was a good question. Pok's reputation was well known. He was behind the hack of Worldwide Pictures a decade before. At the time they called themselves the "Guardians of the World." They leaked confidential information about executives of Worldwide including their salaries, damaging emails, and plans for future films.

Worldwide was specifically targeted. They had a film about to be released called *The Guest*, a comedy about a plot to assassinate Min Yang. The dictator was so outraged, he ordered the attack, although the government of North Korea denied all responsibility. Pok rose to notoriety by leading the group and executing the successful hack. The group employed a variant of the Sharnoon wiper malware and basically erased all of the company's computer infrastructure. The film was never released in the theatres and cost the company millions of dollars and unknown damage to its reputation from the leaked emails.

The group ultimately became known as *The Lazarus Group*. They were behind the Crymeariver ransomware crypto worm that targeted computers run by Microsoft Windows. They hijacked business computers and then demanded a ransom paid in Bitcoins. Many of the companies paid the ransom because it cost less than fixing the problem and being without their computers until it could be fixed.

The Lazarus Group became more sophisticated in their attacks every year. In reality, they were already successful and didn't need my services.

"Why do I need your services?" Pok asked me again when I didn't answer right away.

"You don't," I finally answered.

That response took him by surprise as his eyebrows suddenly raised.

"I don't need you, either," I added.

He still didn't respond.

I took the most direct approach. "Now that we understand each other, let's get down to business. I'm offering you my services. You don't have anyone in this building as good as me."

He put his hand to his face and was thinking. This was probably not how he expected the conversation to go. Curly always said to do the unexpected. *Keep your adversary off balance.*

"You never worked for the CIA," Pok eventually said, breaking the awkward silence.

I rolled my eyes.

"Give me a computer, and I'll show you what I can do," I said.

Pok typed something into the computer.

"I have a list of every CIA agent. Your name's not on it."

I knew that wasn't true. There'd been rumors that North Korea had hacked into the CIA computers, but there was no evidence of that. I also knew there was no place with one list, for this very reason. But I decided to play along.

"Do you think I'd use my real name? You didn't, Mr. Pok."

That caught him by surprise. A look of anger flashed across his face as his jaw clenched and his eyes narrowed. I'd hit a nerve. I knew his real identity, but he didn't know mine, which gave me an advantage.

Pok typed something else into his computer. About a minute later, he turned the computer toward me. "Hack into this email," he said, as he slid the wireless keyboard and mouse my way.

"May I use my own network analyzer?" I asked.

"Be my guest," he said.

He had locked me out of access to his main computer network. The first thing I did was unlock it. The screen was not facing him, so he had no idea what I was doing. He'd find it, but it would take several days.

In less than a minute, I was in the emails. I turned the screen back toward him.

He stared at the screen for several long seconds. His mouth was slightly opened in amazement, even though he tried hard not to give away that he was impressed. I'd be in awe of him and his abilities as well if they weren't for nefarious purposes.

This was where I needed to exercise some self-control. I was competitive by nature. Part of me wanted to challenge him to unlock an email faster. That was the competitiveness from playing football all those years kicking in. I resisted the urge. I had bigger goals now.

"Very impressive," he admitted.

"Like I said, I'm the best."

I decided to throw a nuclear bomb into the conversation. "I want to work for the Lazarus Group. That's why I'm here."

No one knew if the Lazarus Group really existed. I didn't know either, but I was highly suspicious.

His eyes gave away the truth.

Excitement pulsed through my veins. This was no ordinary cyber lab. They were not into petty, cybercrime and corporate malfeasance. This was where the Lazarus Group worked from. I was certain of it. This lab was the biggest threat to national security of any that had ever existed.

I have to get into their computers!

The Lazarus Group was believed to have been formed to hack into government nuclear programs. Their mission was to steal nuclear codes and take control of nuclear weapons.

North Korea's motives were clear. The United States was threatening them. With less than a half a dozen nukes, the US could take Min Yang out of power in no time. Gaining surreptitious control of another country's nuclear weapons by cyber espionage, gave Min Yang almost unlimited power to demand whatever he wanted from the world.

I maintained my steely stair as Pok fidgeted, giving me more telltale signs that he was hiding something and that I was on to him.

"Ahh, . . The Lazarus Group. Do you believe in unicorns as well, Mr. Hardy?" Pok asked sarcastically. He was definitely lying. His eyes flittered to the left. His head tilted, and his voice inflections changed.

"I'll believe in one when I see it," I replied, staring straight ahead, my eyes affixed to his.

And I've just seen one.

"I have a question for you, Mr. Pok." I said.

He remained silent, probably not willing to admit his real identity even though the silence was just as telling.

"The Lazarus Group and The Judas Group. Why do you use biblical names?"

7

Iranian Embassy
Pyongyang, North Korea

Hamid Ahmadi, the Iranian Ambassador to North Korea, paced back and forth in his office. Amin Sadeghi, the Director of the MOIS, the Ministry of Intelligence and Security for the Islamic Republic of Iran was on the speaker phone.

Amin was demanding answers that Hamid didn't have.

"I don't know why Assad didn't make the drop," Hamid said nervously.

"Where is he?" Amin asked in an elevated voice.

"I don't know," Hamid said, using all his power to keep his voice from quivering.

"When did you last see him?" Amin asked more as an accusation than a question.

"This afternoon," Hamid answered. "I gave him the papers in Wonsan. That's the last I saw of him."

The papers were in a satchel. They contained the nuclear codes and passwords to Pakistan's nuclear weapons program. A North Korean cyber lab had hacked into Pakistan's server and stolen them. With those codes, Iran could commandeer control of all of Pakistan's weapons and launch them against targets in Israel and US bases in the middle east. Iran had promised North Korea several billion dollars for the information. A substantial down payment had already been made in exchange for the papers. The brilliance of the plan was that Pakistan would get the blame and the US retaliatory response. The whole scheme could never be tied back to Iran.

Now Assad and the papers were missing.

Assad was supposed to meet a contact in Wonsan early that evening and transfer the satchel. The contact would then smuggle it to Iran through Russia. Everything had gone according to plan until Assad didn't show up for the drop.

Amin was in a panic. They had both tried Assad's phone for several hours without a response.

"Do you trust him?" Amin asked.

"He's your man," Hamid countered, risking raising Amin's ire even further.

"You're in charge of the operation in North Korea. I'm thousands of miles away. I can't control what happens on the ground. All you had to do was deliver the papers and make sure he got them to the contact."

"Which I did. What happened afterward was beyond my control."

Hamid silently cursed.

This was a disaster in the making. He wasn't going to take the blame. Hamid paused to wait for Amin to voice an agreement, which never came.

"Assad has been an agent for years," Hamid continued after sitting down, thinking that might calm his nerves. "It seems unlikely that he would steal the satchel and just disappear. He'd be looking over his shoulder the rest of his life. Plus, he's loyal to the state and to Allah. It's been years since we've had a traitor among us. There has to be another explanation.

"You're right. He's my best agent," Amin said. "Why would Assad steal the codes? Who would he sell them to?"

Hamid poured himself a drink of water. His hand shook as he raised the glass to his mouth.

"I can go to Wonsan and look for him," Hamid said, although he didn't want to. It would be an hour and a half drive. He had dinner plans, which looked like they were about to be cancelled.

"Stay by your phone," Amin said. "I don't want you to risk missing a call from him."

"Could it be the Americans?" Hamid asked shuddering at the thought and feeling the blood drain from his face.

"That's always possible," Amin said furtively. "We've taken every precaution on our end. Who knows about the damn Koreans! The infidels are always trying to tap into their communications. The General assured me there would not be a problem."

"From their perspective, there wasn't," Hamid countered. "They're going to insist this is not their problem. They delivered the codes. Once they were in our hands it's our problem."

"We must find Assad!" Amin said. Hamid could hear the desperation in his voice. Amin reporting to his superiors that they lost the codes was like Hamid having to break the news to Amin. It wouldn't be pleasant.

"I don't even know where to start looking," Hamid said. "We're just going to have to hope he turns up."

"Call me as soon as you hear something," Amin said.

"Of course. You do the same."

Hamid hung up the phone slowly. It was going to be a long night.

***

The next morning, Hamid's phone rang. He answered it on the first ring. "*Annyeonghaseyo*," Hamid said into the phone, using the informal greeting of hello.

"Ambassador, my name is Ji-ho. I'm the Senior Colonel of Police in Wonsan."

North Korea had two domestic law enforcement agencies. The secret police, officially called the Ministry for Protection of State security and the local police, officially called the Ministry of People's Security. Based on his title, Ji-ho would be the highest-ranking police authority in the city of Wonsan.

If he was calling, it couldn't be good.

"How may I be of service to you, Colonel?" Hamid asked, dreading the response.

"Do you know Assad Fathi?" he asked.

Hamid's heart sank.

"Of course," Hamid answered, not wanting to give away too much information until he knew the reason for the call. If Assad had been arrested, it was better to keep a distant association, even though he had diplomatic immunity. In North Korea you were guilty until proven innocent. Hamid had read that there were only twenty not guilty verdicts in the North Korean judicial system over the last year. Even Iran had more than that.

"Why do you ask?" Hamid asked, trying to be proactive in the conversation.

"Assad is dead. His body was found on a walking trail early this morning by a hiker. Shot to death."

Why was Assad on a mountain trail? He was to meet his contact in a restaurant by the sea.

"How did you identify Assad?" Hamid asked, wanting to ask about the satchel but waiting for the right time.

"His passport and papers were in his suit coat pocket."

No mention of the satchel.

Assad had entered North Korea on a business visa and the higher ups in the DPRK were fully aware of his identity and presence.

"Do you have a suspect?" Hamid asked.

"We don't at this time. It looks like a professional hit to me. The shot was precise. It went right through his heart. Whoever shot him was proficient with a gun. There's no other evidence at the scene."

Here came the most important question as Hamid finally got up the nerve to ask. "Did you find anything else on him? A briefcase or satchel?"

"No," Ji-ho said. "We didn't find a weapon either. The scene was completely cleaned of evidence. The only thing we know is that he was having dinner at a restaurant down by the boardwalk. He abruptly left shortly after his meal was brought to the table. Mr. Fathi didn't even finish his meal, nor did he pay for it."

"That's strange."

"Somebody led him away from his meal, to his execution. Are you aware if Mr. Fathi had any enemies?"

"I was going to ask you that question," Hamid answered. "Why would someone kill Assad? Do you think it was a robbery?"

"His wallet was still in his pocket," Ji-ho answered. "He had a watch on his wrist and a ring on his finger. A robber would've taken those."

"That rules out a robbery," Hamid said, playing along. He already knew that the satchel was the real target. It had to be a professional. Assad was too skilled to be killed by a local robber.

But who was the professional assassin who hunted Assad down and stole the satchel, and why did he kill him? That was obvious. Assad wouldn't have given up the bag easily. He died a hero protecting the bag. But how did the assassin even know what was in the bag?

He had more questions than answers.

"There's one surveillance camera in the area," Ji-ho said. "We're checking it to see if it caught any images of the killer."

"Please let me know, Colonel, if you find out anything. I'm concerned that an Iranian businessman would be targeted for assassination."

"I'll let you know as soon as I have more information," Ji-ho said.

"Thank you."

Hamid hung up the phone and called the Director on his direct, secured line.

"Assad is dead."

"I know. I just heard," Amin said.

Hamid was surprised, although he realized immediately that he shouldn't have been. The reach of the MOIS never ceased to amaze him. They usually knew things before he did.

"I just spoke with an investigator," Hamid said. "No satchel was found."

"This is a disaster."

"Should I contact the General?" Hamid asked. He was referring to Im Song, the man who coordinated the transfer of the codes and was one of the highest-ranking members of Min Yang's inner circle.

"You'd better," Amin said. "I have to go break the news on my end."

Hamid was glad that Amin was no longer using a threatening tone with him. A somber resignation had set in over him.

"How can we find that satchel?" Hamid asked. "Someone has it. The investigator said it was a professional hit job."

"The Americans!" Amin said almost shouting. Hamid heard something slam down on the other end. His fist or some object in his office.

"Most likely. The investigator said that there is a surveillance camera near where it happened. Assad was having dinner, and someone interrupted him. He left without eating or paying. He was killed up on a mountain trail."

"We have to get our hands on that video surveillance tape," Amin said. "It might shed some light on what happened."

"How can we do that?" Hamid asked. "The investigator won't give it to me."

"The North Koreans aren't the only ones who can hack into a computer," Amin said. "I'll get my own people working on it. Most surveillance tapes are stored on the cloud. Let's just hope this one is."

"Good idea. Let me know how I can help."

"Go to Wonsan," Amin said. "Ask around. See if you can find out anything. Somebody saw something. I want whoever did this hunted down and shot like a dog."

"Director, I'm an ambassador," Hamid retorted nervously. "I'm a diplomat. I'm not trained to take on an assassin."

"I'm not talking about you," Amin said roughly. "I'm sending two men. Omid Froohan and Jaffar Abdi. They are two of my best killers. Make all the arrangements for their arrival. Let the Koreans know so they aren't harassed. We must find that satchel."

"I'm leaving for Wonsan, now," Hamid said. "We'll find whoever is responsible for this."

"Inshallah," Amin said.

God wills it.

8

The term *hacker* had always been a somewhat controversial term. Some cyber criminals argued that they were the good guys, waging war against the big corporations and those who oppressed the poor and polluted the environment. Others said they were just pushing the boundaries of knowledge, with no intention of doing anyone any harm. They preferred the term *unauthorized user*.

I'd always considered myself a soldier in a battle between good and evil.

After spending the last ten hours with the notorious Gi Man Pok, the most infamous hacker who ever lived, I could see where the lines were blurred. Under any other circumstances, we would be the best of friends. Like me, he didn't do it for the money. He did draw questionable ethical lines, refusing to participate in schemes that stole money from the poor, but willing to steal what did not belong to him, nonetheless. More than once, he insisted that he only stole from those who could afford to lose it and from financial institutions he believed were the real criminals in the world; the corporate elite who accumulated wealth on the backs of oppressed people.

"I'm like that American hero, Robert Hood," he'd said.

"Robin Hood," I corrected.

"Right. Right. Right." Pok said the word *right* a lot, inserting them between the words fairly often. Not unlike teenagers who inserted the word *like* in almost every sentence whether it needed it or not.

Such were the rants I listened to most of the night, mixed in with diatribes espousing the virtues of communism and socialism.

"Everyone in North Korea gets free health care, right?" he had argued.

I held back answering, just nodding occasionally.

"All the people get a minimum guaranteed income. Right? Every month," he said defensively several times.

That guaranteed income is below the poverty line I wanted to argue back but bit my tongue. Almost every American had a cell phone, cable television, a refrigerator, and most other basic conveniences that a large portion of the world didn't have. While our system of democracy wasn't perfect, we built the most prosperous country in the history of the world. An opinion I kept mostly to myself.

"What's criminal," Pok said, "is that there are so many millionaires in America. Right?"

"Everyone in Venezuela is a millionaire," I countered. "But no one can afford a loaf of bread!" He may have just been trying to get a rise out of me. If he was, then he succeeded.

His arguments would've actually held some weight if he didn't practice his vast skills on behalf of the most oppressive government in the world. One that consistently persecuted and ruled its people with the ruthlessness of a Stalin, Lenin, Mao, or Hitler. Only Min Yang and his family were billionaires in North Korea. A few elites and oligarchs lived in luxury. Everyone else barely eked out an existence.

Pok made some vague attempt at justifying his criminal activity that fell on deaf ears with me. As time went on, the lines of good and evil re-formed in my mind and helped me to confirm my moral superiority and justification for what I intended to do, which was to bring his organization to its knees.

By the morning, I had grown to despise the man, even more than I did before I met him.

I no longer even admired his skills. A serial killer might be good at killing and not getting caught, but his abilities were not to be lauded.

Pok went to get us some breakfast, which was great because I was starving and tired. The night before, I only grabbed a couple hours of sleep on his couch. I wanted to go lie back down but had work to do before Pok returned.

Halee, sleep when you're dead, Curly had said during one of his many training exercises where we had to go days with only a few hours of sleep.

I'd feel better when Pok got back with coffee. That would give me a burst of energy. At the moment, I appreciated the time he was away. It helped me to formulate my plan.

As far as Pok was concerned, we had become the best of friends, and he had come to appreciate my skills. I had little to no compunction about keeping up the ruse and even formulated a thought about possibly kidnapping and delivering him to the CIA. The world would be better off without the menace preying on society, no matter how altruistic he thought his motives to be.

I ruled out that option. Gaining access to his computer was my primary focus. He'd given me limited access to his computer network. I could get in now, but the risk of getting caught was greater. When he got back, I would take complete access—with or without his permission.

My work was interrupted by an alert that came up on his computer.

I opened it, but not before looking around to see if anyone was watching me. From my vantage point, I had a clear line of sight to the elevators and would know when Pok arrived back at the building, so I decided to open it.

The alert signified a potential hack to his network. More than likely, he got thousands of them every day. I wondered what was so important about this one.

I started investigating. Several minutes later, I discovered that someone was trying to hack into the Korean Internet service provider, Star JV. Apparently, Pok had the responsibility of protecting North Korea's government-controlled internet called Kwangmyong, along with his task of attacking foreign websites. To use a football analogy, Pok played on both sides of the ball. Both offense and defense.

Min Yang was known to heavily surf the internet, and it became clear that Pok had the responsibility to protect him from his sometimes reckless behavior. It probably kept Pok up at night.

General phishing scams weren't much of a threat to North Korea. The government only gave permission for roughly thirty businesses to even have a domain. Most commoners had no access to the internet and might not even know about its existence, so the risk of malware and email scams and viruses infecting individual computers was low. The Supreme Commander was one of the few who ventured out onto the net far enough to become a prey for hackers.

This particular alert was interesting to me. I also saw it as an opportunity to show Pok more of my skills. First, I needed to discover the source. Pok arrived right after I did so.

"Here are your four egg sandwiches," he said almost mockingly, like he couldn't believe I could eat four at one time. "And your three cups of coffee," he added with a chuckle.

"What?" I said, taking the bag from him. "I'm still a growing boy."

Pok was older than me, but only by a couple years. I figured him to be twenty-eight or twenty-nine. Like most Asian men, he barely weighed a hundred and fifty pounds, soaking wet. From my experience, Koreans ate like birds. Not surprisingly, he finished his one sandwich, shortly after I finished my four.

"Someone's trying to hack into your system," I said. "You got an alert."

Pok exploded out of the side chair on the other side of the desk and bolted around to where I was sitting and demanded I get up.

"You opened the alert!" he said roughly. "No one gave you permission to look at my personal information."

"Settle down," I said, with anxiety rising in me. I needed to calm him down. "I already identified the source for you."

He ignored me as he read the alert. His fingers typed furiously. I walked to the other side of the desk to give him privacy and also to try and remain calm. With the coffee and his sudden outburst, adrenaline flowed through me like a volcano about to explode. I couldn't let him see my concern. Maybe it was a mistake to open the alert. I might've blown all the goodwill I'd built up overnight.

I decided to press the issue further to make him think I didn't do anything wrong. I got up from my chair and walked behind the desk and looked over his shoulder.

"You go back and sit down," he shouted, putting his hand up to block the screen.

"All right," I said, lackadaisically. "But I can save you a bunch of time. I already know who's trying to hack your system. By the time you find out, they'll already be gone."

"I know what I'm doing. If I don't hurry, they'll get in."

"They're already in," I said. "You're too late. I can even tell you what they're looking for."

"That's impossible," Pok argued. "That alert only came in a few minutes ago. It takes several hours to find the source, even if it can be found. Most hackers are getting good at hiding their identities."

I shrugged my shoulders.

He continued typing with a purpose.

"Do you want my help or not?" I said, sarcastically.

"No. I don't need your help. I should have you arrested for even looking at the alert."

"The Iranians are the hackers."

He stopped typing. His eyes went from the computer screen, to me, then back to the screen without even moving his head.

"How do you know that?" Pok said.

"I told you. I already found them. If we hurry, we can find out what they're looking for before it's too late." I'd lied earlier when I said I knew what they were looking for, but Pok didn't catch the inconsistency of my words.

He stopped typing and stood to his feet, making a motion with his hand for me to take his place.

Several keystrokes later, I was at the source.

"See," I said. "This is an Iranian computer trying to hack your system."

"That's incredible," Pok said with his mouth opened and his eyes widened in amazement.

"Let's find what they are looking at," I said.

More keystrokes for several minutes led me closer to the source.

"There... in the Azure Cloud," Pok said.

"Do you want me to stop them or let them keep going so we can find out what they're looking for?"

"Let's follow them around," Pok replied. "But don't lose them."

"They're snooping around Wonsan. What's in Wonsan that the Iranians would be interested in?" I asked.

"I don't know," Pok said. "That's strange behavior, right? The Iranians are an ally. We never see a hack from them. Are you sure someone is not pointing to them, but it's originating from another source? The Americans maybe?"

A computer hacker had many ways to disguise his activities. A common practice was to make it look like the hack was coming from a different source.

"They are using the Tor network, but I know how to get around it," I said. The Tor Network used multiple tunnels across the globe and bounced the signal around various servers, making it hard to track. It still had to originate at one source and with one Tor browser. Iranians weren't as sophisticated as the CIA in tracking, so they were easy to catch. That's why I could find them so fast.

The question of why the Iranians would be looking for information in Wonsan was still unanswered, and I was curious. I opened up another browser and began searching for information.

"Don't lose the Iranians," Pok said with urgency.

"I won't. I'll find them. But look at this," I said. I had entered a search for chatter related to Iran and Wonsan over the last twenty-four hours.

Pok read what I found out loud. "An Iranian MOIS operative, was killed in Wonsan. A professional hit job. The CIA is suspected." Pok looked at me suspiciously.

"Don't look at me," I said jokingly, raising my hands in the air in a fake surrender pose. "I never did field work. I prefer working out of an office where I don't get shot at."

That wasn't true. I was happiest when I was in the field. Like in college. I preferred football practice and games to sitting behind a computer. It just happened that computers were what I was good at. In training, Curly said I had the second-highest score in hand-to-hand combat and weapons proficiency.

"Who was first?" I had asked.

"Jamie Austen" Curly said. The woman who was now my girlfriend, maybe someday my wife.

My thoughts turned back to the computer as I rushed back to find the Iranians.

"Here, let me take over," Pok said, motioning for me to get out of his chair. "You're doing fine. I'm just more familiar with our internet. I can make it go faster."

Pok attacked the keyboard like I attacked the four egg sandwiches. He gave me a running commentary along the way.

"They are looking for a security camera. In the Wonsan Tourist

Zone," Pok said. "There's only one in the area, right?" he asked as if I would know.

"It's on a construction site," he said. "The time of the murder was last night."

Pok laid out the details methodically.

"He was killed on a mountain trail," I said remembering the information from my search.

"There are no security cameras on the trail," he added. "Only down by the boardwalk."

Pok paused, clearly thinking. Then he began typing again.

A few more keystrokes later, he said, "The Iranian operative was last seen eating dinner at a restaurant."

A half a minute later. "Here we go," Pok said almost under his breath. "I found the camera."

He rewound the video. I was impressed with the ease in which he maneuvered effortlessly around the internet. I tended to pound on the keyboard. Probably because my hands were so much bigger than his.

He stopped and pointed excitedly.

"Look right there!" Pok said. "That's the man."

"How do you know?" I asked.

"He's middle eastern. How many Iranians are having dinner in Wonsan around that time? None. I imagine."

"At least one," I said, correcting him.

A lone man sat at a restaurant on a boardwalk. A bag that looked like a satchel sat at his feet. The image was grainy, but we could see enough to know he was middle eastern. He also had that look of an operative. I'd seen it many times. Curly worked our tails off trying to knock that look out of us.

"No way!" Pok said. "I can't believe what I just saw."

I couldn't believe it either. A young girl walked right up to the table, stole the operative's satchel, and walked away. The man got up and followed her. The camera captured their movements until the girl started running out of the screen.

That same man was found dead several hours later.

Who killed him?

And who was that girl?

9

Pok knew more about the situation with the young girl stealing the satchel than he was letting on, which raised my curiosity even further. The whole thing made no sense. Pok was right. Iran was an ally. Why would one of their agents be killed in North Korea? And why would the Iranians need to hack into North Korea's computer system to access the security camera? Surely, they could get whatever information they wanted from the North Korean investigators.

The only explanation was that there was some highly valuable and sensitive information in that satchel.

But what did I care? *Not my problem.* One less Iranian operative walking around on this earth was a good thing. God bless whoever killed him. I had more important things to consider. If I got my own computer, I'd investigate further.

I was about to take a big step toward that end right now.

"What can I do for the Lazarus Group?' I asked Pok. "I think I've proven my abilities."

"You should be the one answering that question," Pok responded. "What *can* you do for us? I'm not sure."

"I can get you in places you can't go," I said.

"Such as?"

There was a long moment of silence. I was sitting in the chair across from Pok on the other side of the desk. He was in front of his computer.

"Pick a company you want to access," I finally said.

I hoped he chose one on my list.

"The CIA," he said.

I laughed out loud.

"I want to be alive tomorrow," I answered.

"I thought they don't know where you are?" Pok retorted.

"If I hack into the CIA, they'll know it's me," I said. "I'm the only person in the world, capable of doing it."

There was another long moment of silence. "But... Every time I turn on a car, I'll wonder if it's going to blow up. Even worse, I'll wonder if some drone at 35,000 feet, that I can't see, is going to blow me to smithereens. Right now, I'm not on their radar. I want to keep it that way."

"You asked for a company," Pok said flippantly.

"How about we start with something a little less ambitious?" I said.

"You pick a company."

Perfect.

Just what I wanted to hear.

"FCI," I said. FCI was Financial Capital Investments. The largest hedge fund in the world.

This time Pok was the one who laughed out loud. "Now who's the one being ambitious!" Pok said sarcastically. "I've been trying to get into them for years."

"How about I transfer a million dollars from one of their investment accounts into your bank account just to prove it to you?"

"I'll believe it when I see it."

"Prepare to be amazed, Daniel-san," I said in my best Chinese accent. "I need a computer and one hour to hack into the site."

"Who's Daniel-san?" Pok asked with a puzzled look on his face as his mouth twisted to the side.

"Mr. Miyagi? The *Karate Kid*? Don't tell me you've never heard of that movie." American movies were banned in North Korea, but I figured he'd seen at least a bootlegged copy.

Pok shrugged his shoulders, clearly not understanding the joke.

"Never mind," I said, waving my hand dismissively. "Where do you want me to do my work?"

"You can use my computer," Pok said.

All the better.

***

Pok wanted to look over my shoulder.

"No way I'm going to show you my secrets," I said adamantly. "We haven't even discussed the terms of our relationship. This is like a job interview. We're checking each other out. The million is a free-bie. A goodwill gesture on my part."

"If you can steal a million from FCI any time you want, why do you need to be paid by me?"

"A fair question. I have bigger plans for us than just stealing money."

"Like what?"

"One step at a time. Let me prove to you that I can access FCI, and we can go from there."

"How do I know it's not a trick?" Pok asked nervously.

"You still don't trust me," I said jokingly. "I'm offended."

"You'll get over it," he retorted.

"When a million dollars shows up in your account, you'll know it's not a trick."

"I locked my computer, so don't even think of trying anything," Pok said. "You can get on the web, just not on our site."

I wanted to say that I could get on their site anytime I wanted. How did they think I found their facility to begin with? Instead, I just said, "I don't want to be on your site."

As soon as he was out of the sight of the computer screen, the first thing I did was unlock his computer. It took an extra minute of my time from the one hour. Pok was watching me nervously. I asked for some water, and he refused to go and get it. He had someone bring it in.

It was an anxious hour for both of us.

***

"I'm in," I said an hour later.

I could've said that after ten minutes but pretended to work for the full hour to make it look more realistic.

"I don't believe you," Pok replied.

"See for yourself," I said, starting to turn the screen toward him. Instead, Pok stood up from the chair on the other side of the desk and walked around it so he was behind me. On the screen was the site structure of the website for Financial Capital Investments.

Or at least it appeared so to Pok.

He let out a noticeable gasp of delight. I let him control the mouse as he navigated around it, acting like a kid in a candy store.

FCI managed 150 billion dollars in assets. From Pok's perspective, he had just struck gold.

"Pick a letter between A and Z?" I said to Pok taking control of the mouse.

"A," he said.

"A it is." I began typing and pulled up the investment account for Mr. Richard Adams. The balance in his account was over ten million dollars allocated among several investments.

Pok examined the page carefully.

Richard Adams didn't exist and neither did the account. But Pok didn't know that. What he was looking at was a fake copy of the real website. I hoped there weren't any obvious mistakes on the web page.

"You're amazing. I'm impressed," Pok said.

You have no idea how impressed you should be. Now if Brad Rice will cooperate, we'll work some magic.

Brad Rice was my handler with the CIA. Two years ago, I went to him with an idea for a software program. He rejected the idea and said it couldn't be done. For a year, I spent every minute of my spare time working on the program. With limited resources, the best I could do was a rudimentary skeleton of the idea. When I showed it to him, he was so impressed he took it to the CIA security council and got approval for me to build the software program with a team of ten programmers and a four-million-dollar budget.

The result was a computer virus so lethal we had to work out of our own computer lab, with a separate server. It was like working with a pandemic virus at the Centers for Disease Control. Precautions had to be taken to make sure it never ended up on the web until the time was right, the program was fully developed, and safeguards were in place to control it.

It took us a year to finish it. When it was completed, I named the program *Kryptonite* because it was the Achilles heel to any computer system. Applied properly, it could permanently destroy any known computer system in the world.

The reason it took us so long to develop was that we had to reconstruct and build the websites of more than a thousand companies across the web as a front to hide the destructive virus underneath. Meticulous care was taken to build the sites to the exact dimensions of the real websites so that our facsimile was indistinguishable from the real thing. Like an art forger, creating a replica of the Mona Lisa. To pass as the real painting, it had to be perfect.

We had never used Kryptonite. The CIA was waiting for the right time. It seemed as good a time to me as any.

FCI was one of the companies on our list which was why I was glad I got to choose it. We duplicated their entire website including graphics and logos and created several thousand fake customer accounts as well. Once Pok gave me access to his computer, I logged into the Kryptonite program, and pulled up the FCI webpage.

Since I unlocked Pok's computer, if I gave Kryptonite permission, it could access the North Korean server and view everything happening, undetected. With a few strokes of the keyboard, Kryptonite could destroy the entire North Korean lab. More than likely, the CIA would want to mine the lab for information before destroying it.

I hadn't yet given the CIA permission. More trust needed to be earned with Pok so I didn't get arrested. Since Mr. Robert Adam's investment account was fake, so was the ten million dollars in investments. That money didn't exist. I needed the CIA to approve a transfer of one million dollars from a designated CIA account into the account Pok designated.

The moment I logged into Kryptonite, someone at CIA headquarters in Langley, Virginia was scrambling to notify a supervisor, who would no doubt be on the phone shortly to the Director of the CIA and probably Brad, since I logged in under my ID. I glanced at my watch. 9:45 a.m..

Not ideal. North Korea was thirteen hours ahead of Virginia, so it was 8:45 p.m. the night before. Hopefully, someone could be reached who could authorize a transfer. Protocols were in place for such a contingency. The CIA didn't want an officer in the field, hanging out to dry, while someone in Virginia was at a baseball game or a movie or having dinner.

I just needed for them to cooperate so I could continue the ruse and gain Pok's trust further. I stalled for time, giving Langley time to get in touch with the right people.

"I need your wiring instructions," I finally said to Pok. "What account do you want the money to go into?"

Pok reached in the drawer and pulled out a list that appeared to be several accounts. He wrote down a routing number and account number.

The website had a process for filling out the transfer of money.

"There's a fifteen-dollar fee if you want the money instantly deposited," I said to Pok, laughing.

"I'll take it out of your commission," Pok said with anticipation building in the room.

The anticipation was both his and mine. I was as anxious as he was to see if the CIA would really transfer the money. If they didn't, I was in serious trouble.

I acted like I was checking and double checking the numbers.

"Are you ready?" I asked.

I hit send. Now, all we could do was wait.

10

Arlington, Virginia
11:05 p.m.

When the phone rang, violently awakening him from an intense dream, Maxwell Grant wasn't happy. The red digital letters on the clock confirmed what he had suspected. He'd only been asleep for four hours.

"This better be important," he muttered to himself. He rolled his nearly three-hundred and fifty-pound frame to a halfway seated position, rubbed his eyes with the palm of his hand, cleared his throat, and grunted out a greeting.

"Yeah," he said gruffly.

"Director, this is Brad Rice. I'm sorry to bother you at this late hour."

By his own admission, Grant was an unlikely choice for the position of Director of the CIA. The un-consummate politician, Grant's personality was abrasive, brusque, rude, crude, and basically socially unacceptable for a position that required tact and diplomacy. The President trusted him which was why he had the position.

"Not as sorry as I am," Grant said, almost to himself. "What's going on?"

"I don't know."

"Well, remind me to fire you first thing in the morning, and hire someone who does know," Grant said roughly and only half kidding. He'd never fire Brad, but that didn't mean he didn't feel like doing so at that moment.

"You know about the possible data breach with the Pakistani nuclear codes," Brad said.

"You're the one who briefed me on it!" The words came out more vitriolic than Grant intended, but they might have the desired effect. "I think I'll go ahead and fire you tonight since you've clearly lost your short-term memory. Either that or you think I've lost mine."

"You also know that an Iranian operative was killed in North Korea yesterday," Brad added, not acknowledging the rude comments.

"Brad," Grant said slowly. "Let me ask you a question. Do you think I'm stupid?"

"I'm sorry?"

"Do you think I'm stupid?"

"No sir. I think you're brilliant."

"Then why are you calling me in the middle of the night, to tell me things you already told me today?"

Brad never called. He was one of his most trusted men. It must be important if he was calling this late at night. That didn't mean he wouldn't give him a hard time. It was time for him to get to the point.

"I just wanted to remind you of the facts, sir," Brad said, apologetically.

Grant's one pet peeve was being unnecessarily bothered at home especially at night. He got up early and went to bed even earlier which wasn't ideal for a CIA Director. Most of the bad actors in the world were in hemispheres several hours ahead of Virginia time, and, more often than not, most crises arose in the middle of the night. Grant's directives were for his employees to handle it themselves, if at all possible. That's what he paid them for, he insisted. If it was a real emergency, then they shouldn't hesitate to call. Brad was testing the limits of his patience.

"I don't need reminding," Grant retorted. "I'm well aware of the data breach and the dead Iranian. I'll sleep better tonight knowing there's one less Iranian spook in the world. That's *if* I ever get to sleep. Is that what you called to tell me?"

"No sir. Alex Halee just accessed Kryptonite. From a North Korean server."

The Director sat straight up in his bed. Suddenly, fully awake. "What the hell is Halee doing in North Korea?"

"I don't know."

"He's your man! You don't know what your operatives are doing?"

"You know Halee."

"Did Halee kill the Iranian?" the Director asked, suddenly connecting the dots. It became clear why Brad felt the need to remind him of the Pakistan security breach and the dead Iranian. It's possible that all three were connected.

"I don't know, sir. But that's an assumption that wouldn't be out of the realm of possibility."

Grant rubbed his face roughly. His mind raced. Processing and analyzing the data points. The consequences were mind blowing if he allowed his thoughts to go to their logical conclusion. He tried hard to rein them in and process them separately. He was good at analyzing facts and spitting out solutions that usually seemed to work out for the best.

A Junior World Chess Champion, Grant had the uncanny ability to see the complex world as chess pieces and keep the United States two moves ahead of everyone else. His sharp mind allowed him to assimilate facts quickly and process a successful strategy even his most ardent critics were amazed by.

"Somebody hacked into Pakistan's nuclear server and stole their codes," Grant said, speaking out loud. "North Korea is one of many possible suspects. So are the Iranians. But we don't know who's behind the hack. An Iranian operative was found murdered in North

Korea. There was chatter of a satchel missing. Now, Halee is trying to access Kryptonite from a North Korean computer."

"Those are the dots, sir," Brad said. "I'm trying to decide if the dots should be connected. If not, it's a pretty big coincidence."

"Of course, they're connected! I don't believe in coincidences," Grant bellowed, anger building inside of him the longer the conversation continued.

"Halee is supposed to be in South Korea," Brad said, defensively.

"Damn it!"

"I sent him there to find the North Korean cyber lab. Apparently, he found it and for whatever reason decided to pay it a visit."

Grant got out of bed now. Paced the room. He was probably going to have to go to the office.

"Is Halee dumb enough to go to North Korea on his own?" Grant asked.

"You know the answer to that question as well as I do, sir."

"Are we sure Halee is definitely in North Korea?" Grant asked, not hardly believing what he was hearing. For a moment, he wondered if he was still dreaming. "Any chance he's just pointing his computer there? The man is a magician on a computer. A master illusionist. It could be a ruse."

There were a lot of unanswered questions that made it hard to come to any conclusions. Grant hated making assumptions, even though his job required him to do so almost every day. Very few things were certain in the world of espionage.

"It's possible, but I don't think so," Brad said, hesitantly. "If it were anybody else, I'd say no. But it's Halee we're talking about. I think he found the lab, snuck across the border, and found a way to infiltrate it. My analyst says the request is coming from the North Korean lab. It's the same lab we believe the Judas Group is acting out of. God only knows how he could've infiltrated it and still be alive to tell about it!"

"Any chance it's not Halee?" Grant asked. "Could Kryptonite be hacked?"

"The person logged in using Halee's passcode. I think it's him."

"He could've given it to the North Koreans under duress."

"I don't think Halee would cave. Not this quickly."

"When did you last hear from him?" Grant asked.

"Two days ago. He messaged me that he found the North Korean lab. He sent me the location. It's about thirty minutes south of Wonsan."

"The Iranian was killed in Wonsan," Grant said.

"Yes sir."

"Like I said, I don't believe in coincidences." Grant paused. "The North Korean lab stole the codes and sold them to Iran. The operative was in North Korea to pick up the codes."

Grant was thinking off the top of his head. It helped him to verbalize it. Brad was as good as anyone in his knowledge of the field. He would have some input.

"Halee discovered the missing codes and learned about the handoff," Grant continued. "He went to North Korea, stole the satchel. That's why it's missing. Then he killed the Iranian. I don't understand why the hell he didn't get out of dodge right then. Why hang around and try to infiltrate the lab?"

"It doesn't make sense, sir," Brad agreed.

"We should let it play out," Grant said. "If Halee is accessing Kryptonite then let him. Let's see what happens. If he somehow infiltrated the Judas Group, there would be a treasure trove of information to mine."

"It's not as simple as that," Brad said.

"Why not?"

"Halee is wanting to transfer a million dollars from Kryptonite to a North Korean account that is controlled by Gi Man Pok."

"What!" Grant exploded in vitriol. "You're just now telling me that piece of information. You might've led with it."

"He sent in the request a few minutes ago. That's why I called you," Brad said, not responding to the outburst. "What do you want me to do?"

"That changes things," Grant said. "We need to verify that it's definitely Halee before we do that. Is there any way to get in touch with him?"

"I've tried," Brad said. "I called his hotel and his cell phone several times. I sent him emails. My guess is he went into North Korea without them. In case he was captured. The devices have sensitive information on them. If Halee's in North Korea, he doesn't want them to think he's still with the CIA. That would get him killed in a matter of minutes. I'm assuming he's trying to convince them that he's gone rogue and the money is his way of proving it. His way of gaining their trust."

Grant processed the information. This was a hornet's nest about to get stirred up. Ever since the US declared North Korea and Iran part of the "axis of evil," every action had significant ramifications. If the world learned that a CIA officer gunned down an Iranian operative inside North Korea, the world outcry would be overwhelming.

"What do you want me to do?" Brad asked.

"Deny the request."

"We could get Halee killed, sir." Brad raised his voice as the tension of the call reached an apex.

"It's his own fault! No one gave him authorization to go to North Korea. If he's stupid enough to do so, then..." Halee was a valuable asset. He genuinely liked the kid and was impressed with his abilities. But not enough to risk his own career over it.

"I don't disagree," Brad said. "Still we can't hang him out to dry. If we give him the million, and he's able to infiltrate the North Korean cyber lab, we could set them back by two years. If he killed the Iranian and took the nuclear codes, he'll deserve a medal when he gets home."

"It's too big a risk. He's on his own. He got himself into this mess, he'll have to get himself out of it."

Brad began to voice what was probably going to be a further objection, but Grant cut him off. "Deny the request!" Grant said adamantly.

"Yes sir."

"I'm going back to bed. Although, I doubt I'll be able to sleep. Call me if anything else comes up."

11

Masikryong Hotel
Wonsan, North Korea

Hamid Ahmadi, the Iranian Ambassador to North Korea, sat in his hotel room trying to make sense of what had happened in Wonsan two days before. He met with the investigator, viewed the security camera, and questioned the waiter at the restaurant, along with a shop owner who saw Assad chasing the young girl down the boardwalk with the satchel in her hand.

The pieces started coming together in his mind. He had to get his thoughts crystallized before Amin Sadeghi, the Director of the MOIS, called, demanding answers.

Only one thing made sense, but he hated to verbalize it to his boss for fear of creating an international incident. This crisis had made its way to the top of the Iranian government. Word was that the Ayatollah himself, the Supreme Leader, was aware of the events and wasn't happy.

Surely, no one was blaming him. He'd know more from the tenor of his upcoming call. He was ready to defend his actions if necessary. All he did was deliver the codes to Assad. He was miles away when Assad was ambushed, and the satchel stolen.

Regardless of how the events unfolded, he couldn't help but feel a sense of dread. Like his life was in danger. From whom, he wasn't sure. The North Koreans, possibly, if they were behind the missing satchel, which was the working theory at the moment. Perhaps, an

American assassin on the loose in North Korea, determined to kill everyone responsible for the transfer of the codes, including him. Maybe even his own government. If they blamed him in some way.

The drive to Wonsan from Pyongyang had been fearful. He continually looked in his rearview mirror for any sign of a shadowy threat. The North Koreans were ruthless when someone came in their crosshairs. Min Yang and his band of killers made retribution against enemies—routine in North Korea.

The American assassin, if one existed, could strike at any time, and who knew who he might be targeting. The Iranian government would do it by ordering him home. Once there, he would just disappear. Death wouldn't be immediate, though. It would be long, drawn out, and painful.

His first choice would be the American assassin. That would be quick and relatively painless in comparison. There might even be an opportunity for a deal. An exchange of information for his life. He'd never betray his country under normal circumstances but wouldn't hesitate if it meant saving his life. Especially for something he didn't do.

Actually, his first choice would be to stay alive. Blaming the infidels of America was usually the best way to ensure that. The hatred in his government for Americans ran deep. However, the evidence all pointed to a different conclusion. One he would share with Amin as soon as he called. Sharing those thoughts were risky, but he felt like it was the right thing.

As if on cue, his cell phone rang. An unknown international number appeared on the caller ID.

International calls were forbidden in North Korea, but as a formal diplomat he was given an exception. The call could be closely monitored by the government, although it took them days to decipher phone calls and create transcripts, if they even bothered. The powers that be were more concerned about cracking down on illegal phones smuggled in from China than they were about foreign diplomats of allies such as Iran. High tech devices that jammed the communications and tracked the illegal phones had been deployed all across North Korea with some degree of success. He was certain they wouldn't bother with his phone.

Even so, just in case, they spoke in Farsi, a native Iranian language, knowing North Korea wouldn't have a translator readily available to decipher that language.

"We've been double-crossed," Hamid said, getting right to the point after the formal greetings.

"By whom?" Amin asked.

"By the North Koreans."

"That's impossible!"

"It's very possible. I've seen the video from the security camera."

"So, have I," Amin retorted. "All it shows is that the satchel was stolen by a young girl."

"I know who the young girl is," Hamid said. He'd been sitting on the edge of his bed. After saying that, he walked over to the window and looked out onto the street. The Masikryong Hotel was a luxury hotel in Wonsan. He could've requested a room with a better view but chose the street view on purpose. From his vantage point, he could see who might be parked on the street, watching the hotel. So far, he hadn't seen anyone, although he'd heard that American spies weren't easily detected.

"Who is the girl?" Amin demanded to know.

"She's the daughter of Min Yang's cousin. I recognized her from a party that was held at the Presidential Palace complex. Her father holds a high position in the regime."

Nothing was said for what seemed like a minute as that information sank in.

"Why would the North Koreans use a girl to steal the satchel?" Amin asked.

Hamid had anticipated that question and had an answer ready. "The perfect ruse," Hamid said. "Think about it. Assad is a trained agent. If a man approached him, he'd be suspicious. He'd never consider a little girl a threat to take the satchel."

"That was a question that has bothered me," Amin said. "I've been wondering how Assad could've fallen for such a trick. It's obvious now. Your explanation makes sense."

Hamid breathed a sigh of relief.

"But the girl couldn't have killed Assad," Amin added.

"The way I figure it," Hamid said, "the girl stole the satchel and led Assad up to the mountain where he was ambushed. They didn't know there would be a security camera nearby or that we would ever see it."

"Why even transfer the codes if they were going to steal them back?"

Before Hamid could answer, Amin came to his own conclusion. "They want us to think it's the Americans!"

"Exactly! Why would we suspect the Koreans? They're the ones who sold us the codes."

"Those snakes! They stole the codes, sold them to us, then stole them back before we could use them," Amin said angrily. "After the money changed hands. How do we even know the codes existed?"

"I saw them myself," Hamid answered. "Remember, I delivered the satchel to Assad. I inspected the papers before I transferred them to him. They seemed legitimate to me."

"They must pay!" Amin said. "My men are arriving tomorrow. Have you made all the arrangements?"

Hamid had. The plan was for the men to arrive by plane under aliases and tourist's visas. They would stay in the same hotel he was in.

"Yes. Everything is all set. What do you want the men to do?"

"Kill the entire family! In retribution."

"Including the girl?"

"Especially the girl. But not until they get the satchel back. We'll show the Koreans they can't steal from us."

"Do you think that's wise?" he asked, realizing that questioning Amin's judgment was risky.

"You may be right. We need to rethink this. Tell them to make it look like a professional hit. Like the Americans did it. Keep up the ruse. Tell the Koreans we believe the Americans are behind Assad's killing."

"Do you still want the girl killed? She's just a child."

"Yes. That will anger the Koreans even more. Not that there's anything they can do about it. The most they can do is rattle their chains and spout off a bunch of threats that the Americans don't take seriously. At least the Americans are scared of us."

There was a long pause in the conversation that Hamid did not dare interrupt.

"Tell them to get the satchel back and kill the girl and her parents. As soon as possible," Amin finally said.

Hamid wanted to object but didn't dare say another word. At least he was off the hook.

For now, anyway.

***

Bae was mad at herself. Still. Even though it had been two days since she stole the satchel from the businessman eating at the restaurant. Just thinking about it caused her hands to shake.

The images were still seared in her mind. She'd been chased up the mountain, shot at, and came within inches of losing her life. And for what? A satchel full of a bunch of worthless papers, and meaningless numbers. The only other thing she found in the satchel of any interest was a small device about the size of her thumb. It said USB on the back.

She had no idea what it was for nor did she care.

At first, she swore off ever stealing again. After thinking about it further, she concluded that she liked it and would only steal from North Koreans who weren't businessmen. She'd still avoid mothers with kids and college students, but everyone else was fair game.

Bae flexed her shoulder. It still hurt from the fall over the fence as did the painful scratch on her side. The thing that wasn't healing was her bruised ego. She thought she was better than that. Where did she mess up? The plan had been flawless, or so she thought.

The only conclusion she could reach was that the papers were more important to the businessman than most things were to people who she'd stolen from in the past. Not that she'd never been chased before. No one liked having their bag stolen. It's just no one had ever cared enough to pull out a gun. Carrying a gun was illegal in North Korea unless you were a member of the police or military.

That made her curious which was why she hadn't destroyed the items in the satchel. Someday, she might be able to make some sense out of the papers and understand why they were so important to the man.

She shuddered every time she thought about the gun.

Truthfully, though, she liked it.

If she were honest, it had been exhilarating. The chase. The gunshots. Fleeing for her life. Hiding in the bushes and the rocks. Somehow, she'd come out on top. She was still alive. The businessman wasn't.

That should mean something. A question formed in her mind. She asked her father the question that night at dinner once she got up the nerve.

"Father, what would I have to do to be a spy?" she asked.

He laughed at her. "That's a silly question. You're only thirteen."

"That's not silly," her mother said. "Answer her question, darling."

"A spy is a very prestigious position in North Korea. They are on the same level as Generals. You must do well in school. Then there is a special school you must attend."

"Where is the school, daddy?" Bae asked. She knew her dad had a high-ranking job with the regime; but she didn't know what it was or what it entailed.

"It's a secret spy school," he said, changing his voice to make it sound mysterious. "It's just outside Pyongyang.

"What do you learn there?"

"Things like firing a weapon," her dad answered. "Using explosive devices. Hand-to-hand combat skills. Physical fitness. You also have to learn Japanese and other languages."

Bae sat in amazement, her heart beating faster at the thought of learning those things.

"Can girls be spies?" Bae asked.

"Have you ever heard of Kim Hyon-hui?"

She shook her head no.

"She's one of the most famous North Korean spies. She went to the south and blew up an airliner. Killing a lot of people."

"Wow!"

"Anyway, study hard and do good in school, and maybe you can be a spy someday."

Bae decided right then and there.

That's exactly what she was going to do.

12

The Lazarus Group Cyber Lab
North Korea

The transaction request cannot be processed at this time.

I stared at the screen and muttered angrily under my breath, even though I half way expected it. I could hear the conversation in my head between my handler, Brad, and Director Maxwell Grant. Brad would be arguing for the release of the million dollars. The Director would be skeptical.

"This is an unauthorized mission," I could hear the Director say. He was probably in bed asleep when the phone call came. He'd be in a bad mood from being awakened.

"I trust Alex," Brad would argue. "This is the opportunity to hack into the North Korean cyber lab and unleash hell on their system. It's worth the risk."

The Director was a good guy, but he did things by the book. He was willing to stick his neck on the line for an officer if he had all the facts. In this instance, he had almost no facts. I couldn't blame him. This was my fault. They didn't know what I knew. They didn't even know for certain that the request had come from me.

If they could see me now. I had my fingers on Gi Man Pok's computer. No one in Langley would believe that was possible. All they had to do was agree to the million, and they were inside a North Korean cyber lab's computer system. They'd pay ten times that amount if they had that information.

The imagined conversation back in the United States raged in his head.

"Deny the request!" I could hear Director Grant say, the words rattling around in my mind. "Halee got himself in this mess! Let him get himself out of it." The Director's decision would be final. That's probably how it went down. I was sure it pained Brad to do it, but he had followed his boss's instructions and denied the transaction.

Now I was in deep you know what. My mother taught me to never say the words out loud even if I was thinking them.

I surveyed my options again. Again… because I'd spent the last ten minutes thinking about this very scenario. *What would I do if the request was denied?* I hadn't come up with a good solution then, and I didn't have one now. I saw Pok walking back toward his office where I sat in front of his computer agonizing over what to do.

I had to come up with something fast or I'd be led out of that building in handcuffs in a few minutes. Or worse, I'd find myself in a gunfight with twelve soldiers with Type 88 assault rifles.

I wasn't armed.

You're always armed, Halee, I heard Curly remind me in my head.

It's not the same. They have assault weapons and I don't.

I didn't have time for it, but the conversation raged on, nevertheless.

I did the math. Each assault rifle had at least thirty rounds in it if they were modified. Maybe as much as a hundred and fifty rounds. Eighteen hundred bullets to my none. I liked their odds better than my own.

I told you to abort the mission, I heard Curly say.

How did that help me?

Pok walked back into his office. He had taken a restroom break.

"Is something wrong?" he asked as I didn't get the look of exasperation off my face fast enough.

"The transaction was denied," I said. "I did some digging and any transaction over a 100K, requires passcode verification. His password is encrypted. It's going to take me some time to break the code."

Pok crossed his arms and put on a fake smile of disgust. "Why am I not surprised?"

"It's a minor setback," I said, seeing all my efforts flying out the window.

"I didn't believe you could do it anyway, and I was right." Pok said it with an increased pitch in voice, obviously sharing my frustration. He nervously tapped his fingers on the table, which increased my nervousness, if that was possible.

"Look," I countered. "I've been thinking about it. We shouldn't have been trying to take out a million the first time anyway."

Pok rolled his eyes and clenched his fist.

I needed to defuse the situation and fast. "Hear me out," I said. "If we steal a million, it will send all kinds of red flags through the system. They'll know they've been hacked."

"Yeah. So. What's your point?"

"Don't you want to steal more than a million? The fund is worth 150 *billion* dollars." I was sure to stress the billion. "Once I know how to get the passwords on these accounts, we can take a lot more money at once."

I could see the wheels spinning in his mind. The argument might be winning the day.

"I proved to you that I could get in the system," I argued. "You yourself admitted that you've been trying to do it for several years. With no success. I was able to do it. That should mean something."

My voice was higher pitched now as I spoke with increased urgency.

Pok shook his head. "No! No! You've proven nothing. The only proof is money in the bank. You want to prove yourself? I want to see money in my account. If you can't do that, I'll have you arrested. I was a fool for ever trusting you to begin with."

"Look at this," I said, turning the computer screen toward him. Robert Adams' account was still on the screen along with the red letters, *the transaction request cannot be processed at this time*. I clicked out of that. I didn't need for either of us to be reminded of that failure.

The screen flickered and we were back to Robert Adams fake overview page. I clicked on the documents tab. "Look at his statements. He has multiple $9800.00 transactions." I had gone into that page and put those transactions in while Pok was away and while I was waiting on Brad's approval of the million. For this very contingency.

"He's avoiding the ten-thousand-dollar disclosure limit," Pok said.

I wasn't sure if Pok would know that, but he did. Banks were required to report all transactions over ten thousand dollars to the IRS. Many people got around that by doing multiple transactions under the ten thousand dollars to avoid scrutiny. Robert Adams didn't exist and neither did the transactions, but Pok didn't know that.

"Right," Pok said. "So, what's your point?"

At least we were still talking. As long as there weren't guns pointed at me, I still had a ray of hope of getting out of this situation alive.

I hesitated. Unsure if my plan would work. My idea was to send another transaction request through. For $9,800.00. It would require Brad's approval back in Virginia. I had no idea if he would give it. If he didn't approve it, all hell was going to break loose in the lab. Maybe I could escape before the soldiers came after me. If not, I'd have to fight my way out.

Time for me to decide.

"I'll make the request for $9800.00," I blurted out, before I had finalized the decision in my head. "That won't require a passcode. That's better, anyway. Robert Adams probably won't notice the transaction. Neither will FCI. No one will know we breached his data. Then we can access as many accounts as we want. All at once. We'll steal billions before they know what happened."

I studied Pok for a long moment to see if the argument was winning the day.

"I like the idea," he finally said. "Make it happen. Let me know when it goes through. I'll check my account. If the money's there, we're in business. If it's not..."

"It will be there," I said assuredly, although deep down I wasn't confident at all.

Pok left the room as I began frantically typing on the keyboard. A few minutes later, Pok was back and so was Combover guy along with a couple of his armed friends. I looked up from my work and gave Pok a glare of disapproval. He ignored it.

The request was ready. I hit send.

Combover guy was grinning through his rotten and stained teeth. I tried not to give away my disdain for him. A jolt of panic went through my body when I realized that the safety on his gun was no longer off and his finger was locked on the trigger. Someone had obviously pointed it out to the idiot.

I looked back at the request and said a prayer. Then silently sent a plea to my handler.

Brad don't let me down.

***

CIA Headquarters
Langley, Virginia

Brad couldn't take his eyes off the computer screen. He was staring at the Kryptonite software program which was pulled up on his computer. If Alex made another request, he wanted it to come directly to him. His emotions fluctuated between anger and fear. Anger that Alex seemingly went off the reservation and did something as stupid as go into North Korea with no backup, no coordination, and no advanced planning. Fear that his life was in grave danger.

It was the most irresponsible thing he'd ever seen an officer of the CIA do.

He looked at his reflection on the computer screen. What he saw on his face gave away one of his many conflicting emotions. The look surprised him. What he saw was a smile and bright eyes. He was beaming with pride that Alex had been successful.

It was the most amazing feat he'd ever seen an officer of the CIA do.

Infiltrating a North Korean cyber lab, with no backup, no coordination, and no advanced planning was nothing short of miraculous. No one but Alex could've pulled something like that off. Well... maybe Alex's girlfriend Jamie. But no one else that he could think of.

His officers were like his children. When they were on an operation, he had trouble sleeping at night, worrying about their safety. Even though Alex didn't get his permission to go on the mission, that didn't mean Brad didn't care about the fact that he was in harm's way.

If it had been up to him, he would've paid the million. An officer like Alex was worth ten times that. No. A hundred times. That was the point. Alex's value to the Agency couldn't be measured in monetary terms. But it wasn't his decision. The Director probably made the right call under the circumstances. That didn't make it any easier.

The hardest part was not knowing. The waiting. He might not ever hear from Alex again. If Alex was arrested, he'd disappear.

They'd never know where they took him or what his fate was. The call to Jamie would be excruciating.

Don't get ahead of yourself.

This was a constant battle for Brad. His imagination always ran wild when his officers were in danger. He tried to envision in his mind what they were going through and what they were thinking. If he put himself in their predicament, it would help him understand the situation better and maybe make a better decision. He'd been in the field for twelve years and had been shot at more times than he could remember. Even wounded more than once. Brad had done things without headquarters approval. Nothing like what Alex did, but still, he could relate.

His computer screen roared to life bringing him back to reality. A new transfer request had come in. On Kryptonite. From Alex.

$9,800.00.

That was brilliant! Clever. Alex never ceased to amaze him. He pictured what was going through Alex's mind sitting in front of a similar computer in the North Korean lab. Alex had been forced to improvise. The North Koreans would have been furious that the million-dollar request was turned down. Alex probably made an argument that a million was too much anyway. He probably made up some excuse about needing a passcode or something.

Let's start smaller, he heard Alex tell them.

Under the ten-thousand-dollar banking limit.

An ingenious plan.

"What should I do?" Brad said, not realizing he was talking to himself out loud.

The options were running through his mind. He should call the Director.

Brad shuddered, his entire body spasmed. The thought of waking up the Director again wasn't a pleasant one. Grant was already worried about exposure to the Agency. A million dollars was a drop in the Agency's thirty-billion-dollar budget, but still enough money that it would draw oversight scrutiny. An unauthorized mission into North Korea was a bigger problem than the money. If they approved the request at any amount, they became complicit in the scheme, even if they weren't to begin with.

Brad understood the dilemma. The best thing for him to do was pass the decision off on the Director. Let him put his neck on the line. Brad picked up his cell phone and started to dial the number but stopped himself.

The amount was under ten thousand dollars. Well under his expenditure limit. Brad could make this decision on his own. He didn't need the Director's approval. Didn't Grant always say for them to make the decisions themselves? That's what he paid them for, the Director had drilled in them.

Brad looked at the screen, then at his phone, and then at his screen again.

"I'll pay the $9,800 out of my own pocket if it comes to that," Brad said.

The decision was made.

His hands hovered over the keyboard as he still hesitated.

What if it was a trick? A hacker. If this backfired, Brad would be in a world of deep trouble. Right now, it was Alex's problem. Approving the request could be seen as going against the Director. Brad was only a few years away from getting his pension.

He began typing. None of that mattered. He wasn't the one sitting in a North Korean lab with his life on the line. He wasn't going to risk Alex's life to protect his career.

Brad typed a few keystrokes and hit send.

Request Approved.

13

Bae couldn't remember ever being this happy.

Since she announced out of the blue her inner desire to be a spy two days ago, there'd been a noticeable change in her father's attitude toward her. An only child, Bae had always gotten the distinct impression that her dad was disappointed that she wasn't a boy.

In North Korea, having sons who could serve the Party Centre in various capacities, especially the armed forces, garnered favor, and respect from the regime. While never spoken aloud, her father let his displeasure be known in other ways. Mostly, disinterest and absence. Bae couldn't remember the last time they'd done anything as a family, or when her father had actually touched her with any hint of affection.

Her mother overcompensated by doting on her at every opportunity. Shopping was her primary feeble attempt at filling the void. Bae's closet was full of designer clothes, shoes, and even costume jewelry. Most of which she never wore. She preferred faded jeans, sneakers, and a tee shirt. Her beautiful shoulder-length, shiny, jet-black hair was almost always pulled back in a ponytail, much to her mother's displeasure.

Bae shunned makeup and hair care products even though she had a shelf full of them in her bathroom. Her mother had long since given up trying to paint her nails, brush each other's hair, or play dress up. The numerous dolls and teddy bears—attempts by her mother to bring out Bae's feminine side—were all stored in boxes in the attic, having not been touched in years.

She'd heard the term *tomboy* in school one time and thought the description fit her perfectly. Bae considered that she might be subconsciously trying to win her father's approval by acting more like a boy and less like the prissy girl her mom wanted her to be.

In many ways, she wished she were more like her mother. Stunningly beautiful, her mom was feminine in every way. Having been brought up in North Korean royalty, she learned to be prim and proper, never unkempt, and always ladylike. Bae was taught manners but forgot them at inopportune times, especially at the dinner table which was where her mom insisted on a certain decorum.

She couldn't force herself to meet her mom's standards, even though she tried. To her mother's credit, other than at the dinner table, she didn't force it on her. But Bae could see the disappointment and disapproval written all over her mother's face.

So really, she felt like she was letting down both of her parents. In a way, she never measured up to either of their standards as opposite as they were. Consequently, she always felt a sense of inadequacy which, now that she was a teenager, had turned into rebellion and resentment.

Her father wasn't the only one who rued not having a boy. Bae would've given anything to have a brother. That way, her parents would at least have one child they were proud of.

All that miraculously changed when she dropped the bombshell at the dinner table that she wanted to be a spy. She heard her parents arguing about it later that night through the paper-thin walls of their bedroom.

"She's just thirteen," her mom argued. "She couldn't possibly know what she wants to do when she grows up. Not yet."

"They admit girls into spy school as young as fourteen," her father said. "I talked to Colonel Chung-ho. He thinks Bae is a perfect candidate."

A perfect candidate. A jolt of excitement shot through her like an electric current.

"Of course, he does," her mom countered. "Bae is young and beautiful. They train these girls to be prostitutes and seduce foreigners so they can spy on them. They want to teach her how to have sex with men," her mom said, raising her voice.

Bae felt her face blush when she heard that part of the conversation, not fully comprehending what her mom meant. *What is a prostitute?* She knew what sex was. Girls at school were obsessed with boys, and she heard a lot of chatter about sex. Boys and trashy talk were of no interest to her, so she rarely participated in those conversations. But if that's what she had to do to be a spy, then she'd do it. That's how bad she wanted it.

"Not all girls become prostitutes," her dad countered. "The regime has all kinds of spies. She might go to America. To college. She'll be educated. Bae can travel the world."

"It's dangerous."

"It's an honor to die for our country," her dad retorted. "Besides, Bae can take care of herself. She's not your normal thirteen-year old. She's special."

She didn't know what to think of the conversation. To hear her parents expressing so much concern for her and paying her so many compliments was stunning. Her mom said she was beautiful. Her dad said she was special. Where was this coming from? She didn't think they cared about her at all.

The conversation went on for nearly an hour. Bae learned a lot through it. She'd have to leave home and wouldn't return for several years—if ever. The school had living and training quarters at a secret location in the mountains. She'd be given a new name. Of all the things she heard, that was the only thing that bothered her because she liked her name.

One thing she did glean from the conversation was that a spy was highly prestigious and high ranking in North Korea. On the same level as Generals. Upon graduation, she would immediately move to the highest civilian rank. Her parents would be compensated with money and favors from the regime.

"I'm proud of Bae," her dad said as the conversation came to an end.

That settled it in her mind. Those were words she never thought she'd hear.

Her dad was proud of her.

***

The next day, her father came home from work early and called Bae down from her room. "Bae, I have a surprise for you," he said. Her mom was also summoned, and Bae found them together in the family room.

What could it be?

She was so excited. This was two days in a row her dad was paying attention to her. He could go days without even speaking to her. She bounded down the stairs and into the room, with a smile that had been permanently fixed on her face the entire day, now heightened by the anticipation of a surprise. A surprise for *her*. Something that had never happened as long as she could remember.

The house was modest but smartly furnished compared to other houses. In the family room was a couch, love seat, and two chairs along with a bookcase filled with reading material approved by the regime. An extra room just for leisure was a luxury only the privileged class enjoyed. In most households, every room was packed with family and relatives, sleeping on the floor, crowded into every available square foot of space. From talking to her friends at school, Bae knew how lucky they were.

Her dad stood at one of the chairs with his leg straddling it and his elbow resting on his knee. His chin was up, and shoulders were back, pride obviously beaming off his face and demeanor.

"I spoke to Colonel Chung-ho," he began. "He gave me a brochure for the spy school," he said as he handed Bae a nicely bound, four-colored brochure.

She opened it with more anticipation than she ever remembered feeling before.

"We have to fill out an application, but he thinks you'll get in," he continued. "You have everything they're looking for. Beauty, brains, and ambition."

Without thinking about it, Bae ran to her father and threw her arms around him. He caught her and flung her around in a circle. Something he hadn't done since she was a little girl.

"He said I have beauty, brains, and ambition," she said shyly, looking over at her mother who nodded approvingly, her own sweet smile affixed to her face.

"What's in the box, daddy?" she asked. "Is it my surprise?" On the coffee table was a box about two feet long and two feet high.

"Open it."

Bae tore into it like a starving hyena.

"What is it?" Bae pulled out a shiny bright object and held it in the air with both hands.

"It's a computer," her dad said. "Colonel Chung-ho wants you to learn how to use it."

They sat on the couch and she put the computer on her lap, carefully, like she was holding a rare piece of fine crystal in her hands. She lifted the top of the computer and stared at the dark screen and ran her fingers along the top and sides.

"It's called a laptop. I'll show you how to use it," her dad said.

Her mother sat beside her and looked at the computer as well. Bae knew that very few people in North Korea were allowed to have computers. Her dad had one at work, but he had never brought it home.

"Let's go upstairs and get it set up," her dad said, taking the computer in one hand and her hand in the other.

They went up to her room, cleared her desk, and set the computer in the center. They plugged the cord into the outlet and powered it up. Bae almost burst out of her skin when the screen roared to life. She'd never seen anything so magnificent.

For the next two hours, her dad patiently showed her how to use it. It felt like the world was suddenly at her fingertips. Just as importantly, she felt as close to her dad as she ever had. They laughed and had the best time.

After he left, she stayed up half the night, unable to pull herself away from the best gift she'd ever received. Bae went to the closet and pulled out the satchel she'd stolen from the middle eastern businessman. Out of all her backpacks, this one was the nicest by far.

With great care, Bae took out the papers with the numbers and threw them in the trash can. The computer fit perfectly in the satchel with room for the cord and all the accessories. She kept the USB stick that was inside when she first stole it. At school she learned that it was called a thumb drive and fit into a computer. Sometime soon, she'd try it on her new computer.

When she couldn't keep her eyes open any longer, she fell into bed and was asleep almost instantly. The satchel with the computer lay on the pillow next to her.

***

Kalma International Airport
Wonsan Kang-won-do, North Korea

Omid Froohan and Jaffar Abdi, arrived on a flight from China around ten o'clock at night, an hour past their intended arrival time. International flights to North Korea were limited to China and South Korea and were notoriously unreliable. The two members of the Iranian Artesh, the equivalent of the army in most countries, flew from Iran to China and caught a commuter flight directly to Kalma Airport where Hamid Ahmadi, the Iranian Ambassador, met them on the road outside baggage claim.

They weren't hard to spot. Froohan and Abdi were both seasoned fighters who fought in the deserts of Iraq, Syria, and Turkey and in the mountains of Afghanistan. Their rough and hardened exteriors caused Hamid to shudder.

Over the years, he'd met many soldiers. These men were as imposing as any he'd ever seen.

Iran had seen its share of war. Hamid's career path had always been as a diplomat, so he never saw combat action. These two men had seen more death and destruction than most people could see in a hundred lifetimes, and it showed on their faces. Strong and burly, they walked with a purpose. Their suspicious eyes flittered around nervously, looking for threats even though they were perfectly safe in North Korea.

"Salaam," Hamid said to the two men when they emerged from the baggage claim area, each carrying one small bag. After exchanging the standard greeting for peace, they shook hands and greeted each other with a kiss on the cheeks. Even the most hardened fighters welcomed a fellow Iranian warmly and in an effusive manner. A custom important in the Iranian society.

Hamid opened the trunk to his car, and the men each set their bag inside. In the trunk were the weapons. Iran was allowed to have weapons at the embassy for protection but weren't allowed to carry them in the country. Hamid was taking a risk having them in his possession outside the embassy. A necessary risk, in that the fighters couldn't bring weapons with them on the flight.

Omid opened the weapons bag and pulled out two PL-15 Russian made handguns. The rifles were left in the bag. He handed one to Jaffar and they quickly hid them in holsters under their suits. Hamid started to object but thought better of it. Even though carrying weapons in North Korea was strictly prohibited, especially by foreigners, these were not men to argue with.

The drive to the hotel was made in silence. When they arrived, Hamid pulled into the parking garage and parked away from any cameras or other cars. He handed them an envelope.

"Inside is your room key," Hamid said. "There's also a map to the house where the girl lives. You'll find a picture of her in the envelope as well. There's also a description of the satchel."

The men didn't speak. They just nodded with an occasional grunt.

"The satchel is probably not at the house," Hamid continued. "Our guess is that the girl handed it off to a third party. You must get that satchel back. Or at least its contents. There are papers with codes and numbers on them. And a USB thumbnail drive. We especially want that back."

The USB flash drive held all the passcodes and nuclear codes for the Pakistan weapons program.

"I don't have to tell you how important it is to get that satchel back," Hasid said.

Their instructions were to kill the parents, capture the girl, and torture her if necessary until she told them who she'd given the satchel to. They were to then kill the girl and dispose of her body in the woods or a nearby lake. Hamid saw no reason to go over those gruesome details again.

The men grabbed their bags and the rifle bag out of the trunk, and abruptly turned and walked toward the hotel, leaving Hamid standing there with his mouth still open.

Hamid was glad they were gone and hoped he never had to see them again.

I would hate to be that family.

14

CIA Headquarters
Langley, Virginia

"Brad, we have a problem," Rhonda, Brad's assistant, said.

Brad was Alex's handler at the CIA. Similar words spoken by Jim Lovell on the ill-fated Apollo 13 mission had become commonplace when someone wanted to communicate a problem. Often used jokingly around the Agency. From Rhonda's tone, Brad knew she wasn't joking.

After he authorized the $9,800.00 payment to the North Korean account, he decided to stay in the office even though it was just after midnight. The situation on the other side of the world still made him uneasy, having no idea what in the world Alex Halee was up to.

"What part of the world?" Brad asked.

"North Korea."

Brad felt his heart skip a beat.

"What kind of problem?"

"We're shut out of Kryptonite," Rhonda said soberly.

"What? That's not possible." Brad began furiously typing on the computer on his desk. His login and password didn't work. His mind began racing through the reasons why that might be the case. Only two came to mind. Alex locked him out, or the North Korean's had hijacked Kryptonite and taken control of it.

There was no plausible reason for Alex to do so. The second option sent terror shooting through his veins as the realization hit him like a pile of bricks.

They'd been tricked. It was the only explanation. He slammed his fist down on the table.

"What's the damage?" Brad asked.

"None yet," Rhonda answered immediately. "Our firewall is holding, but we're being bombarded with hundreds of computers trying to hack into our main server through Kryptonite.

That settled the issue. The North Koreans had definitely commandeered Kryptonite. Alex was probably dead, or worse, being hauled off to a jail as they spoke. Brad put both hands to his head, hardly able to fathom what had just happened.

Dozens of safeguards were built into Kryptonite to prevent access to the CIA main computer. That's why Alex had insisted it be designed on its own servers. Brad scrolled through his mind looking for a connection that would provide an opening to the Koreans.

The wire transfer!

The $9,800.00 came from a CIA account which was accessed by his computer. The question was not if they could break through the firewall, it was how long it would take them. A question he needed to ask.

"How much time do we have before they break through?" Brad asked, ducking his head some as if he was bracing for the answer.

"Forty-eight hours, tops," Rhonda said.

"Get our best people in here, right now!" Brad barked orders one after another. After a few more instructions, Rhonda ran out of the room.

He rubbed his eyes roughly. How could he have been so stupid?

The clock on the wall read 3:33. An ominous sign, whatever that meant.

He picked up his phone.

He's still asleep!

Doesn't matter. He has to know. I just made the biggest mistake of my career.

He hit send and called the Director's number.

***

The Lazarus Group Cyber Lab
North Korea

"Wake up Alex," I heard a voice say roughly.

At first, I was confused. Groggy. After Pok confirmed the receipt of the $9,800.00, I curled up on the couch in his office to catch some shuteye.

"Get up, Alex! Now!" I heard Pok shout.

Why was Pok calling me Alex? My name was Joe Hardy. In my sleepy state, I couldn't make the transition between my alias and real name. A shove in my chest with what was obviously an assault rifle brought me to my full senses. I'd been sleeping soundly and didn't hear the office fill up with people who, once I opened my eyes, I saw and turned my head and focused.

Instinctively, I rolled over slowly and blinked several times to adjust to the light shining in my eyes. Sudden moves with an assault rifle pointing at me wasn't a good idea. Three assault rifles actually, which wasn't good.

Eleven rifles total if I included the eight in the hallway. There were twelve at the entrance when I first arrived. That meant one was still guarding the entrance to the building. Combover guy was out in the hall, grinning widely.

I sat up slowly with my hands raised in the air, ready to strike if I saw an opening.

Don't even think about it.

We were in an enclosed room. The three gunmen were standing over me with every advantage. I'd be dead before I blinked twice. Pok was on the other side of the desk, taking away any possibility of me seizing him and holding him hostage until I was safely out of the building.

If there was an MSO to my situation—a Mission Success Odds—they were extremely low at the moment. Once my mind finished assessing my situation, I began to process what it all meant.

One question stood out above the others forming in my mind. How did Pok know my name? A sheepish grin of victory was dominating his face. Anger rose inside of me as I wanted to wipe it off with one strike. If I could get my hands on Pok, one hit to his face would send that smile to the other side of his scrawny little head.

"You look surprised, Alex Hardy," Pok said.

Good. He doesn't know my full name.

I wanted to feign ignorance but realized it was a useless strategy. It would only make me look stupider than I already felt.

"I was just beginning to like you," I said sarcastically.

By this time, I was sitting up. I crossed one leg over the other, leaned back on the sofa and put both arms up along the back of it. If I relaxed, maybe the men with the guns would as well.

"I've never liked you," Pok said with the veins on his neck throbbing in anger.

"When did you know it was me?" I asked, thinking the longer I kept him talking, the longer I was still breathing.

"The moment I laid eyes on you! The great Alex Hardy. You think you're better than me. Look at you now."

Pok didn't realize that I had unlocked his computer and set up a link between Kryptonite and his server. Langley would be working furiously as we spoke, mining his server for information, setting up all kinds of bugs. I was careful to not let my face give anything away. I may be screwed but so was he and his operations.

Admittedly, my getting screwed meant death, but I could take some satisfaction in having accomplished something on this mission.

What was Jamie doing right now?

Probably sleeping.

That's what I should be doing. Sleeping in a five-star hotel in South Korea. A large sigh suddenly escaped my lips right before a question followed it.

"So, what do we do now?" I asked. "Maybe we can work out an arrangement."

Pok let out a deep diabolical laugh which surprised me for a man of his slight size and build. Obviously fake, but impressive for someone of his puny stature. I wanted to say as much but thought the better of it.

"We have no arrangement," he said laughing again.

"Is this funny to you?" I asked. "What's funny about 151 billion dollars in the FCI fund? I tell you what; I'll split it with you."

"The arrangement is that you are going to spend the rest of your life being tortured at the resort in Hyanghari," Pok said. The Koreans called their secret prisons, resorts. A lame attempt at humor, I assumed.

One good thing was coming from this. Pok had just given him some intelligence information. The CIA had never been able to confirm the existence of the Hyanghari prison. Pok just did so.

I also suddenly felt better. Pok had given me some new information about my fate. The intent was not to kill me right away. As long as my heart was still beating, I'd always have hope of getting back to America alive. Maybe not in one piece, but living, and with one piece of intelligence. Two actually. I confirmed that Pok was still alive, and I knew his location. I wanted to keep him talking to see what else I could learn.

"Since we're just shooting the breeze, and considering we're apparently never going to see each other again, I have a question for you," I said.

Pok looked at me skeptically as his eyes narrowed and his lips pursed. "Why should I tell you anything?"

"What was in the satchel?" I asked.

"What satchel?" His eyes gave away that he knew what I was talking about. He was stalling for time deciding if he should answer that question.

"The satchel the young girl on the security camera stole."

"None of your business."

"Oh, come on!" I said casually, raising my voice slightly. "I'm the one who discovered the Iranians hacking into your system and gave you the information. You wouldn't even know about the girl if it weren't for me. You at least owe me that. And what difference does it make? I'm going away for a long time. Who am I going to tell? The rats in my cell?"

Pok laughed at my joke, easing the tension some.

"I guess you're right. It doesn't matter. And from one hacker to another, you'll appreciate this. It will give you something to think about while you rot away in prison. Haunted every day by the fact that you have this information and can't do a thing about it."

"Now you really have to tell me. You've got me curious," I said flippantly.

"Nuclear codes. That's what's in the bag."

I sat straight up in the chair causing the men with guns to react. One had a gun in my face. I pushed it away. Pok had already given away the fact that his higher ups wanted to interrogate me. If one of these lowlifes were to kill me before that happened, they would take my place in Hyanghari. There was a limit to how far I could push it, but I had some leeway and would take every liberty I could to exercise some control over the situation.

"I don't believe it!" I said strongly. Challenging the information was the best way to get him to share more. The smug look on his face told me he was the one who had stolen the codes. This was actual intelligence that was more important than even hacking into his system. Anything related to Iran and nuclear weapons got everyone's attention back in the states.

Pok let out another laugh. Not as diabolical as the first. More of a girly giggle. I really disliked this man. It would almost be worth it to throw caution to the wind, jump across the desk and snap his neck before the gunmen outside the room could react. The three in the room couldn't stop me. I could disarm them in a matter of seconds.

"The nuclear codes are from the Pakistani server," Pok said. "I stole the codes, passwords, locations, and I'm in their system if they try to change them. We sold them to Iran. Brilliant actually," Pok said his voice trailing off and his stare now off in the distance as he looked out the window.

That gave me an idea. If I could disarm one of the men and turn the gun on the other two in the room, I might be able to kill all of them before they killed me. Another wild idea went through my mind. Two chairs were on my side of the desk. I could grab one and throw myself through the glass window.

Would I survive the fall? The chair might cushion some of it. We were three stories up. I needed more time to plan my moves. Pok was talking now. Giving him more time to say something else I could use against him made more sense than flying through the air to my probable death.

"Who's the girl?" I asked.

"I don't know," Pok said. Truthful. He showed no signs of deceit. "The Iranians are looking for her as we speak. They paid good money for the codes, and she stole them. Kind of funny if you think about it. I wouldn't want to be that girl when the Iranians find her."

That changed things. I had to find that satchel. And the girl. I suddenly had a deep affection for her. Anyone who had the guts to steal a satchel from an Iranian operative was okay in my book.

I needed a better plan. Falling three stories was too dangerous. Making my move outside the building, in the open space, made more sense.

"Doesn't matter," Pok said. "I have control of Pakistan's nukes. I could launch them right now at the US if I wanted to."

Those words sent a chill down my spine. This raised the stakes. I had to stop Pok. Staying alive became my top priority. Not just for my benefit but for the possible millions who could be killed if the Iranians got their hands on those codes.

Pok must've sensed that he had said too much because he suddenly shut up. By his body language. I could tell he wasn't going to say any more. His arms were folded, and the scowl on his face told me our conversation was over.

"Get him out of here!" he said, standing to his feet. I stood as well. I wanted out of there as much as he wanted me gone.

"It's been nice meeting you, Pok," I said. "I'll see you again real soon." I said it in a threatening enough tone that he backed away from me.

I headed toward the door.

"Alex!" Pok shouted.

I turned and looked his way as three guards and I all stopped in unison.

"Have you considered why it was so easy for you to unlock my computer? You're good but not that good," Pok said, trying to laugh diabolically again causing him to violently cough several times.

Then it hit me. I knew exactly why as I started walking again.

Brad and the Director would be pretty angry with me right about now.

15

The new computer had opened up a world to Bae she didn't know existed. Especially after her dad set her up with an email account. A friend at school, Seong, also had email, and the two exchanged messages almost every day. Having had her account longer, Seong took it upon herself to teach Bae everything she knew about the internet and emailing.

The abbreviations Seong constantly included in the conversations, intrigued Bae as much as anything, and she desperately wanted to learn the "cool" internet lingo. The two also used the emails to practice their English, although their conversation today was more abbreviations than words.

WUD?

She asked Seong what she was doing. Seong taught her not to use punctuation marks, and Bae immediately realized her mistake after she sent it. She couldn't get out of the habit, and not adding a question mark went against everything she'd been taught by her mother, who was a stickler for proper writing and grammar.

HW, Seong emailed back. She was doing her homework.

I'm done with mine. Bae responded.

Today was Saturday and Bae had finished her weekend homework the night before. Her dad was at work, and she was counting the hours until he came home. A strange feeling, since she never remembered looking forward to him coming home before.

My dad will be home soon, she told Seong so she'd know why she signed off quickly, which she would do when her dad got home.

My parents are lame, Seong wrote. Her dad worked in construction. An important position to the Regime which was why her family was given access to the internet.

LOL.

A couple of days ago, Bae might've agreed. Now she didn't feel that way about her parents.

I teach you some new abbreviations, Seong's message read.

Bae's heart started beating faster. She loved learning new things on the computer.

POS. KPC. PIR. PAW. The message came from Seong with no explanation of their meaning.

Bae stared at the computer screen trying to figure them out.

? IDK what you mean.

She waited patiently for Seong's response which took a couple minutes to arrive. The Internet was extremely slow in North Korea, especially outside of Pyongyang, the capital city. The computer let out a dinging sound when she got a new message.

POS is parents on site. KPC is keep parents clueless. PIR is parents in room. PAW is parents are watching.

Those made her laugh out loud, although Bae wondered what the point was. Her dad could look at her emails anytime he wanted. She'd never put anything in writing that she didn't want him to see. The rules were explained to her with a stern warning that he would take the computer away if she violated them. While Bae had a rebellious streak, the last thing she would do was risk losing her computer privileges. This was the best thing that had happened to her in a long time. If ever.

Instead of responding, she just sent Seong another *LOL* along with a *BFN*. Bye for now. Better to not say anything that might get herself into trouble. As if on cue, a ding on the computer signaled that she had another email. This one was from her dad.

Do you want to get some ice cream?

A burst of excitement warmed her insides.

Yes! Bae couldn't help but put the exclamation mark on the message.

Get your bike ready. I'll be home soon.

She sent him a smiley face. Another thing Seong taught her to do. She packed up her computer. Although unnecessary, she never left the laptop on her desk unattended. Every time she was finished with the computer, she meticulously cleaned the keyboard and screen and packed it neatly in the satchel and hid it under her bed.

Not from her parents so much—or from anyone really. Crime was nonexistent in her neighborhood. It was more for her peace of mind, knowing her most prized possession was safely stored in her room.

Seeing the satchel sent a slight chill through her as she remembered the man she had stolen it from, and how close she came to getting shot or worse. That was the worst part of using the satchel. The memory of the most traumatic event of her short life still haunted her at times.

Once the computer was safely stored, she put the memory of the man out of her mind, left her room, and went down to the garage. Her other most prized possession was her motorcycle, a Yangyong 125cc model, made in China. Her dad drove a Taedong River Motorbike which was the most popular in North Korea. Individuals weren't allowed to own motorcycles in their own names until a decade or two before, and her dad bought the Yangyong as soon as it became legal. When he got the Taedong a couple years later, he gave the smaller bike to Bae for her twelfth birthday

Motorcycles were her dad's preferred mode of transportation to work. Most roads outside of Pyongyang weren't paved and full of potholes and ruts. The main roads were only slightly better maintained. Therefore, bikes were the best and cheapest way to get around.

She never felt more alive than when she was on her bike. Especially riding with her dad. Riding bikes was one of the few things they did together. It made her feel close to him, even before when they weren't as close. They'd spent many a Saturday riding through the countryside.

When she wasn't riding with her dad, she had to stay off the main roads or the North Korean police would pick her up and haul her down to jail. Bae dreaded the thought of calling her dad to come and bail her out. Bail wasn't the right word. The policemen were corrupt. They earned the equivalent of $5.00 a month. Yet they were wealthy in comparison to most people because they took bribes at every opportunity. Her dad had drilled into her that she should stay away from the police. They'd pull her over even if she weren't doing anything wrong.

"They can't be trusted," her dad had said.

"But we're in the privileged caste," Bae said more of a question than a statement. She didn't understand why the police would bother them. Her mom was a cousin of the Divine Leader.

"That's exactly why you can't trust them," he said. "We have money. Most people don't. They are corrupt and will try to steal from us if they get the opportunity, knowing we can pay."

So, Bae had a deep distrust for the authorities. So far, she'd never had a run in with one and was careful not to break any laws on the bike. Ironic, considering the risks she took stealing backpacks. For some reason, she didn't see that as a big risk. Not like operating a heavy and expensive machine. Like the computer, she cherished the bike, not willing to do anything to risk it being taken away from her.

Maybe when she graduated from spy school, the police would

leave her and her family alone. She'd be considered above them in the caste system, which was everything in North Korea.

The roar of her dad's motorcycle coming around the curve up the mountain to their house left her breathless in anticipation. Her bike was already out of the garage and was ready to go. Her dad motioned for her to wait and then went into the house and came out a couple minutes later, out of his dress clothes and without his business backpack. He had on jeans, a black leather jacket, and riding boots. He looked like a movie star.

He gave Bae a kiss on the cheek before getting on his bike, almost bringing a tear to her eye.

"I'll race you down," he said as he straddled his bike and brought up the kickstand.

Bae gunned the engine and took off, hearing him yell, "Hey!" as she sped off laughing. It wouldn't take long for him to catch up. His bike was twice as fast, although she was as good a rider and knew the roads like the back of her hand.

They lived on a mountain overlooking Wonsan. Their home didn't have a view of the ocean, but the ride down did once they came out of the dense forest. The sun was at its peak and shimmered off the crystal blue sea. She dared to gaze upon it for several seconds, even though the road was rough. Mostly she kept her eye on the road, so she didn't ruin the front axle by banging it into a huge pothole.

Her dad hung back purposefully letting her win the race as she reached the bottom first.

They came to a stop in the road, and he pulled alongside her, giving her a nod for her good riding and win.

He acted like he wanted to tell her something, so she leaned toward him to hear what he said over the roar of the bikes. "I'll race you to the ice cream shop," he said as he revved the engine and took off, leaving her in his dust.

Her engine stalled. Bae cursed under her breath. When she got it started, an all-terrain vehicle passed through the intersection. She stared hard at the two men in the vehicle. They looked like the man at the restaurant. The one who shot at her. They returned the stare, but she was wearing a helmet with a face mask, so she was sure they couldn't see her face.

She breathed a huge sigh of relief when they didn't turn onto the road that led to their house. Her mother was there alone. She tried to force the feeling of dread out of her. Just because they looked like the man at the restaurant didn't mean they knew him or were after her. How could they? No one had seen her take the backpack except that one shop owner. Still, the men were acting suspiciously. They were driving slowly. Looking around like they were lost. The looks in their eyes were pure evil. Like the man on the mountain. These men looked even scarier.

Bae gunned her engine and started moving, even though the men's vehicle hadn't cleared the intersection. She wanted to catch up to her dad as soon as possible. As soon as she was with him, she tried to put the two men out of her mind.

***

They ordered two ice creams on a stick from the outside window and sat down on a bench to eat them. Her dad took a lick and said, "You're a really good rider."

"Thanks," Bae said with a wave of her hand. These compliments from her dad were making her feel special. For years, she ached for this kind of attention. She wondered if it would last.

"No seriously," he said. "You're really good. That's a skill that'll come in handy at spy school."

The mention of spy school brought a smile to her face. She brushed a couple strands of hair out of her eyes and said, "You think they have motorcycles at spy school?"

"I imagine so. Spies have to get away from the bad guys sometimes. Motorcycles are the best way to do it. A bike can go places a car can't go. Probably easier to get away if you're being chased."

The talk of bad guys brought the image of the two men back to Bae's mind. It must've shown on her face.

"Is something wrong?" he asked.

"Did you see the two men in the truck?" Bae asked.

"I did," her dad answered.

"They looked scary to me."

"They were Arab," her dad answered. "Probably Iranian."

"What are they doing here?"

"I was wondering the same thing. I didn't see a government minder in the car."

"What's a government minder?"

Her dad finished the last bite of his ice cream stick and then shifted positions, bringing one foot up to the bench where he rested his elbow on it. "A government minder is an escort or a guide. Foreigners aren't allowed to drive a car in North Korea without one. Those men could be arrested if they're caught."

"Who do you think they were?"

"Probably related to the mafia. Anyone who leaves without his minder is arrested on the spot and charged with espionage. It's a very serious offense. Of course, they can always get out of it by paying a bribe. The mafia has plenty of money to pay the bribes."

Bae looked around to see if she saw any sign of the car. They were sitting outside with a good view of the road.

"Oh well," she finally said. "It's probably nothing."

"Don't worry about them. They won't bother you."

They finished their ice cream and headed back home. Bae's head was like it was on a swivel as she was constantly on the lookout for those men. She didn't let herself relax until they pulled into the driveway a few minutes later.

"Leave the bikes out," her dad said. "We might take them out again."

They walked into the house, but not before Bae took one last long look down the driveway.

16

Since her dad said they might go for another ride on the motorcycles, Bae decided not to get her computer out of the satchel. Instead, she slid it out from under the bed and put it on the desk to set it up later. The heat of the day was subsiding, so she opened the window to let a gentle breeze cool the room.

The house didn't have air conditioning. Only the very wealthy in North Korea had it. In fact, their home and everyone else's was owned by the government. There was no rent or mortgage. Everyone in North Korea was assigned a job and a place to live based on their status. Bae's parents had instilled in her how lucky they were compared to most people. Consequently, Bae never felt the need to complain about some of the common conveniences she heard about in other countries that were lacking in North Korea.

What she really wanted to do was take a nap. She'd been up half the night on the laptop, and felt a yawn come over her. Sleeping during the day wasn't something she'd ever been able to do, so she just grabbed her music player, slipped the headphones over her ears, closed her eyes, and laid down on the bed.

A noise interrupted her calm.

Shouting.

Coming from downstairs.

It startled her. She could hear it clearly even with her headphones on. That's how loud it was.

Bae bolted out of bed. Her heart had gone from a calm, steady beat to racing faster than her motorbike.

The door to her bedroom was closed, so she opened it gently not to be heard. The shouting had grown even louder. She recognized the dialect. Whoever it was sounded like the middle eastern man from the restaurant.

She got on her knees and inched over to the railing where she peered cautiously over the side.

Horror engulfed her. The terror caused her to want to shriek at the top of her voice, but she swallowed it.

The two men she had seen in the car were in the foyer of the house, just inside the door. Both had guns pointed at her mother whose eyes were wide in shock, her arms clutched around her body as she cowered in fear.

Her mom kept saying, "I don't know what you want. I don't understand you."

The men didn't speak Korean. They were shouting at her in a language Bae couldn't understand either. The man's tone was threatening. Rough. Filled with hatred. The men were big and strong. One grabbed her mother's shoulders and shook her, flailing her tiny frame around like he was holding a doll.

She let out a shrill scream. "Please. I don't understand you. Take whatever you want," her mom begged. "Just don't hurt us."

"Ka-bang," one of the men said pushing her mom roughly, knocking her to the ground. Ka-bang meant *bag* in Korean.

Mom picked herself up back up to her knees and put her hands in front of her, pleading, begging.

He kept repeating the word "Ka-bang" over and over again. He raised his hand to strike her mom, but she cowered down as she scooted back away from him further down the hallway, almost out of Bae's sight. Bae was behind them, so they couldn't see her without backing up and looking up the staircase toward the second floor.

"I don't know anything about a bag," her mom said.

"Ka-bang," he shouted, grabbing her mom's hair.

"Dowa juda," her mom cried. Her cry of *please* didn't faze them. "Dowa juda," she said again with even more urgency. Her mother was crying for help.

Bae crawled back to her room. The men wanted her satchel. She'd give it to them.

She grabbed it off the desk. It made her pause. The papers from the satchel had been thrown in the trash can. They were long gone. The flash drive was still in it, along with her computer. She started to unzip the bag to take out the laptop.

Before she could, she heard her dad's voice. He was shouting at the men.

An explosion of sound ripped through the house.

A crack like a firecracker went off, echoing off the ceiling of the hallway and into Bae's room. She let out a muted yell as she tried to scream but couldn't force the air out of her lungs.

"Mom!" she said under her breath, not wanting to give away her position.

Bae ran out the door of her bedroom to the railing and peered over it again, this time from a standing position. She saw her mom lying on the ground. Her body contorted in an unnatural position. Blood was in a pool coming from her head.

A sudden rush of air-filled Bae's lungs in the form of a gasp. The urge to let it all out at once in a scream was so intense that Bae had to put her hand over her mouth to prevent it. The sight of her mother laying on the floor motionless, caused tears to fill her eyes so quickly, her vision blurred.

A pain shot through her heart like she'd been stabbed with a knife. Grief, fear, and anger were all at once competing for dominance. Grief was winning to the point that she was paralyzed and unable to move.

Her dad's scream brought her back to reality. The men were down the hallway out of her sight. They were shouting at her father. He was shouting back. A scuffle ensued. She could hear what she thought was her father being thrown to the ground. He was no match for the two huge men.

She had the satchel in her hand. The realization hit her that it wouldn't make any difference. They were there to kill them all and take the satchel.

Dad.

She heard him beg for his life.

Indecision came over her. She carefully sneaked down two stairs and leaned over the rail so she could see what was happening.

Her dad lay on the ground. The men stood over him. Their eyes met. Bae tried to block out the image of her dead mother from the scene and focus her eyes on her dad.

"Ka-bang," the man said to her dad roughly.

Her dad began to sob. He pleaded with the men to not harm his daughter. But they didn't understand him, and he didn't know what they were saying. She turned her head away, not able to bear to look at the scene unfolding before her.

This was a nightmare. She wished she were dreaming.

If Bae took the bag down there, they would all die. Maybe she could use it as a trade. That was foolish. They'd overpower her in a second. The only way to stay alive was to leave there with the bag.

"Geoeol," one of the men said roughly to her dad. "Girl," he was saying. He wanted her dad to tell him where she was. How did they know about me? Somehow, they knew she'd stolen the satchel.

"Bae! Run for your life," her dad shouted catching her eye again.

One of the men raised his hand above his head and brought it down violently against her dad's face.

Bae scurried back up the stairs. She didn't see the blow but heard her dad cry out in pain.

"Geoeol! Ka-bang! Geoeol! Ka-bang!" The man kept shouting the words, alternating between girl and bag. Bae knew what he wanted. The impulse was to run down there and give it to them, but her dad's next words stopped her.

"Save yourself, Bae. Run. Take my bike."

Bae ran back to her room and closed the door. The shouting downstairs intensified. She clutched the satchel in her hand, unable to fathom that the bag had caused so much pain and destruction to her family. Anger flooded into her like a tsunami.

I will not give it to them.

She put the satchel on her back, went to the closet, and slipped on her shoes. The window was still open, and she was through it and down the side of the two-story house in seconds. She'd done it many times, sneaking out at night to steal backpacks.

A muffled sound came from the house. It sounded like the branch of a tree snapping.

Was it a gunshot?

The men were no longer shouting at her dad. She strained to hear her dad's voice.

Nothing.

A sudden eerie silence.

The reality hit her with the force of a truck slamming into her at full speed. Her dad was dead. He had to be. Out of the corner of her eye, she saw movement in her room. A man stuck half his body out of the window and looked around. She hid behind a bush.

The man went back inside as Bae let out a slight yelp and used the opportunity to run around to the front of the house to the driveway where both of the motorbikes still sat. Her dad told her to take his. She'd only ridden it once. Hers was more familiar, but not as fast. Her dad was right. His bike would get her away from the house faster.

His helmet wouldn't fit so she had the presence of mind to grab hers and slip it over her head before mounting his bike. She tried to straddle it but was in the wrong position. It was too heavy for her. Maybe it had been a mistake to take his bike.

The second time was easier. Bae reached over and grabbed the right handle with her right hand. With her knees bent slightly to gain more leverage, she kicked her right leg high over the side, until she was in the right position on the unfamiliar bike. It almost fell over as she struggled to hold the added weight upright. It would've if not for the kickstand.

Her legs barely reached the ground. Leaving the kickstand in place, she was able to steady the bike while she started it.

The motorcycle had a start button which she fumbled to find. Bae's hands were shaking so hard she had to force them to steady. Finding the button, the bike roared to life as soon as she pushed it. Her right wrist twisted to rev the engine to warm it.

With her left foot she steadied the bike leaning it slightly while she kicked up the stand with her right foot. At the same time, she pulled the clutch lever, pressed the shifter down to first gear, and released the clutch slowly while gently twisting the throttle, careful not to stall the engine.

Even though the bike was started didn't mean she could keep it upright. So many things could go wrong. The bike could topple over from the weight. She could stall the engine. Giving it too much power could cause her to veer out of control.

The men inside, no doubt, heard the sound of the bike starting and would be out of the house in no time. There was no time for her to go to her bike.

Making her dad's bike work was her only option.

Bae twisted her wrist, giving the motorcycle gas. The bike started to move. This was the critical time as a motorcycle doesn't start out in a straight line. She had to get the speed up fast enough to where counter steering would keep the machine upright. Immediately the machine's added power reverberated through her hands as the machine responded to the commands of her right hand that controlled the throttle.

Even over the sound of the roar of the engine, she could hear the shouts behind her along with several popping sounds. That caused her to let out a squeal muted by the helmet.

They were shooting at her!

A bullet clanged off what sounded like the back fender. Several whizzed past, making a strange sound like a wasp buzzing around her head. Rocks and dirt skipped up off the ground. She hit the throttle harder, and the bike responded to her command, immediately giving her more speed. So much that she almost didn't make the first curve.

The back wheel slid to her left and it took all her strength to hold the steering into the slide. She came precariously close to the ditch, but the bike straightened at just the last moment before she would've crashed. The next section was straight, so she gunned it even though she was going downhill. The forest alongside the road was like a blur out of the side of her helmet as it flashed by.

At the next steep curve, Bae slowed considerably to make sure she maneuvered it safely. Over the next two miles, she skillfully steered the bike down the mountain, avoiding the potholes, taking the corners with more speed as she became more comfortable.

Her eyes were filled with tears. So much so that it blurred her vision again which was the biggest problem she suddenly faced. Bae didn't dare take her hand off the wheel to lift her visor to wipe them off.

So, she tried to fight them back.

At the bottom of the mountain, she reached the T in the road. The same spot she'd seen the two men earlier. She should've told her dad everything at the ice cream shop. Maybe he could've protected them.

Too late now.

Bae looked in both directions. Not for other cars, but unsure which way to go. A turn to the right led her out into the country, away from the city. There were many places to hide. But the roads weren't maintained properly, and there were no people around.

She remembered the mistake she made with the man at the restaurant. Going up on the mountain rather than staying down around the shops. When she made that decision, she was alone with him. There was no help around. Had she stayed on the boardwalk, she may have been able to get someone to help her. The man wouldn't have wielded a gun with other people around.

So, she turned to the left. Back toward the city. The roads were better. There were people there who could help her. She could go to the police.

Could she?

"Never trust the police," her dad's words echoed in her ear.

It created confusion in her. She'd just seen her parents murdered in cold blood. But she stole the satchel. The men would get arrested but so would she. The police might even blame her for her parent's death.

It was risky.

Still, she was sure she made the right decision. Going back toward the city was the safest thing to do. The men might not be able to find her in the maze of streets. Hopefully, she had enough of a head start to where they could never find her.

Where would she go? What would she do? Who would help her? Her mom's family?

All of that would have to be sorted out later.

She gunned the motorcycle and sped away from the intersection. Just as she did, the two men pulled up to the same intersection. A few seconds later and she would've been out of their line of sight.

They turned left. In the same direction.

Bae let out a scream. She twisted the throttle and the motorcycle jumped. The front tire came off the ground slightly.

She looked down at the speedometer.

70. 80. 90.

Too fast. She looked in her rearview mirror.

Not fast enough. The men were still gaining on her.

17

The longer the chase went on, the more comfortable Bae felt on the bike. Even to the point that she began trying evasive moves to lose the men. A couple times, she almost did lose them.

Something her dad said when they were having ice cream came back in her mind. *Motorcycles can go places that cars can't.*

Wonsan had many places a bike could go that a car couldn't. The streets of Wonsan scrolled through her mind like a movie as she tried to picture the many curves and turns and figure out which one would be best. The boardwalk was the obvious one, but there were too many people around. Theoretically, the men in the car could drive on the boardwalk. They seemed desperate enough to follow her anywhere.

Seconds before, she took them down a one-way street, and they didn't hesitate to follow her. There weren't any cars coming, and they navigated the road safely only having to dodge one car. That was part of the problem. There was little to no traffic on the streets. She recently read on the internet that there were only 300,000 cars in all of North Korea. Most were owned by the government. The police force had some cars as did the army. About ten percent were owned by civilians. The elite mostly. Her family had one car and two bikes which was more than most.

Most people took public transportation, which left the streets mostly bare.

She muttered her frustration to herself. Had there been more cars on the road, she could have weaved in and out of traffic and lost them in the maze of vehicles. The best scenario would be a traffic jam. A motorcycle could maneuver between the line of stopped cars and leave the men behind.

Bae tried several things to shake them, even driving on the sidewalk at one point, but the men matched her every move. The lights were an opportunity to make an evasive move, but the rare times one was red, the men followed her through without hesitation.

The satchel was still on her back. Bae considered throwing it to the ground. But something of tremendous value was in that bag. Her parents had died for what was in there. She wouldn't give it up easily. In fact, she was ready to throw caution to the wind. What did she have to lose? With her parents gone, what was there to live for? She would become a slave of the state, forced into child labor camps by the regime. A fate worse than death.

With her mother dead, she'd lose her status with the regime. She'd never get into spy school now. The only thing willing her to live was revenge. These men would pay. She didn't know how. But she had something valuable in the bag that they wanted, and she was determined to keep it from them.

So, the cat and mouse would continue a little longer.

It would be over when she said it was over. On her terms. They might catch her. Probably would. But she wasn't going to make it easy for them.

***

The ride from the North Korean cyber lab to Wonsan was a good two hours. Over rough and hilly roads. My back hurt from the uncomfortable position I was forced to lay in. The guards at the cyber lab had thrown me into the back of a van with my hands cuffed behind me. My pleas for them to cuff my hands from the front fell on deaf ears. I knew the ride would be uncomfortable.

I'd seen many action movie heroes in a similar situation. The depictions were unrealistic. In a movie, the CIA operative would open the back door, jump out the back of the van, and roll on the ground. Then take off running without even a scratch from the fall.

That didn't happen in real life. If I went flying out of the van, even at a low speed of thirty miles an hour, landing on the hard surface of the road would be painful and debilitating if I weren't killed outright. I was crazy enough to do it, but wise enough to know that my MSO was just slightly above zero. And we weren't traveling thirty miles an hour. We were doing at least sixty. I wished they'd slow down. The bumpy road was infuriating me by the minute.

The second option in movie escape scenes was even more unrealistic. In the same position, James Bond, or some other notable spy would commandeer a weapon from one of the guards in the back seat and then shoot the driver. I had no doubt that I could do that very thing. I could free my hands, surprise the three guards in the back, who were totally clueless, take one of their weapons, aim and fire, and the driver's brains would be splattered on the windshield.

A scenario I'd seen many times in the movie and could picture in my mind.

Then what?

The van would veer out of control and crash with no one driving it, but I didn't have a seat belt on. What were my chances of survival from slamming into a tree, an embankment, or another car? If we rolled over, I'd be flung around the inside of the van like a crash dummy. If I survived the crash, so would one or more of the guards. The weapons would be thrown around the van. Who knew which one of us would retrieve a weapon the soonest?

The best solution was to wait until the van stopped and I was safely out and on solid ground. Not that my options were that much better. If the men were unarmed, beating them up and disarming them would be much easier. Taking out five without one of them getting off a shot was highly unlikely. They were each carrying assault weapons which could shoot thirty rounds in a couple seconds.

While a movie star can be shot at a thousand times and never be hit once, it didn't work that way in real life. Even an idiot firing an assault rifle will hit something if only by sheer numbers.

At least, thinking about those options was making the tedious ride go faster. And it took my mind off the utter failure of my mission. Pok had gotten the best of me. He tricked me from the beginning. I don't know why I fell for it. The first thing I was going to do when I got rid of the guards, was go back to the lab and set things right. Pok would pay with his life.

Even more importantly, I had to figure out a way to disarm the computer before they could infiltrate the CIA system. Thirty-six hours was about how much time I figured I had.

City lights suddenly came into view.

Another option formed in my mind.

We were approaching Wonsan. Almost certainly, I was being taken to a local police station. From my memory, it would be a small hole in the wall, a makeshift house with one, maybe two, cells at the most. Being the weekend, if I were lucky, there'd only be one guard. With a handgun strapped to his side. Poorly trained.

That's where everyone was initially processed. Even political prisoners. People arrested didn't stay there long. The next day, the secret police would come and take me away for interrogation. Maybe on Monday since it was the weekend, although North Koreans didn't observe the Sabbath. Most were atheist. Sunday was like any other day, but some still took it as their day off.

After a lengthy and painful interrogation, a judge would find me guilty of espionage, and I'd be sent to one of the notorious prison camps which were numbered. Camp 22 or 25 would be most likely. They held the "enemies of the state." More than 50,000 people were housed in those camps. Very few were foreigners. Who, besides me, was stupid enough to conduct an espionage operation in North Korea? Most of the prisons were filled with locals who made some kind of misstep.

Truthfully, I didn't know where they'd send me. No American spies that I knew of were ever captured. Until now. Something I wasn't proud to admit.

"Hey fellas," I said breaking the silence and the monotony of the ride. I could hear guns rattling as the guards stiffened.

"Can we stop and get a hamburger?" I said. "I'm hungry."

No one said anything.

"Do you have a McDonalds? I could go for a big Mac and fries. Have you ever had McDonald's French fries? I hear they put sugar on them. Have you ever heard that?"

"Dagchyeo," the driver said. He had just told me to shut up in the rudest and most vulgar way possible in the Korean language.

"It's my treat," I said.

One of the guards turned around from his seat and hit me in the stomach with the butt of his gun.

"Hey!" I vehemently protested. "I just offered to buy you dinner and you hit me. That was totally unnecessary."

I was actually glad he did. The banter woke me up from the monotonous drone of the van engine. My senses were alert again. Along with anger that raged inside from him hitting me. I needed that rage to repay the favor in a few minutes when we arrived at the police station, which I knew was coming up.

Sooner than I thought. The van slowed.

18

Two cars were following Bae now. As if she didn't have enough troubles.

When she ran through a red light, a police cruiser saw her and was now on her tail, with his blue lights flashing and siren wailing. The Arabs had dropped back, still following, but far enough away that the policeman wouldn't notice.

They ran the red light too! Why didn't you stop them?

Bae's indecision caused the situation to escalate further as she didn't stop right away. Now, the cruiser was crowding her, trying to force her off the road. She thought about speeding away and leading them both on a chase, but if she couldn't shake the one, how could she lose both of them?

As the cruiser got closer, she couldn't resist the impulse. One flick of the wrist and Bae was able to put distance between them, obviously taking the policeman by surprise. Ahead was a park. Bae turned into it and got off the road, cutting through the middle, winding through the trees. The cruiser stayed on the main road that made a circle all the way around back to the main entrance. He was racing parallel to her and trying to reach the other side before she did.

The road took a turn which took the policeman out of her sight momentarily as she veered to the right, away from where he was driving. Her only thought was to get away. In the middle of the park, just ahead was an abandoned railroad bridge. If she could reach it before the policeman, she could ride in between the rails to the other side. He wouldn't be able to follow her.

Before she could reach it, the Arabs appeared out of nowhere. They'd taken the circle going in the other direction. They must've sensed her plan because they blocked the entrance to the trestle. Bae let out a scream of frustration as she had to come to a complete stop, or she would've hit their car.

One of the Arabs flashed a gun.

Bae shrieked and turned the bike sharply to the right, sliding the back end almost parallel to the ground. She had to put her right foot down to steady the bike. Her knee almost buckled under the weight of the machine, and she cried out in pain.

Fear was burning a hole inside of her. What should she do? What would happen if they caught her?

I have to get out of here—now!

The policeman was back in view, coming up quickly from the other side. Bae was trapped and had no choice but to go back to the road. She gunned the engine, leaving a trail of rocks and dust behind as she sped back toward the entrance.

Which would be better? Should she take her chances with the Arabs who killed her parents and were likely going to kill her, or the police who would put her in a corrupt system that would take away her freedom and probably send her to a child labor camp? The choice was between being eaten by a tiger or a lion. Neither option was a good one. What she really wanted to do was find the nearest cliff and drive over it. The Arabs would never get their satchel, and she'd put an end to what seemed like a hopeless situation.

But there was still some fight left in her. But how long could she keep this up? She was already exhausted from the stress of the chase.

Bae reached the exit first. Once on the main road, she decided to slow the bike down and also her heart that was racing. Tears were streaming down her face. She lifted the flap on her helmet and made a feeble attempt to brush them away. Should she just give up?

What would her dad tell her to do? If only she could talk to him one last time.

Before she could decide, the police cruiser suddenly sped up to where he was right on her tail. The flashing lights reflected off the mirror then the face mask of her helmet, startling her. She whipped her head around to look, but he was coming so fast, her eyes were barely able to focus, temporarily blinding her with the bright flashing lights. The siren was so loud it was deafening.

The last thing she saw before everything became a blur was his face. His eyes were widened like saucers, like a crazed maniac. His mouth was as wide as a full moon as it seemed like he was shouting wildly inside the car. Two hands gripped the steering wheel as he was rocking back and forth, clearly enjoying the interruption to his probably normal, mundane existence.

That made her decision for her. She had to get away from the madman and take her chances with the Arabs.

Without warning, the cruiser hit her from behind. Bae lost control. The back wheel was suddenly in front of the bike as she did a one-hundred and eighty-degree turn. Somehow, Bae managed to keep it upright. She was not going that fast.

When the motorcycle came to a complete stop, Bae hit the throttle. The back tire spun in the gravel. The bike kicked itself into neutral. The tire was completely flat from the collision.

Bae threw her hands into the air in exasperation. "You ruined my bike!" she yelled at the policeman.

The policeman was out of his car in a flash. His gun was drawn and in her face before she could react. He shouted instructions for her to get off the bike and onto the ground.

Bae turned the motorcycle off. Unable to hold it upright, it fell to the ground as she jumped away. The man told her to put her hands in the air. Ignoring the instructions, Bae unstrapped the helmet and took it off her head and shook her hair out. The police officer was screaming at the top of his lungs now, but she didn't hear him. Something else had her undivided attention.

An even greater threat.

The Arabs drove by slowly, and stared at her. She glared back. Bae wanted to stick her tongue out at them but realized how childish that would look. At the moment, she had the upper hand. She had the satchel and was on her way to the police station where she would be out of their reach. If she had her way, they'd never get the bag.

The police station was the best option. There, she could talk her way out of this mess. Once they knew about the murder of her parents, they would understand why she ran. She'd explain everything. The satchel. Two men who murdered her parents. If they didn't believe her, they could go to her house and see for themselves. Her family was privileged. Part of the family of the Divine Leader. Loyal. She had been invited to spy school. They would have to believe her.

For now, she would do whatever the officer said.

The Arab man flashed the gun again. Bae could see the indecision in his eyes as they flittered back and forth, and he raised the gun, then lowered it back down.

"Get on the ground," the policeman shouted waving the gun in her face.

"Gladly," Bae said as she flopped to the ground, face down, making herself less of a target.

The officer took the satchel off her back.

"Be careful with that," Bae said. "It has my computer in it."

He slapped her across the back of her head. The blow stunned her, almost knocking her unconscious. For a moment, she saw stars.

"Don't trust the police," her dad's words sliced through the daze of the blow.

She immediately regretted revealing what was in the satchel. Most things on a person when they were arrested were confiscated. The computer and the bike would be long gone once they got to the station. Better to not say anything about her parents or their house. The police might come and ransack it if they know no one was alive to protect it.

The man pulled her to her feet roughly and ordered Bae to put her hands together where he secured them with a zip tie. He moved the bike off the road completely, inspected it, letting out a creepy moan of approval. Apparently, he liked what he saw.

He searched her body. Apparently, he liked that as well, as he got a little too grabby. Bae pulled away. The man raised his hand to slap her again, but she cowered and turned her head.

He forced her into the back seat. The satchel was thrown roughly onto the seat in front. Thankfully, he got in the front, started the cruiser, and drove away. For a moment, Bae wondered if he was really going to take her back to the station.

The Arabs were parked just down the road and were looking their way.

The entire drive, she kept looking back at the Arabs. They were there. Stalking her like a lion stalking prey. Waiting for the right moment to pounce.

When the cruiser pulled into a parking space in front of the station, Bae let out a huge sigh, even though the Arabs pulled into another space across the street a block from them. She started to warn the policeman but decided against it. He might force a confrontation. Bae knew he was no match for the vicious trained killers in the other car.

Bae was numb. So many emotions had risen to the surface that she had shut down. She wanted to cry again but held back the tears, not wanting to give the officer the satisfaction that he'd hurt her.

He ordered her out of the car.

She hesitated. Would the Arabs use this opportunity to make their move? The two men could break the policeman apart like a matchstick. The Arabs could shoot both of them, grab the satchel, and be on the road before anyone knew what had happened.

When she didn't get out immediately, the man grabbed her by the hair and pulled her out. She fell to the ground. He ordered her to stand. It wasn't easy standing with her hands tied, but she managed to get to her feet. Once upright, he shoved her from behind, although it wasn't necessary. Bae was already walking rapidly toward the door of the station.

As she did, a van pulled in.

Were they with the Arabs? A wave of panic flashed through her body. Bae was relieved to see the men inside were Korean. She had to wait for the policeman to open the door since she didn't have use of her hands. When he did, she bolted through the entrance where she felt safe for the first time in over an hour.

19

So much for best laid plans.

The van pulled into a parking space at the police station, and I had already planned my moves in detail. The drive over had given me plenty of time to think about it.

There were five guards, so it was five against one. Not exactly, if I planned it right. Most likely only one, maybe two guards would open the back trunk to let me out. Why would it take all five? The men were more confident in their abilities than that.

That improved my odds considerably. Two against one.

Once out of the van, I'd take the opportunity to stretch my legs. That would be a normal thing to do. The other guards would probably follow my lead and do the same thing. My hands were still cuffed behind me, but that particular style of handcuffs was easy to break free from with the proper technique. Two seconds was all I needed.

Once my hands were free, one perfectly timed elbow to the side of guard number one's head would incapacitate him in one motion. A carefully placed kick to the groin to guard number two would cause any man to double over and drop his weapon. I had to remember that the two guards were considerably shorter, and I'd have to adjust my angle to make sure the blows were delivered on target.

Both men's guns would be on the ground. I'd grab whichever was closer. Once I had a gun secured, the other three guards would be easy to eliminate as threats. They'd be at the front of the van. I'd be at the back. The doors to the van might even be at just the right angle to block their views.

A few minutes from now, I'd be driving away in the same van that brought me there. Back to where it had come from. The cyber lab. It took two hours to get here. It would take less time to get back. Where Pok awaited. Unsuspecting. Not knowing that I was about to rain the full wrath and fury of my skills on him.

Everything was going as planned. Two guards were in the back opening the door to let me out. They had no idea what was about to happen to them.

The first thing I did when I got out of the van was scan my surroundings. Even before I stretched my legs. The precaution was as second nature to me as opening my eyes when I first woke up in the morning.

What I saw stopped me in my tracks. Across the street was a suspicious vehicle. Out of place in relation to its surroundings. Curly, my handler at the CIA, had taught me to trust my instincts. That I would see things subconsciously before all the facts registered in my conscious mind.

The car was backed into a space facing the wrong direction. No shops were open, and no other cars parked near it. It stuck out like a sore thumb as the saying goes. The biggest tell was that the men sitting in the car weren't Korean. They were middle eastern. That might not be out of place in New York City, but in North Korea that was something you never saw.

Of course, they were probably as shocked to see me as I was them. As unusual as it was to see two Iranians in North Korea, it was even more unusual to see an American. I gave them a long stare, and they did the same to me. From the looks of them, they were trained fighters. Not spies per se, but they had the look of hardened Iranian National Guardsmen. The type we saw in Afghanistan, Syria, and Iraq.

My focus on the men was interrupted by a commotion next to the van. I only caught a glimpse of the back of her, but it looked like a policeman was leading a young girl into the station. By her size, she looked to be of similar age and build to the girl who stole the satchel in the security video. The policeman had a satchel in his hand, dangling low to the ground, giving me even more confirmation.

It didn't take much to put the two together. The Iranians were after the girl and that satchel. If I was right, the Pakistan nuclear codes were in that bag.

I couldn't believe my luck. If I could call it that. Now it wasn't five against one. I had the five guards, the two Iranians, and at least two police to overcome in order to steal that satchel. Still, there was a real opportunity to keep the nuclear codes out of the hands of the bad guys.

Nine to one.

They were all armed. I wasn't.

Yeah, I was really lucky.

Luck is when skill and preparation meet opportunity, Curly always said.

Besides, you're always armed, Curly's voice rang out in my head for at least the hundredth time in the last twenty-four hours.

That was true. Three guards with assault weapons stood less than four feet from me. All I had to do was commandeer one of those weapons, and I was armed. Outside in the open wasn't the place to do it, so I scrapped my original plan, and let them take me inside.

I assumed that would escalate the situation for the Iranians. They would presume that I was there to steal the satchel. However, they wouldn't storm the place with seven gunmen inside. They'd wait for the five-armed guards to leave. That made sense to me as well. The guards from the lab wouldn't hang around long. I was a nuisance to them. They'd want to get back on the road and to the lab and to their homes as soon as possible.

Once they were gone, all I had to deal with were two policemen and the two Iranians. The two Koreans were likely poorly equipped and inadequately trained. CIA reports said that some local police didn't even have ammunition for their weapons. I hoped that wasn't the case because I needed one of their weapons to fight the Iranians.

Four to one. I liked those odds better.

Only two to one, if I could overpower the policemen inside and steal one of the vehicles and get away before the Iranians knew I was gone.

But... There was the girl. She was in grave danger. I couldn't leave her behind. That really complicated things.

All of a sudden, I didn't feel so lucky.

***

The inside of the police station was just like I envisioned it. The entrance opened into a small room with one desk and one chair. The obligatory pictures of the Yang family were on the wall, otherwise, they were completely bare. The lighting was poor, and the furnishings below adequate for even a third-world country.

A door led to a back room that was a makeshift prison or holding cell, roughly twelve by twelve. One long bench was fastened into the wall. The floor was concrete and what paint was on the walls was cracking and peeling. I could see mold growing in the corners and leak spots in the ceiling tile. Fortunately, it wasn't raining or cold.

The girl was sitting on the bench with her hands secured in front of her by a zip tie. She huddled in the corner of the room, with her legs up on the bench and her head between her legs. Petrified. Her whole body was shaking.

One look at me only made it worse. She scooted even further down the bench, into the farthest corner, and curled up into a tighter ball, with her head turned away, not wanting to make eye contact.

The guards pushed me into the cell roughly and closed the door, which was nothing more than poorly designed, makeshift bars with a lock. When it shut, it sent a loud, clanging sound echoing through the room. The bars were in such disrepair, a good shaking might send them tumbling to the floor.

I sat down on the bench, but away from the girl, giving her some space. The guards were talking to the policemen in the other room, explaining who I was.

She looked up and turned her ear slightly toward them like she was intently listening to their conversation.

"He's an American spy," one of them said.

When the guard said it, the girl gave me a furtive glance like she was checking me out.

"Do you speak English?" I asked her.

She nodded yes.

"Don't talk in Korean. I don't want them to understand what we're saying. Can you do that?"

The girl swallowed hard and took her feet off the bench and put them on the floor. She was small. Black hair. Dark brown eyes. Beautiful features. She was better dressed than most Korean children. Probably came from a higher-class family. It made me wonder what had gotten her into this predicament.

"What's your name?" I asked.

She didn't answer but recoiled back in her almost fetal position.

"I saw you steal the satchel," I said.

Her eyes widened in amazement. "You were there?" she said barely above a whisper. Her lips contorted in puzzlement. I could understand why. At six-foot-four and two-hundred-thirty pounds, I was hard to miss. She probably wondered why she hadn't seen me there.

"No. But I saw it on a security camera," I said in a gentle, unassuming tone. I needed to gain her trust.

"Are you really an American spy?" she asked inquisitively, her voice grew stronger as she gained more courage.

"You're in real danger," I said, as I scooted closer to her. "There are two Iranians outside who want to kill you and steal the satchel."

"I know." The girl looked off in the distance. Her face showed the strain. There was no telling what she'd been through over the last couple of days. This girl had an innocence about her. I was guessing that she didn't know there were nuclear codes in that satchel when she stole it.

"You and I have a mutual problem," I said. "As soon as those five guards leave, those Iranians are going to come in here and kill both of us."

The girl flinched. I don't think I was telling her anything she didn't already know.

"That policeman out there can't protect you," I said. "But I can."

"How are you going to do that? You're in handcuffs. Locked in a cell. Same as me." The girl held her hands up in the air.

"That's no problem. I can get out of the handcuffs. But I have to know that I can trust you. I want to help you."

"How do I know I can trust you?" she asked.

"That's a fair question," I answered. "You don't. But you don't have a lot of options at the moment."

"Start by answering my question. Are you an American spy?"

The girl had a sassiness about her.

"Think about it," I said. "Why else would I be here? I didn't come to North Korea on a sightseeing expedition. But I need your help."

"I'm going to be a spy," she said almost smugly. "I'm supposed to go to spy school when I turn fourteen. My dad got me in."

I saw her wince when she mentioned her dad. What was that all about? Now wasn't the time to ask.

"Really!" I said in a surprising tone although I meant for it to be complimentary.

"I'm tougher than I look," she said, clearly taking offense. "Why should I help you?" Sometimes, I forgot that even young kids were indoctrinated with a hatred for Americans. We saw it in the middle east. Many American soldiers lost their lives when a young child approached, and they let their guards down only to find the kid had a bomb strapped to his chest.

I needed a way to get through to this girl and fast. An idea came to mind. "Do you want your first spy lesson?" I asked.

"Sure," she said, her demeanor suddenly changing.

I turned my back to her so she could see my handcuffs. "I'm going to teach you how to get out of hand restraints."

The girl scooted closer to me as I began to move my hands in a circular motion.

"What are you doing?" she asked.

"The cuffs have links between the two wrist restraints. I'm twisting them so that they kink up. This is the hardest part."

"Why are you doing that?"

"When I get the links in the right position, they will actually lock up which tightens the handcuffs but weakens the links. Like this," I said as the chains suddenly froze up.

The girl was soaking it up like a sponge.

The five guards left. The policeman that brought the girl in left as well. We were there with just the one guard. That meant the Iranians would make their move soon. I needed to hurry. They'd wait a few minutes to make sure the men didn't come back.

"Watch this," I said to her. Once the links froze, I gave the cuffs a violent jerk and the chains broke.

"Wow!" she said. "That was awesome!"

I stretched my hands to the ceiling and rotated my shoulders in a circular motion to loosen them up. The cuffs were still around my wrists but at least my hands were free.

"What about me? Can you get me out of mine?" The girl held out her hands. "I don't have the same ones you did."

"Stand up," I said to her, "and put one foot on the bench."

She did as I said.

"In the future, if someone puts a zip tie on your wrist, flare the bottom of your wrist out, and put your thumbs together, like this." I looked back over at the guard. He was busy at his desk, oblivious to what we were doing.

"Like this?" she asked.

"No. Put your hands in a fist with your thumbs up."

She tried it.

"It's harder to do now because you're already restrained." I demonstrated it for her in more detail. "Flare your wrists out. Then when they secure the ties, when you relax your hands the zip tie will not be as tight. Then you can wriggle your hands free."

"What do I do now since they are already tight?"

"I can take them off for you," I said.

"No! I want to learn how to do it."

I liked the girl already. She reminded me of Jamie, my girlfriend back home. Stubborn and independent.

"Bring your hands up over your head. Flare your wrists out as far as you can making the zip tie as taut as possible."

"I don't know what you mean by taut. You mean teach. Like you are teaching me."

"No. Taut." I spelled it out for her. "Stretched. So, it's really tight."

She did it.

"Like this?" she said with a grimace.

"It may hurt a little. Are you sure you don't want me to break the ties for you?"

"I said I wanted to do it myself." The girl raised her voice for emphasis.

"Shh," I said. "Don't let the guard hear you."

I stood up so I was next to her.

"Bring your arms down. Really fast."

She started to do it, but I stopped her. "You want the zip tie to be really tight. So, flare your wrists out. Bring the tie down against your knee. Really hard. Right here. The bony part." I pointed to the top of her kneecap which was jutting out.

"I'm ready," she said. The girl moved her back leg to get more leverage. She raised her hands over her head, took one look at me, tightened her lips together and then brought her arms down in one quick motion. The ties slammed against her knee. She let out a yelp. The zip lock gave way, leaving the tie dangling loosely on her wrists.

She let out a squeal of delight.

I was amazed. It had taken me four tries to learn how to do that. She did it on the first one. I nodded my approval.

"What do we do now? she said.

"I have a plan," I said.

"What is it?"

"You're not going to like it."

She frowned and curled her nose, in an obvious show of displeasure. Just like my girlfriend Jamie does, when she's disgusted with me.

"Here's my plan," I said as we huddled close together so I could explain it to her.

20

"I'm not doing that," Bae said adamantly.

"We have to figure out a way to get the guard into the cell so I can disable him so we can get out of here," I said.

I was free from my handcuffs and Bae was free from her zip tie, but we were a long way from being out of the woods. Between us and freedom were the bars that locked us in, a North Korean policeman guarding the exit, and the two Iranians outside the police station who were intent on killing us.

Bae was resisting my plan.

"I'm not going to flop around on the floor like a sick monkey," she said, rolling her eyes.

"You said you wanted to be a spy." I couldn't suppress the huge grin on my face. "This is your chance. Sometimes you have to do things you don't want to do."

Bae crossed her arms in front of her in defiance. "Why don't you do it then? Why does it have to be me?"

"The guard doesn't care anything about me," I said. "He won't open the door if I'm sick. You're a young girl. From a rich family. He'll open it for you, and I'm the only one who can disable him."

"I'm not doing it," Bae said, pouting her lip.

I guessed she wasn't going to change her mind. "You are so stubborn!" I said in a whisper so the guard couldn't hear but with enough emphasis for her to know I was angry.

Time was of the essence, and I was losing patience. We both still sat on the bench and I moved closer to Bae, and crowded her in an attempt to intimidate her. "We're sitting ducks in this jail cell. If the Iranians make their move, we're dead."

"What do I need you for anyway? I've done fine on my own."

"Looks like it," I said sarcastically. "You got yourself thrown into prison. You have two Iranians right outside the door, itching to kill you."

"Well... From what I can see, you got yourself thrown into prison too. You must not be such a good spy."

She had a point.

"What's your plan then?" I asked.

"The guard will protect me," she retorted.

I laughed out loud. "That guy couldn't protect a bug from a grasshopper. You don't know these Iranians. They're good. And they're angry with you. They won't just kill you. They'll kill your family."

I saw her wince again. Maybe they had already killed her family. That's why she was running.

"Look. I may not be able to protect you either," I said softening my tone. "But I'm the best chance you got."

Bae stood and put some distance between us. "Tell him you have to go to the bathroom or something if you want to get out of here. I'm staying put."

I threw my head back in exasperation. The bathroom idea had crossed my mind, but the guard wouldn't open the door for that. He'd tell me to relieve myself in the corner. I had to think of something else.

Before I could, the argument became moot when the guard suddenly appeared at the door, opened it with a key, and walked inside.

***

Within seconds, we both knew what he wanted.

Evident by the lustful look in his eyes and the creepy grin that showed his rotten, stained teeth, or at least what was left of them. He barely noticed me. I put my hands behind my back so he would think I was still restrained. Bae didn't think of it because she kept her hands in front of her. The zip tie that was binding her hands a few minutes before was on the floor next to my foot. When the guard wasn't looking, I made a lame attempt to kick it under the bench.

It didn't seem to matter to him. He had one thing on his mind. Toothless guy reeked of cigar smoke; and by the looks of his greasy hair, the filthy clothes, the caked on grime under his nails, and the stench that suddenly filled our prison cell, it didn't seem like he had taken a shower any time recently.

He sat next to Bae who promptly scooted away from him as she contorted her face from the smell of the man. He reached out and touched her cheek with the back of his hand. Gently. Seductively. Like she would like it. Bae's face twitched and her body tensed. I could see her hand ball into a fist. *Don't do it, Bae*, I wanted to say. *I'll take care of him.*

"Don't touch me," she said, glaring at the man.

He took her arm and jerked her to her feet. Bae tried to resist, but he was too strong. He dragged her across the room toward the door. I wanted to move, but the angle wasn't right.

"Aren't you going to do something?" she said to me in English. I was, but I needed to wait until his back was to me. Even if he never turned away from me, I would still have to react. There was no way he was leaving the room with her.

Bae screamed. Fought him with everything she had. He seemed to be enjoying the battle he knew he'd win with his superior height and weight. This wasn't the first time he'd done something like this and probably liked it when his victims put up a struggle.

Bae needed to quit fighting. She was making things worse. Her petite frame and inexperience made her vulnerable to getting hurt. The greasy man gave her several opportunities that an experienced fighter would've taken advantage of that would've disabled him. But Bae didn't have any idea what to do.

She needed to quit fighting for another reason. The policeman's vile smell was being stirred up from the battle, like a witch's brew. I almost gagged.

As expected, he started getting the upper hand. Greasy man had hold of her arms. Bae was feisty but was losing the battle. Her legs were braced against the ground. The guard was pulling her, and she was sliding across the concrete floor like she was water skiing. Finally, he let her go, and Bae ran back against the back wall.

He was on her in a second. This time he grabbed her around the waist. Bae let out a shriek and tried to wiggle away, but he was too strong.

His back was to me.

Perfect.

Like a cat, I bolted from my seat. In no time, I had my forearm around his neck. I slammed him backward. A loud crunching sound echoed through the room as his head cracked when it hit the floor, knocking him out immediately. His body convulsed twice and then went limp.

I helped Bae to her feet. She had fallen when I freed her from the man's grip. She was still shaking. "Are you okay?" I asked. She didn't respond.

I dusted both of us off in a feeble attempt to get the remnants of the man off of our bodies. The only way I was going to get the smell out of my nose was to get outside which I was anxious to do anyway.

"We have to hurry," I said as I knelt down next to the policeman. The guard's gun was in a holster. I checked it for bullets and found it full, so I took it. He had another magazine on his belt. I took that.

I started rummaging through his pants.

"What are you looking for?" Bae asked.

"His keys," I said.

"You mean these?" Bae held up some keys and shook them in the air.

"How did you get those?"

"I took them off his belt when he was sitting next to me."

"You're amazing," I said. "You might make a good spy after all."

Bae shrugged her shoulders, but a smile formed, clearly moved by the compliment.

I took the keys from her hand and inspected them. One appeared to be to his police cruiser. The key to the handcuffs wasn't on him. I'd have to pick the locks later.

"Let's go!" I said.

We went into the main office where I looked for another weapon. A Russian-made RPK-74 assault rifle was propped against the wall. It had seen better days. It also didn't have any ammunition in it. It would have to do. The Iranians wouldn't know the magazine was empty, and just the sight of it would give them pause.

I went over to the window and peered out, careful not to be seen. The Iranian's car was still parked in the spot, but they weren't in the front seat. A wave of panic went through me.

They were in the back with the trunk opened, clearly preparing to make a move. The guard had come into our cell in just the nick of time. Saved his life as well. For now, he just had a bad concussion. Had he waited a couple of minutes later, the Iranians would've been inside, and we'd all been dead.

Them behind the car was another stroke of luck. We might be able to get to the police cruiser without being seen. If they didn't see us, they might not follow the vehicle when it pulled away. They wouldn't have any reason to believe we were the ones in it.

Bae had the satchel on her back. I nodded in agreement.

"Here's what we're going to do," I said. "I'm going to open the door slowly. You go first. I'll follow you. Go to the driver's side and get in the back seat. Stay down. Don't let them see you."

I examined Bae's eyes closely for any sign of fear. None was evident more than could be expected under the circumstances. She raised an eyebrow confidently, then pursed her lips in determination.

I gave her one last instruction. "If the keys don't work for whatever reason, you take off running. Toward the woods. Don't look back. I'll hold them off. Whatever you do, don't let them have the satchel. Destroy it."

I opened the door slightly, and she slivered through it without hesitation.

The cruiser was two spaces down from the front of the building. Bae was in the car in a flash. I followed shortly after she was safely in. The Iranians didn't see her but saw me. I heard one of them yell and point in my direction. They came out from behind the back of the car and pulled their guns and started toward us. I waved the RPK-74 in the air, and the Iranians jumped back behind the protection of their car.

The police cruiser was unlocked, thankfully, so I opened the door and jumped into the driver's seat. I put the key in the ignition and prayed for it to start. When it did, I quickly put it in reverse, pulled out of the space, and sped down the road. I didn't know the roads, so I didn't know where we were going. All I knew was that we were headed south.

The lab was south.

It didn't matter. The lab would have to wait. I had to put it and Pok out of my mind for the moment.

The Iranians would have to be dealt with first. They settled in behind us as we drove down the road to a confrontation that was soon coming. I needed a plan, and I needed it quickly.

21

"You did good back there," I said to Bae after she finally told me her name. "You're going to make a good spy."

"Thank you," she said as she smiled broadly. "So, did you. You knocked that guy out with one move. That was amazing!"

Bae was now in the front seat, the satchel at her feet. I was curious to get in it and see what was there but didn't want to force a confrontation. She was still leery of me, and I didn't blame her. Even though I saved her life, she may have thought that I did so to get my hands on the satchel. I had more work to do to earn her full trust.

"You're welcome. But I did it for me," I said with a grin. "I couldn't take that man's smell for another second."

"I know!" Bae crinkled her nose. "Ewww. That man was gross. And he had no teeth. Yuk!"

It felt good to let out a little tension. If only for a moment.

Bae's tone turned more sober. "That man would've raped me if you hadn't been there."

"I'm just glad I *was* there," I said.

"I tried to fight him off," Bae said with a far-off look, "but he was too big and strong."

"Size has nothing to do with it," I said.

"What do you mean? He was a lot bigger than me. I was no match for him."

"A blow to the right spot, and any man will fall to the ground.

There were several times when you could've disabled him if you knew what you were doing."

"Will you teach me?"

I didn't answer right away. The Iranians in my rearview mirror had more of my attention. They followed us away from the police station and then dropped back and were keeping a safe distance away. Probably just out of the range of the RPK-74 assault rifle. Showing it to them had done the trick. They were hesitant to attack us. For now. They'd make their move as soon as we were outside the city limits which would be soon.

"Can you show me some moves?" Bae asked again excitedly, sitting up in the seat.

"I will. But not right now. I'm worried about losing the Iranians."

Bae turned in the seat and looked behind us. "I thought we did lose them," she said.

"Do you see those headlights?" I asked, pointing.

She nodded.

"That's the Iranians."

"How do you know it's them?" she asked.

"I just know."

"Why are they so far back then?"

I said, "Let's find out. Do you want to learn some more spy moves?"

"Sure."

At the next street, I turned right.

"Keep your eyes peeled for those headlights," I said.

Bae turned around in the seat, so that she was facing behind us, peering over the headrest.

"There they are," she said excitedly. "They turned too."

At the next street, I took another right.

"Watch for the car," I said.

"It turned again," Bae shouted a few seconds later.

I took another right.

The Iranians turned again and kept following us.

Another right and I was back on the main road.

"You were right," Bae said. "The car followed us the whole time."

"That's a good move to detect if someone is tailing you. Make four consecutive right-hand turns. Nobody does that unless they're following you. We call it losing a tail. If I were really trying to lose them, I would've executed the turns faster. I was just showing you how to find out if someone is following you."

"Oh... Why didn't you try to lose them?" Bae asked.

"These guys are professionals. We aren't going to get rid of them easily. These are basic moves I'm showing you."

"Now they know you know they're following us. If I said that right."

"I wanted them to. If they know I'm on to them, that'll make them hesitate to make a move. There's another move that will detect if someone's after you, but I don't want to do it now. It's too dangerous."

"What's that?" Bae asked.

"Pull off on an exit and then get right back on. If the car matches your move, then you know they're following you. You can also just pull off the side of the road. If they pull off as well, then they're a tail. Also, you can speed up and slow down. If the car matches your moves, then you're being followed."

"How do you lose a tail?" Bae asked.

"Good question. There are several ways."

"Will you teach me some of them?" she asked.

"If you stop at a light, that's a good place to lose a tail. When it turns green, don't move. Just stay stopped. This works really well if there's another driver stopped at the light going in the other direction. As soon as it turns red, then floor it. You have to get through the intersection before the other driver does. They'll block the person following you."

"That makes sense. The Iranians were chasing me on my bike. I should've done that then. I just ran through the red lights. That's why the policeman stopped me."

I figured Bae had a run in with the Iranians before I met her. She's lucky to have survived it.

"Another thing to do is turn off the road at the last second. If the person is tailing you, he won't have time to react."

"You sure do know a lot about being a spy," Bae said.

"Well… I've been doing it for a while."

"Do you think we can lose them?" Bae asked.

Before I could answer, the Iranians made their move. Their headlights were suddenly illuminating the inside of our car. Losing them was no longer an option. I knew it was going to take every bit of my abilities just to get us out of this alive.

"Put your seatbelt on!" I shouted to Bae.

She let out a shriek as the Iranians came up on us fast. They hit us in the rear end, trying to cause us to spin out. The police cruiser fishtailed but held the road. The tires weren't completely bald. I sped up to try to take advantage of their lost momentum.

A shot rang out. Barely perceptible. Most people wouldn't even notice it, if they didn't know what a gunshot from a moving car sounded like. I began to serpentine back and forth on the road. No other cars were in sight.

Bae gripped the door handle until her knuckles were white.

I sped up and slowed down to keep the Iranians off balance.

It's nearly impossible to get off a good shot when both cars are moving, especially on a road as bad as those in North Korea. I had to constantly avoid the potholes to keep from damaging a tire. Even then, that didn't mean the Iranian couldn't get off a lucky shot. But I felt better that they were behind us and not beside our car.

As if on cue, the Iranians sped up and tried to get beside us. I was able to block them. They tried again. This time I let them. When they were right beside us, the Iranian in the passenger seat leaned out the window and tried to steady the gun to get off a shot. At just the right moment, I slammed on the brakes, and his shot went careening harmlessly off into the field to our right.

Now I was behind them. I sped up rapidly and hit the Iranians at just the right angle to send them into a spin. Bae was amazingly quiet. Either paralyzed in fear or in control of her emotions. I wasn't sure, but it helped that she wasn't screaming in my ear. That would be a distraction I didn't need at the moment.

The Iranians didn't go into the ditch like I'd hoped but were facing the wrong direction when they came to a stop. I used that opportunity to speed away. Putting some distance between us was my top priority.

I gave Bae more instructions even though the road was getting most of my attention. "Another way to lose a car is when you go around a curve, take a side road if one is there. Don't do it unless you're out of their sight and the road goes somewhere. Otherwise, you'll get trapped on that side road. If it works, they'll continue on, and you can go back the way you came. Let's look for a road."

"What about a railroad crossing?" Bae asked.

"What about it?"

"There's a train just ahead," she said pointing at it. We'd been running beside train tracks for several miles. A train was just ahead, going in the same direction. We were coming up on it from the back.

"I know these roads," Bae said. "My dad and I ride our motorcycles out here all the time. If you hurry, you can beat them to the crossing. If you can get across to the other side of the tracks before they do, they'll have to wait for the train to pass, and we can get away."

"You're brilliant!" I said, flooring the car even more. It hesitated but eventually built up more speed. The sedan groaned and creaked under the strain. I felt like I was playing a video game trying to dodge all the ruts in the road.

"How far is the crossing?" I asked, as I saw the Iranian headlights again in my rearview mirror. They were back on our tail and gaining. Their car was newer and faster than ours.

"Just a couple of miles ahead. You're going to have to hurry to beat the train to the crossing"

Another mile and the Iranians had already caught up to us. The crossing was our best option if we could make it.

I pushed the car to its limit. The crossing was now in view. So was the front of the train. I assessed the angles in my mind. If I got to the crossing too late, then we were stuck on the road with the Iranians. It seemed like they were gaining the advantage. If I arrived too early, we would both make it through the crossing before the train, and I didn't know the road on the other side. If I arrived at just the wrong time, our bodies could be plastered on the front of the train along with our car.

Picturing it all in mind, I slowed down slightly.

"Why did you slow down?" Bae asked.

I didn't answer. I had to concentrate. The margin of error was in the milliseconds, and I didn't want to calculate incorrectly, or we'd end up dead. Too much was on the line for that to happen. I had to get that satchel to the CIA. And I had to stop Pok before he hacked into the CIA server and accessed all the secret information.

Slowing down didn't give away my plan to the Iranians. They'd be confused. That's what I wanted. The crossing was getting closer. If I timed it right, the Iranians might overshoot the crossing altogether.

"Hang on," I shouted to Bae.

I turned the wheel sharply, putting the car into a slide, steering into it with all my strength. When I regained control, I gunned the engine. It was a race to the crossing. The train was coming fast. The crossing wasn't flat. It wasn't even a crossing like what I was used to seeing in America. There were no lights or gates. The makeshift dirt road was at a slight incline and then went over two sets of tracks. The road on the other side went down another incline where the road made a sharp curve.

The car bounced wildly when we hit the tracks. For a moment, I thought the car would stall, but it continued on. The sound of the train was deafening. The earth shook, and the car vibrated so much that we were shaking like we were on a roller coaster at an amusement park ride at Disneyland.

I thought we had more time to spare. I panicked and hit the accelerator. The car jerked forward, and we were catapulted down the hill on the other side of the tracks. We cleared the tracks just a half second before the train blew through the crossing, trapping the Iranians on the other side.

Now I had a different problem. Just on the other side of the tracks was a sharp curve. Off the curve were cliffs, with a huge drop off.

"Hang on!" I shouted.

I slammed on the brakes, and the car skidded to a halt. Just feet away from a plunge to our certain death.

We both just sat there. In silence. My hands gripped the wheel and my knuckles were as white as Bae's.

"That was too close," I said, my voice cracking.

I heard Bae let out a deep sigh.

When I got my wits back about me, I assessed the car. It had stalled. I started it and started driving away. A loud thumpity-thump sound was coming from one of the tires which was obviously flat.

I pulled the car ahead, so it was just around the curve, out of the line of sight. I grabbed the gun out of the center console and got out of the car and leaned back on the hood.

"What are you doing?" Bae said.

"Waiting for the Iranians," I said.

22

What happened to the Iranians was a matter of basic geometry. The study of points, lines, angles, and intersections. Solids and spaces. Objects coming together at a common point.

In their defense, the Iranians didn't see what I saw.

How could they? Their view was blocked by the southbound train, which was taking its time getting through the crossing, successfully blocking them from getting to us.

My plan was to fill their car with lead as soon as they crossed over to our side of the tracks. I had twenty-four rounds of ammunition. Curly always said to count them before you go into a gunfight. My hope was that my bullets hit them before theirs hit me or I ran out of ammunition.

If I ran out of ammunition, I was as good as dead. In that event, Bae was to run in the woods with the satchel, and I would hold them off as long as I could. Not an ideal plan, but the best I could come up with under the circumstances.

Their plan was clear as well. To race through the intersection as soon as the southbound train cleared the crossing and catch back up to us. They were probably cursing their luck. Hoping we didn't get away with the head start the train had afforded us.

There were two things the Iranians didn't know. One was that we had a flat tire and were waiting for them on the other side. We had no head start. The only thing I could do was force a confrontation.

In that sense, I had the element of surprise working for me. They wouldn't see me or my gun until they came around the curve.

The other thing they didn't know was that there were two trains. A southbound and a northbound. One on each track going in opposite directions.

My mind was processing the geometric equations like a computer. I could see both trains clearly. The northbound freight train was barreling toward the crossing. The southbound train would be clear of the intersection shortly. At some point the beginning of one train and the end of the other would cross. That was a mathematical certainty. The entire equation could be calculated by any high school student if they knew the distance between them and the speed they were going.

What made the equation more difficult was whether it be at the exact moment I was hoping for. At the crossing. Is it possible that the southbound train could clear the crossing just seconds before the northbound train entered it? Could I be that lucky? The odds were astronomical.

Yet, things always seemed to work out that way for me. Jamie said it was divine providence. That God's hand was watching out for me. Curly, my handler, said that we were in a battle between good and evil. *Stay on the good side and good things will happen*, he had said. Some of my colleagues attributed it to a force of the universe, karma, so to speak. Me? I believed in the God of the Bible and always attributed my good fortune to the protection of the Trinity–God the Father, Jesus the Son, and the Holy Spirit. My mother would be proud that I still remembered some things from my upbringing.

I never believed in God more than I did at that moment when the trains aligned in the exact geometric equation almost exactly as it had played out in my mind. When the southbound train cleared the crossing, the Iranians didn't stop to look to see if there was another train on the second set of tracks. A common mistake often made in the states. I only knew about it because my dad spent time around the railroads and drilled in us crossing safety.

The Iranians almost cleared the intersection before the second train arrived.

Almost.

Divine providence.

Had the northbound train arrived at the crossing one second later, the Iranians would've cleared it. Probably shaken from the close call but thinking Allah had saved them. One second earlier, and the crossing would've been blocked, and the gunfight would've only been delayed by the length of time it took the northbound train to clear the intersection.

As it was, the timing couldn't have been more perfect. From my perspective, not theirs. Good overcame evil. God overcame Allah. Some would say the stars aligned. I didn't believe in that stuff. To me the irrefutable laws of geometry aligned.

A. The southbound train cleared the crossing.

B. The Iranians drove into the crossing thinking it was clear.

C. The northbound train entered the crossing at the exact moment the Iranians did.

B intersected with C at the same time and in the same space.

"If a train hits you, the train will always win," my dad used to say.

The train caught the back end of the Iranians car just enough to send it sideways and with enough force to catapult the car into a violent roll. It sounded like a thousand-piece high school band all playing in the wrong key. Combined with the roar of the train, the noise generated by the two was ear-splitting. The sparks from the impact lit up the sky like a firework's show.

I grabbed Bae and pulled her close to me to hide her eyes from the devastation unfolding before us. The Iranian car flipped over and over again until it finally came to rest on the edge of the cliff. I could feel her peeking around my grip. Like any car crash, it's human nature to have to look. It's hard to resist.

When the Iranian's car finally came to a stop, I told Bae to wait by the car and ran toward the wreckage. I didn't even bother raising my gun. There was no way they survived that crash. The car wasn't even recognizable. As I got close, what was left of the car began to teeter and rock slightly until gravity took over, and it plunged over the cliff. It bounded down the side, rolling several more times until it exploded, sending a large plume of black smoke into the air.

At the bottom of the cliffs was a swift river. The car and its plume of smoke plunged into the waterway, sending a cascade of water in several directions while putting out the flames. The car landed on its top, so its mangled wheels and undercarriage were the only things showing. About twenty to thirty feet down the river, the vehicle sank to the bottom.

My body was numb as I stood on the edge of the cliff, taking in the entire scene, trying to process all the ramifications of what just happened. I dropped to my knees to thank God for saving us.

After the prayer, I had the presence of mind to check my surroundings. No one was around. We were the only ones who saw what happened. The northbound train cleared the crossing, and there was no sign of it slowing down or stopping. The engineer either didn't see or feel the impact or didn't care. He probably had a schedule to keep and figured whoever got hit by the train was in a pile of rubble that someone else could sort out.

Pieces of the car were strewn along the road. I didn't see either of the Iranians thrown from the wreckage, but I looked around just in case, even checking the bushes and ditch that ran alongside the road. Satisfied we were safe, and the Iranians were in their watery tomb, I was suddenly overcome with elation bordering on euphoria, and I let myself celebrate.

Bae ran toward me with a worried look still on her face.

I raised my hand high in the air and gave her a big reassuring smile to let her know everything was okay.

"Give me a high five!" I said lowering it down so she could reach it.

Bae looked at me with a puzzled frown as both sides of her mouth dipped.

I took her hand and raised her arm high in the air. And then slapped it against mine. She caught on and we did it several times.

"Why is it called a high-five?" she asked.

I waved my fingers in the air. "Because we have five fingers. In America we hit our hands together when something good happens."

"Here's what we do," Bae said, taking my arms and interlocking hers with mine. She started prancing around in a circle. We were like children playing on a playground. I could feel the tension leaving our arms.

It felt good to just let go and act like a kid for at least a moment. The thought occurred to me that one of us was still a child. Then I looked at Bae and realized that she was no longer a child. Never would be again, considering everything she'd been through. She was growing up fast. The innocence of childhood was gone forever. Bae had seen things most teenagers would never see.

We danced and laughed until we were out of breath. Then I saw it come over her face as the emotion of the moment was too much, and Bae began sobbing. I took her in my arms and squeezed her tightly.

"It's okay," I said. "Everything's going to be okay. Those men will never hurt you again."

She kept sobbing. Uncontrollably. I didn't try to stop her.

"Those men killed my parents," Bae finally said, trying to choke back the tears.

She then began explaining the whole story. We sat on a rock near the cliffs as she related the events of the last few days. Stealing the satchel. The man chased her into the mountains.

"How did you kill the Iranian?" I asked, fascinated by the entire tale.

"He was chasing me, and he fell. The gun was in his hand and went off. I guess he shot himself."

Divine providence. God was working things together for good before we even met.

Bae then described how the two men came to their house. One of them shot her mom in the head. She didn't see her dad killed but heard the shot and saw him fall to the ground.

"How did you get away?" I asked.

"The Iranians chased me on my dad's motorcycle. I ran a red light and a policeman stopped me and arrested me."

"Probably a good thing. The Iranians would have eventually caught you and killed you."

"If you hadn't come along..." Bae said, not able to even finish the sentence.

"I did come along. God brought us together for a reason." I knew most people in North Korea were atheist. The Yang family portrayed themselves as the only deity to be worshiped. Maybe I'd get a chance to tell her more about God and Jesus. Now didn't seem like the right time. I couldn't imagine the grief she must be going through.

"What was in the satchel that the Iranians wanted so badly?" Bae asked me.

I hesitated, not sure how much to tell her. Then I decided that she deserved to know. She had risked her life to protect the satchel. Then I decided she didn't need to know. The less she knew, the less chance her life would be in danger.

"I don't know," I finally answered, feeling like a real jerk for lying to her.

I changed the subject.

"Do you have any other family?" I asked. "Is there somewhere I can take you?"

Bae shook her head. "I have relatives, but I don't really know them very well. I wouldn't even know how to contact them."

Bae was all alone in the world which created a dilemma for me. The Iranians weren't the only threat facing me. I still had Pok and the cyber lab to deal with. I also had to get the codes in the satchel back to Langley. How could I do that and still take care of her?

I decided to avoid the subject for now. I stood and started picking up pieces of what looked like a plane crash debris field. I didn't want any evidence on the road that might cause people to investigate further. Bae helped. When we were done to my satisfaction, I changed the flat tire, and we got back on the road.

I also decided not to bring up the subject again. I needed time to think about what to do with Bae and how to get the codes from her without her knowing about it.

23

Bae recovered quickly from the emotional breakdown. That was a characteristic of a good spy, Curly always said. *Get back to the mission as soon as possible. Don't dwell too long on your successes or failures.*

In my line of work, I saw a lot of death and destruction. Those things had to be put out of my mind fast. The Agency required us to see a counselor periodically. She warned that such emotional disconnection from reality was detrimental in the long run. Truthfully, I had no emotional connection to the death of the Iranians. My two cents worth was that the world was better off without them.

I wondered what the counselor would say about Bae. A thirteen-year-old should never be expected to get over things that quickly. For that matter, a young girl should not have to go through what she just went through. She should be thinking about boys and homework like all the other girls her age.

Still, Bae was in a good mood, which I was grateful for because it was helping mine.

We were on the road again, headed south. It had been at least twenty miles since I saw any sign of civilization. Overall, I was feeling better about the mission. I had a weapon. The two Iranians were dead, and I didn't have to fire a shot.

I had transportation, although it was a police cruiser which was good and bad. People in North Korea tended to avoid any contact with policemen including eye contact. The bad part of it was that an American man driving a North Korean police car would raise suspicion to anyone who had reason to look our way. The only saving grace was that the windows were darkened, and no one could see inside unless they were coming toward us and were looking through the windshield. That would only be a problem tomorrow during the day.

The biggest problem tonight was that we were both hungry and exhausted. We needed time to re-energize. The obvious place to go was Bae's house. There we could get a shower, a meal, and a good night's sleep. I quickly rejected that idea. No way could I put Bae through the trauma of seeing the body of her dead parents all over again.

Neither of us would get much sleep there anyway. The possibility was real that there were more Iranians out there. If there were, that was the first place they'd look. I didn't voice that concern to Bae, but I did say that we needed to go "dark" for several hours.

"What does it mean to go dark?" she asked.

"It's a spy term. It means that we make ourselves unavailable. Hard to find. You can also say 'off the grid.'" The term was also a military term which meant to cease all communications. It was used on the battlefield when they didn't want the enemy to know their location or intercept their communications. I tended to go dark a lot on a mission. I preferred to work alone and with little supervision. Technically, I went dark the minute I decided to go off the reservation and come to North Korea.

"We need to find some food and a place to stay," I said. "The problem is that I don't have any won." *Won* was the official North Korean currency. "In America, there's a gas station and hotel at every exit," I said.

We hadn't seen anything but shanties and old broken-down homes since we left Wonsan. The poverty out in the rural areas of North Korea was staggering.

"One of the bigger villages will have a store," Bae said confidently.

"That doesn't change the fact that I don't have any money," I countered.

"We could rob the store," Bae said.

"We only steal from bad guys," I retorted, raising my voice. "That's the first rule of being a spy. You don't hurt people."

"Tell that to the Iranians," Bae said, chuckling.

I couldn't help but laugh out loud. "You know what I mean. We only hurt the bad people."

Bae's shoulders sagged, and she slumped down in the seat a little, probably feeling guilty or even some shame. She stole backpacks from innocents all the time. That's what got her in this mess, although, ironically, the person she stole the satchel from turned out to be a really bad guy.

I suddenly felt the guilt as well. What I said to her wasn't completely true. I had stolen from good guys before. If it was a life and death situation, I did whatever I had to do to survive. There had been many times when I'd stolen a car, or some food and water from an innocent if necessary, to complete the mission. Rarely, and only when there was no other option, but I didn't have the right to act like Bae's moral superior.

And I felt another twinge of guilt when I remembered that I had lied to her about not knowing what was in the satchel. This was the second time I hadn't told her the whole truth. In my profession, I did it all the time. For some reason, it bothered me that I was lying to Bae.

Before I could explain further, she held up an object in the air that was difficult to see inside the dark car.

"We have this," she said, waving it in the air.

"What's that?" I asked.

Bae opened it and started rummaging through it. I turned on the center console light to see what she was doing. I checked first to make sure no other cars were around. The last thing we needed was to be spotted on the road because I had the center light on.

In her hand was a wallet.

"Where did you get that?" I asked.

"I took it from the policeman. The one back at the station."

I remembered Bae going back into the cell while I was in the office securing a weapon. I looked in just in time to see her give the man a swift kick in the ribs, and then wince from the pain in her foot. It made me smile because the man deserved it. Apparently, she also went back there to get his wallet. That was good thinking. The policeman might have a few day's bribes in there.

"Have you been holding out on me?" I asked jokingly, while giving her a poke in the side with my finger.

She shrank away and let out a giggle. "There's more than 45,000 won in here," Bae said holding the currency in the air. That was equivalent to fifty US dollars, which didn't sound like a lot, but in North Korea, that was three to six months of wages for the average person. He had more than a few day's bribes. That might be a month's worth.

"That's enough money for something to eat and a place to stay," Bae said.

A few miles down the road around a large and windy curve a town appeared. Not a town really, in that the sum of it was all in a one block area. Right in the center of that block was a convenience store. From the looks of it, the store might be the nicest building in the entire village. We pulled into the store but parked in a space where the vehicle wasn't in plain view from inside. Bae would have to be the one to go in. I'd wait outside with my gun in case she ran into any trouble.

"Go inside and get us some food and something to drink," I said. "Also ask if there's a place to stay nearby. A motel or something."

Bae was gone for a long time. After about ten minutes, I wondered if she'd slipped out a back exit to get away from me. In some ways, I wished she would. That would make things easier. But she was growing on me. I liked having her around and felt this parenting urge inside of me to protect her. Maybe more like a big brother impulse.

I'd had this feeling before. Curly tried to describe it to us, although he said you had to experience it to know what he was talking about. When you're on a mission with another person, and you get shot at, and come within an inch of losing your life, a bond develops between you and your partner. It was an indescribable bond that wasn't easily broken. I felt that with Bae. Like she was my partner in this particular mission. It was like God brought us together for a reason.

Maybe I was her mentor. She was my ingenue. *Where did that word come from?* I heard it recently. My mind struggled for the definition. I remembered. It meant a young, naïve girl. An innocent who needed someone to take her under their wing and nurture and teach her the things of the world. I was kind of enjoying teaching Bae some things about being a spy.

Whatever the feeling was, when she came out with two large bags of groceries I let out a sigh of relief. Clearly, I wasn't ready for our relationship to end.

She had a huge grin on her face. Bae got inside the car and slammed the door shut. "I got you a present," she said.

"Do you have to make so much racket? We're trying not to get noticed," I said.

I could see her crinkle her nose at me. It didn't dampen her excitement about my present. She pulled a shirt out of the bag and held it up for me to look at. "This was the biggest size they had. I hope it fits."

My heart warmed, and I could feel the emotion rise inside of me. The shirt was navy blue, with a collar. Not something I would normally wear, but it was the thought that counted. It had the North

Korean emblem on it, which was a circle with a star in the center. I laughed to myself. That would be a good shirt to wear to CIA headquarters one day as a joke. At least it didn't have Min Yang's picture on it. Most tee shirts I'd seen in North Korea had the Divine Leader's name or image on it. If I wore one of those to CIA headquarters I might get shot.

"I love it," I said. "I'll think of you every time I wear it." I meant every word I said. I would cherish the gift forever. "Did you get some food?"

"Oh... I forgot!" she said sarcastically. "Of course, I got some food. And something to drink."

Bae started rifling through the first bag.

"I got some Korean sweet cakes," she said as she pulled out a package, opened it, and handed one to me.

I put it in my mouth.

"Give me another one," I said.

I scarfed two down, barely swallowing. They tasted like donuts. At that moment, I couldn't imagine anything tasting better.

"I got some ginger-flavored crackers and cheese." Her head was buried in the sack, going through each item like she had an order in which she wanted to present them to me. "Oh! I got another kind of cracker. Laver flavored." Bae could hardly contain her excitement.

"What is laver?" I asked. "That doesn't sound like something I would like," I said while I licked my fingers from the sweet cakes.

"It's made from seaweed," she answered.

I made a face and said, "Eww. I've never had seaweed before."

"Then how do you know you won't like it? You're going to try it," Bae said as she went back to her rummaging.

I made a funny sound of disgust.

"Don't be such a baby," she said, suddenly becoming the parent in the relationship. "It's good. It tastes sweet. The other crackers are salty."

"Okay, I'll try it. If you insist."

I had eaten worse things on a mission. There were times when I ate whatever I could get my hands on and was glad to have it. There had been a few times on this mission when I'd been starving.

"I got some Azuke Bean Rice Balls," Bae said in a heavy accent. For the most part I could understand her when she spoke. I asked her to spell out the word.

Instead of spelling it, she just showed me the package. They looked like cheese puffs.

"I also got some Pumpkin baked Monaca Biscuits. And some sweet Red Bean Jelly Bars. I got a dozen of those. Although, you look like you could eat all of them at once."

Now I knew why it took her so long in the store.

"Did you buy one of everything in the store?"

Bae laughed. I loved her laugh. It wasn't deep throated at all. Higher pitched, and it came in short bursts. Like a piccolo.

"Any protein in any of that?" I asked. "Seems like you mostly got sweets."

"I got some protein," Bae said dismissively. She started going through the second bag. "Here's some sliced meat. It's dog meat."

"I'm not eating dog meat!"

"You eat hot dogs!"

"That's not the same thing! Those are not made from dogs. They're made from cows or pigs."

"What's the difference between eating a pig or a dog?" Bae asked.

"I'm not eating dog!" The thought of eating a dog made me gag.

"I'm just kidding. It's ham." Bae roared with laughter.

I joined her.

"What else do you have?" I asked.

"I got two watermelon ice cream bars."

"Let's eat those first!"

"I'm not allowed to eat dessert first."

"Just this one time. Those will melt if we don't eat them fast."

I started the car, pulled out of the store lot, and drove away. Still south. Toward the cyber lab. With no plan.

"I got this to drink," she said. "Omija Berry Tea."

She bought a twelve pack of them. I downed one in seconds. The cool liquid soothed my parched throat and made me forget about the cyber lab and Pok for at least the time being.

"By the way," Bae said. "The store clerk said there's a place to stay just ahead on the right."

We found the place and pulled into the parking lot. We sat in the car and finished eating until we were both full.

It was the best meal I'd had in a long time. The best part was it only cost four American dollars and was paid for by the policeman who was probably waking up from his concussion about that same time.

24

The motel room cost the equivalent of two American dollars. After looking at it, we both agreed we paid too much.

"What are you doing, Alex?" Bae asked me.

"I'm looking for bugs," I said.

"You mean, spy bugs. Like listening devices?" she asked. "Why would there be bugs in our hotel room? No one knows we're here."

"No. I mean real bugs, as in creepy crawly things."

I pulled the bedspread back and looked under the sheets. We asked for two beds but were given one Queen-sized bed. The sheets looked clean. The bedspread looked like it hadn't been cleaned in several years. I pulled it off the bed completely.

"I don't like bugs," I said, shivering my shoulders.

Bae let out a laugh that could only be interpreted as mocking me. "You can stare a gun in the face, but you're afraid of a little ol' bug!"

"No way I'm sleeping on this floor," I said. "My shoes make a crunching sound every time I take a step."

"I'll sleep on the floor. I'm not afraid of a few cockroaches."

"Have you seen any cockroaches?" I asked, looking around the room nervously.

"There's one right behind you!" Bae said in a serious tone. My feet did a little dance as I looked where she was pointing. I didn't see anything. Bae rolled her eyes and walked into the bathroom.

"It has a shower," she said from inside the room, shouting back out to me. "There's a bar of soap in here, but there's not much of it left."

She walked out of the room holding the stub of a bar of yellow soap.

"Don't touch that!" I said. "No telling what's growing on that thing."

She lobbed it at me like she expected me to catch it. I let it fall to the ground. "What are you doing?" I asked. "You're going to have to pick that thing up and throw it away cause I'm not touching it."

"Something is seriously wrong with you," Bae said facetiously.

"I'm a bit of a germaphobe," I admitted.

"What's a germaphobe?" She rummaged through our grocery bags, leaving the soap laying on the floor like a dead mouse staring up at me.

"Somebody who's afraid of germs," I answered. "I'm not really afraid. I just don't like them."

"There's also a toothbrush in the bathroom you can use," she said with a wide grin on her face.

"You're making fun of me now!" I countered.

"I'm just kidding," she said, pulling some items out of the bag. "I got toothpaste and two toothbrushes. Shampoo and soap."

I walked over and looked in the bag. "I'm beginning to like you," I said as I grabbed them roughly out of her hand, "I'm taking a shower. At least the water will be clean."

I inspected the bathroom before taking off any of my clothes. The shower was relatively clean, considering. The towels were tattered and worn, but usable. They had the smell of lye or some kind of bleach which meant they'd been cleaned recently. The shower curtain had seen better days but was functional. The shower head showed signs of rust, but at least it wasn't broken, and water would run through it.

If the motel had running water. I put the odds at fifty-fifty.

I turned on the faucet. The pipes creaked and moaned like a bear being awakened from a winter hibernation. The water did come out but in a weak but steady stream. It took several minutes, but it eventually turned from ice cold to lukewarm. It felt good to get under the faucet and let the remnants of the last few days get washed down the drain.

Occasionally, the water pulsed out, like the fancy massage shower heads in a five-star hotel. I closed my eyes and pretended. I had the uncanny ability to let my imagination put me into more pleasant places and override whatever difficult situation I was in.

I let out a scream. Something ran across my foot. I'd just lathered my hair, and the suds were in my eyes so I couldn't see it.

Bae knocked on the door. "Are you okay?" she asked sincerely.

"I'm not alone in here," I said nervously, trying to brush the soap out of my eyes.

She cracked the door open and said, "What do you mean you're not alone?"

"I think one of those cockroaches is in the shower with me," I said.

Bae laughed mockingly again. "I don't know how your girlfriend puts up with you."

I threw some water over the top of the shower curtain and got a direct hit because she let out a little scream and slammed the door shut.

Truthfully, I was thankful for the shower. I stayed in longer than I should have. When the lukewarm water started turning colder, I thought I'd better get out and save some for Bae.

Still, I took my time before surrendering the room. Brushing my teeth felt as good as it ever had, although the water tasted like it had sulfur in it. My guess was that it came from a well. I was careful not to swallow any of it.

Hanging on the back of the door of the bathroom were two bathrobes. They looked at least twenty years old, signifying that maybe in its heyday the motel had some respectability. Mostly, I was thankful for the robe because it meant I didn't have to put my dirty and smelly clothes back on.

I took the soap and washed my clothes off in the sink and finally surrendered the bathroom, carrying my wet clothes to hang on the long dresser in the bedroom to dry.

"That took long enough," Bae heckled me.

"Shut up! I haven't had a shower in several days."

"I know. I've spent the last few hours with you." She crinkled her nose into a funny face.

I threw my towel at her getting a direct hit. "There's another robe in there," I said as she closed the door behind her. "And a towel."

"Hey Alex," Bae shouted out to me a few minutes later.

I walked over to the door and could hear the shower running.

"Yeah. Do you need something?" I asked.

"Can you hand me the soap that's on the floor?"

"I left the soap in there. And the shampoo."

"I'd rather use the old soap than the soap you used."

"You're not funny!"

She was funny. That sounded like something my girlfriend Jamie would say. The more time passed the more I genuinely liked her.

***

Before we went to bed, I went through my nighttime preparations for whenever I'm inside enemy territory. I propped a chair under the doorknob so no one could enter through the door without me knowing it.

I put my gun on the nightstand and practiced reaching for it from my position on the bed. I couldn't let Bae sleep on the floor, so

I decided that I would sleep above the sheets and she could sleep below them. It wasn't necessary as far as she was concerned. She trusted me, but I insisted.

Bae mocked me again because of all my preparations. She said I didn't have anything to worry about. That all the concern was unnecessary.

"I haven't stayed alive this long by being careless. I'm not going to start now."

"We're in the mountain areas. No one will bother us here," Bae said, settling into her side of the bed. Once she was in bed under the sheets, she let out a slight moan of satisfaction.

I agreed with her. As bad as the room was, I was happy to have it. Better than sleeping in the car or out in the open on the ground somewhere.

"I didn't see any phone lines going to the office," I said, laying on my back with my hands behind my head staring up at the ceiling. "So, nobody can make any phone calls to report us."

"The police don't patrol in the mountains. They stay down in the flatlands where there are more people and more industry. The people in the mountains are really poor. Nothing to steal up here."

"Why is that? I mean... I know most people in North Korea are poor. Why is it worse in the mountains?" I thought I knew but thought Bae might have even more insight.

"The land in the mountains is not fit for growing crops. Most of the food is grown in the eastern flatlands by the coast. Also, the winters are so harsh that you can only grow food six months out of the year, which means they can only harvest one crop per year. The Rust Belt is even worse."

"What's the Rust Belt?" I asked. I knew of the Rust Belt in the United States but had never heard of it in North Korea.

"It's up north. The very top regions of North Korea. Those are the poorest of all. Their winters are even harsher. What little industry they have practically shuts down in the wintertime. When the *koananui haenggun* hit, those people barely survived."

I sat up in the bed and propped up on one arm facing her. "What's the koananui haenggun?" I asked.

"It's also known as the Arduous March," she said solemnly.

"I think I've heard of that."

Bae shifted so she was propped up on one arm, and we were facing each other.

"The Arduous March was the great famine. Although people aren't allowed to talk about it. It's not taught in schools."

"Why not?'

"The regime denies it even happened. It makes them look bad. The words famine and hunger are banned in our society. It implies that the government has failed in some way."

"Why am I not surprised?" I said, somewhat shocked that Bae was this honest with me. If the authorities heard her talking like this, she'd be arrested.

"Almost two million people died!" she said, raising her voice for emphasis.

I could feel my mouth fly open. "Two million people? That's ten percent of your population. How do you even know about it if it's not taught in schools?"

"My parents told me. Even they had a hard time and they were better off than most."

"That must've been horrible."

"The food was rationed," Bae said, shifting positions.

"I'm sure the Yang family had plenty to eat," I said in disgust, wondering if she would be offended by my obvious dig at the Divine Leader. There was nothing divine about him as far as I was concerned. It seemed like she might feel the same way.

"They did, of course," she said, not giving any of her political views away by her tone. "That's why a lot of people in the mountains resent the regime. The way they were treated was inhumane."

Tears welled up in her eyes as she talked about it. I could tell at that point that she was more concerned about the people than defending the regime.

"The Yang's had plenty of food. Then the military. They were fed before my parents even."

"That's how these dictators stay in power," I explained. "I've seen it all over the world. They take care of the military, so they'll stay loyal to them. That makes it harder for people to overthrow cruel despots." I wondered if Bae knew that term, despots.

"Right," she said, either agreeing or just keeping the conversation moving. "The elite were fed next after the military. People like my family. Between the Yang family, the military, and the elite, there wasn't much left over for anyone else."

"How did they divide the rest of the food?" I asked soberly. "Could the mountain people keep what they grew?"

"Everything was seized by the government. Some people hid some, I'm sure. But there were laws made that had to be followed or they were subject to imprisonment."

"I would think the last place a person would want to be was in prison during a famine. Prisoners were probably the last to get fed."

"Actually, children were."

"Children?" I sat up further in bed, hardly believing what Bae was telling me.

"Here was the order. This was an actual decree from the Leader Centre."

I knew that was the name given to the divine leader who was now Min Yang.

"The military was fed first. Then the elites. Then men."

"Men?"

"Yes. Then women."

"I had no idea women were that low in the pecking order."

"Then children. Unless they were under two. The Party Centre decreed that children under two weren't to be given solid food. Of course, people defied the order. But unless the mother could breast-feed the child, he or she would likely die."

"That must've been awful. The mother was starving herself. How could she breastfeed a baby?" I didn't know Bae well enough to know if she was embellishing. It certainly sounded like something the Yang family would do, but I didn't know for sure. I could hardly believe that anyone could be that cold-hearted as to let children die.

"The mountain people suffered the most," Bae explained. "They were left to fend for themselves. That's why there is so much resentment among them."

"Can they grow livestock in the mountains? You know. Cows. Pigs. Animals for food."

"For the most part, we're only allowed to eat meat on public holidays," she said.

"What is considered a public holiday?" I asked, wondering if they celebrated things like Christmas, Thanksgiving, and Easter.

"Min Yang II and Min Yang-il's birthdays are the two main holidays. People can only eat meat on those days. Twice a year. That ham you ate earlier was rare. I'm surprised I found it on the shelf."

I was actually hungry again and had thought about having another snack. The ham with cheese and crackers. I suddenly felt guilty About eating meat twice in one day, when no one in North Korea had meat more than twice in one year.

25

A loud bang on the door woke me from a deep sleep. A split second after my eyes were opened, I grabbed the gun from the nightstand and was out of bed and bounded toward the door. Bae bolted upright in the bed. I motioned her to be quiet.

"Cheongso," a lady said in a heavy Korean accent.

"You've got to be kidding me," I said as I lowered my weapon.

"Cleaning," the woman said again in Korean, banging on the door harder.

"Ajig!" Bae said. She told the lady, "Not yet!"

I took in two deep breaths and tried to slow my heart from the adrenaline that pumped through my veins.

"The mountain people start to work early," Bae said.

"Apparently. What time is it?" There were no clocks anywhere in the room. That must be a luxury for hotels that had at least one star. The thought brought a smile to my face. Surprisingly, I felt well rested and in a good mood.

Bae scooted over to the edge of the bed and reached for her watch. "It's almost nine o'clock," she said. "I can't believe I slept so late."

"You had an eventful day yesterday."

That's why I was so well rested. We slept for nearly ten hours. It was common for spies and soldiers to crash after their bodies were subjected to huge rushes of adrenaline the day before. Sometimes it was hard to get to sleep. Once you did, it was hard to wake up.

I checked my clothes, and they were dry, so I went into the bathroom and put them on. I splashed some nasty water on my face just to shake the cobwebs out of my head, brushed my teeth, and tried the best I could to comb my mussed hair with my hands and fingers.

When I was done, Bae took over the bathroom, and I helped myself to more ham, crackers, cheese, and two of the Korean Sweet Cakes that tasted like donuts. I washed them down with two cans of Omija Berry tea. The morning breakfast also washed the taste of the sink water out of my mouth, hopefully for the last time.

Bae took longer in the bathroom than I expected which gave me time to think of a plan. Today, I had to go to the cyber lab. The problem was figuring out how to infiltrate it a second time. I didn't think there was any way I would ever see the inside of the building again. Word had probably gotten back to them that I escaped from the prison cell, so security would be a lot tighter than before.

The only option was to secure a computer and hack into their network within the range of their wi-fi. The lab itself didn't have wireless for that reason. But I noticed that Pok accessed the system from his phone, wirelessly. There was a possibility I could get in the system through his phone connection if I could get close enough to the building without being spotted.

The problem was that I didn't have a computer. I also had Bae which was another complication. No way I was going to put her in harm's way again. The only thing I could think to do was go back to South Korea, drop off Bae at the American embassy, secure my laptop and cell phone, and sneak back into North Korea.

That would cost me valuable time. However, there were no other options. Computers were illegal in North Korea except for those that were government issued, and I had no idea how to find one of those. A computer store was on every corner in South Korea. The two Koreas were so different.

This whole trip enlightened me to how bad things were in North Korea, and I felt extreme pity for the people who had to live under such horrible conditions. All of which was preventable if one man didn't selfishly control an entire country with such idiocy. Also, hard to believe that some in our country actually wanted America to become communist. They should see what I had seen on this trip.

I couldn't fathom why Min Yang wouldn't let his people come into the twenty-first century. He could still be the dictator. Just let his people enjoy some modern conveniences. The Chinese government was as ruthless and heavy handed as Min. Maybe even more so in some ways. Yet, everyone had a cell phone and computer and could move freely around the country, even fly around the world through their many international airports.

My idea to go back to South Korea wasn't ideal, but it was the best I could come up with under the circumstances, and I was anxious to get moving.

"You said you'd show me some self-defense moves," Bae said excitedly as she came out of the bathroom. "Can we do that now?"

I hadn't told her my plan. I wasn't even sure she'd want to leave North Korea. When I hesitated, a look of disappointment crossed her face and her eyes drooped slightly, as she lost some of the excitement she had come out of the bathroom with. She didn't know it, but this might be my last opportunity, and I promised her.

"Oh, come on!" Bae said, as she put her body into a fighting stance. She bounced around with her fists up, and playfully punched at me in the air.

"Seriously! That's how you're going to fight me?" I said jokingly.

She punched me in the stomach.

"Ow! What did you do that for?" I said.

"Maybe I'll teach you some lessons!" She hit me in the stomach harder.

"Stop it!"

"Are you going to teach me or not?"

She started to throw another punch with her right hand. I anticipated it and grabbed her wrist with my left hand and twisted her arm in a counterclockwise position.

Bae immediately cried out in pain and dropped to her knees. "You're hurting me," she said, and I released my grip.

"Lesson one. It doesn't take much to disable a person. That move will cause a three-hundred-pound man to cry like a baby and beg you to stop."

Bae stood to her feet, rubbing her wrist. When Curly had done that to me, he wasn't so gentle. My wrist hurt for days.

"First thing is that you don't want to stand like someone itching to start a fight."

"How do I stand then?" Bae said like a student would to a teacher when they thought they already knew the answer.

"Just stand like you normally would. You want the other person to think you're not prepared to fight even though you are. So, stand like this." I moved my feet slightly about a shoulder's length apart and put my left foot slightly forward and my weight on my back foot. I took Bae by the shoulders and moved her body, so she was in the same position.

"Like this," she said, putting her fists up and in front of her.

"Drop your hands to your sides."

"I won't be protected. I'll be wide open for a punch."

I turned away and started to pack my things.

"What are you doing?" Bae said with urgency. "Aren't you going to teach me how to fight?"

"I'm not going to waste my time if you're going to argue with me."

Her shoulders slumped, and she sneered, angrier it seemed at herself than mad at me. Sort of like a child who had just been reprimanded.

"I'm sorry. I was just asking. I'll be quiet. I promise."

I stood back in front of her. "Hands to your sides."

She dropped her hands.

"Relax your shoulders." I shook them back and forth to loosen them up some.

"The first rule is to not fight when possible. Anytime you avoid a confrontation, you win even if you know you're better than that person."

"Second rule." I stared into her eyes. Her gaze matched my stare intensity. "Use the least amount of force possible to defuse the situation. Don't let your emotions come into play. You'll have an overwhelming urge to hurt the person. Make them pay for confronting you. Resist that urge. Just because you can kill someone, doesn't mean you have to."

"I get that. No revenge." Bae was a lot more amenable after I had chastised her. That's a good thing. Curly had a harder time with me than I was having with Bae. My girlfriend Jamie was worse than I was.

"Most people want to throw punches with their fists," I explained. "That's how they fight." I simulated a right hook against her jaw. "That's an inefficient way to fight for two reasons. Your knuckles are fragile and easily broken. The head is the strongest part of the body. You're hitting a person with one of your weakest weapons against their strongest defense.

"You're always armed," I continued. "Your body has five lethal weapons on it. First is your heel." I raised my foot and showed her the back of my heel. I had on thick boots with a heavy heel.

Bae wore sneakers. She raised her heel.

"You need to wear different shoes to a fight. Those are fine for everyday life. If you're on a mission, you want to wear a shoe that you can run in but will also do a lot of damage if you kick someone. Lead with your heel when you kick someone. Toes are like knuckles. They are fragile and easily broken. The back of your heel is strong and won't break easily. That's what you want to use. Also, your knee is a weapon. As is your elbow. Feel my knee and elbow."

I showed her how pointed and sharp they were.

"I see what you mean."

"The palm of your hand is what you want to use to throw a punch. Feel how hard that is," I said as I held out my hand.

Bae felt it.

"You said there were five. That's only four."

"You're right. The other is your forehead." I tapped mine. "That's probably the strongest of all of them. But to use it you have to be really close to the person. And you can also do damage to your own brain if you hit the person hard enough. So, avoid that if necessary."

"Avoid a head butt," Bae repeated.

I stared at her for a moment. She was going a little overboard in being amenable. I needed to get her fire back.

"I slapped her on the head."

"Hey! What did you do that for?"

I slapped her on the cheek. Hard enough to get a rise out of her.

Bae balled her fists and went into her fighter's stance.

"See you didn't listen to anything I just said. You let your emotions take over and you fell into your fighting position. You have to always control your emotions. They will get you killed."

"What am I supposed to do if someone hits me? Just stand there and take it?"

"Walk away if you can."

"If that's not an option then what?"

"Then you hurt the person."

"How do I do that?"

"It doesn't take much. All you have to do is hit them where they are most vulnerable. Most people go for the head. That's wrong.

That's the strongest part of the body. Don't do that. Plus, you're a small girl. You'll get out of balance if you lunge at someone's head."

"Where should I hit the person?"

"In the most vulnerable parts of the body. Let's start at the bottom and work up. Toes."

"Toes?"

"Yes. Toes are fragile and easily broken. Which of your weapons would you use to hurt someone's toes?"

I could see Bae thinking as her eyes wandered. "The heel," she answered.

"Very good." I walked around Bae, so I was behind her now. I wrapped my arms around her in a bear hug. "How could you get out of this?" I asked.

She wriggled back and forth, but my grip was too strong. "Don't struggle. Maintain your control. Struggling wastes energy. Remember, a heel is a weapon and toes are vulnerable."

"I stomp on your foot."

"Exactly! And you stomp hard. Viciously. With all your might. Make every blow count."

Bae stomped her foot. I moved mine away. Even with my thick boots, a hard stomp would hurt.

Bae stomped her feet several times.

"Harder!" I said.

"Good! You're doing good."

Bae's eyes brightened from the encouragement.

I took my position behind her again. "Another vulnerable area is the shin. And the knee. A kick to the shin or knee with your heel will drop even the strongest man."

Bae raised her leg and tensed like she intended to do it. I stopped her. "Just simulate it. Slowly." I didn't want her kicking my shin with her heel. I knew firsthand how much that hurt.

She practiced it several times. "Good." I turned her around, so she faced me again. I showed her how to pivot and hit a person in the shin or knee with her heel before they could react. After a few tries, she actually got surprisingly good at it.

"Another vulnerable area in men is the groin."

I could see Bae blush as she turned her eyes away.

"That will put a man down in a second. But it's also hard to pull off. Men naturally try to protect that area. So, the blow has to be a surprise."

"Which weapon do I use?"

"Heel and knee. Let me show you." I moved Bae so she stood close to me.

"If you are really close like this, use a knee." I showed her how to bring her knee straight up in the air and use it as a weapon.

"If you're behind a man, you can kick him like this between his legs. You're not using your heel but the top of your foot which is almost as good."

I demonstrated it to her. She tried it several times until she got it.

"Don't bother with the midsection of your enemy's body. There's a lot of protection there. Focus on the lower body or the head and face. The vulnerable areas in the head are the neck, mouth, nose, eyes, and side of the head. The temple area."

I pointed to each as I mentioned it.

"If you hit someone in the jaw, it might not faze him. It might do more damage to your hand than to his head. But if you hit him in the mouth and break a bunch of teeth, or in the nose, or poke him in the eye with a finger, you'll stop him in his tracks."

For more than an hour, I showed Bae a number of moves which she practiced until she got the general idea. We could've gone on longer, but another loud bang interrupted us.

"Cheongos," the lady said with more urgency.

"I guess we'd better pack and let her clean the room."

Packing didn't take long at all. We had nothing to pack. We were out the door in less than two minutes.

When we opened the door, the maid had a scowl on her face. I put five dollars' worth of won's in her pocket and kissed her on the forehead which brought a huge smile to her face.

"You just gave her two month's wages," Bae said.

"Final lesson for today. Another rule of being a spy. We see enough bad things in the world and bad people. So, help others any time you can."

26

CIA Headquarters
Langley, Virginia

"Have you heard from Alex?" Brad asked Jamie.

Jamie Austen sat in the office of Brad Rice, Alex's CIA handler, having been summoned early that morning for a meeting with no explanation why. She'd learn that asking for a reason was a waste of time. The higher ups would tell her what she needed to know, when she needed to know it.

The purpose of the meeting was probably to give her a mission. Even though Brad wasn't her handler, he sometimes had operations that crossed over into her area of specialty. Jamie was a CIA officer in the sex trafficking division of the Agency. She infiltrated trafficking organizations and rescued girls and did what she could to close down the operations, or at least put a major dent in their effectiveness.

When either she or Alex was on a mission, they always understood the possibility of getting the call they both dreaded. She didn't let her mind go there. Alex was in South Korea. Nothing about his mission was considered dangerous or would put him in harm's way. No more so than driving to the grocery store in Arlington, Virginia, where they both lived in separate condos.

"Have you heard from Alex?" Brad asked.

Now, she wasn't sure what to think. The question could be interpreted one of two ways. Maybe Brad was just making conversation before he got to the purpose of the meeting. Or… there was some problem related to Alex, and, being his girlfriend, she might have some information they didn't have.

Brad was the consummate professional and impossible to read, so Jamie decided to let the conversation play out before she became alarmed.

"Not for several days," she answered.

Brad let the response hang in the air for what seemed like a minute but was only a few seconds—enough time to send alarm bells firing in her head.

"Why do you ask?" Jamie finally asked.

"Alex is missing," Brad replied bluntly.

Jamie's heart did a complete somersault in her chest. "Missing! For how long?" she asked, sitting up on the edge of her chair. This wasn't the first time Alex had gone missing on a mission, so she tried to keep calm.

"Two days," he replied. Brad sat back in his chair, spinning a pencil around and around in his fingers. He wasn't telling her something.

"Did he have any reason to go dark?"

"None whatsoever. This was supposed to be a routine mission. On the scale of importance, what he was doing was extremely vital to our interests, but he shouldn't have run into any trouble. He was working out of the South Korean cyber lab. It's very secure."

"What was the mission?" Jamie asked, knowing Brad wouldn't answer.

"You aren't authorized to be briefed," Brad said matter-of-factly in a monotone, emotionless voice.

"Come on!" Jamie said with some anger behind the words. "It's me. What's so important that I can't know about it? If Alex is missing, I think I have the right to know the details."

Jamie had a high security clearance, but the CIA had a "need to know" policy that was strictly adhered to. Alex couldn't even tell her what the nature of the mission was, and she hadn't asked.

"I'm sorry," Brad said sincerely.

Jamie knew that pushing him further wouldn't help. "Why are you concerned?" Jamie asked. "It's not unusual for one of us to be off the grid for two days."

"We have reason to believe his life is in danger."

Jamie tried to tamp down the panic. How could Brad be so aloof when he said words that serious? He was almost apathetic. She knew he cared about Alex's safety as much as she did; he just sounded so unfeeling about it.

Brad leaned over the desk and said in a quieter voice, "Off the record..."

Jamie was shocked he was doing this. She leaned in. The door was closed, and there was no need for the melodrama, but she knew the body language was Brad's way of saying that secrecy was of utmost importance. She sensed he was about to drop a bombshell on her.

"We think Alex went to North Korea," Brad said.

"What?" Jamie bolted out of her seat and did a couple laps around her side of the room. That was the last thing she expected him to say. It wasn't a bombshell. The news was like a live grenade had been thrown in the middle of the room.

"Are you telling me that Alex is missing in North Korea?" Jamie said, not believing the words she heard coming out of Brad's mouth. The CIA didn't operate in North Korea except by drones and spy satellites.

"That's what we think," Brad said.

Jamie sat back down but then got up again and paced around the room like a caged tiger. Her mind was trying to process the information. Missing in North Korea meant likely imprisonment or death. She tried to keep her mind from going there, but the worse-case scenario kept rearing its ugly head and overriding everything else.

"Do you think he was captured?" Jamie asked hesitantly, dreading the answer.

"I think so. Yes."

Jamie was surprised by the candidness. He must be convinced something horrible had happened to Alex, and he would eventually have to tell her anyway. If Alex was captured in North Korea, he wasn't coming back. Diplomacy might get him back but that could take years and only after Alex was tortured for information to within an inch of his life.

An American student was captured in North Korea a few years ago and came back brain-dead after confessing to being an American spy. He wasn't a CIA asset. The confession was coerced out of him. He was sentenced to twenty years of hard labor in a prison camp but was near death after only two. While he was released through diplomatic channels early and came back to America, he died shortly after his return. North Korea said he died of natural causes and they released him for humanitarian reasons. All of which we knew were lies but had no way of getting justice.

"Why would Alex be in North Korea?" Jamie asked in an accusatory tone.

"I want you to know that I did not send Alex to North Korea," Brad said. "He went on his own. He was supposed to go to South Korea, find the location of the cyber lab in North Korea and come home. That was it. I swear."

Brad was telling her more than he was supposed to. Obviously covering his own hide. This was likely going to the highest levels of the government if it hadn't already. A lot of people were probably already working on containing the fallout.

"That idiot!" Jamie said aloud but mostly to herself. They'd talked about getting engaged when Alex got back. Why would he take such a huge risk? She knew why. She'd done it herself more times than she could count.

"You know Alex better than anyone," Brad said. "He felt like he had a good reason to go there. I think he thought he could infiltrate the lab and activate Kryptonite."

The whole thing suddenly made sense. That was something Alex would do. He'd been frustrated that the CIA wouldn't let him use Kryptonite, despite his many pleadings. He did all that work, and it was just sitting on the shelf. Alex was convinced Kryptonite could turn the cyber war in our favor if used properly.

"Did he activate it?" Jamie asked.

"Yes. But the North Koreans found out about it. We're even blocked from accessing it. We think Pok is behind it."

Jamie let out a groan. Alex was well intentioned, but his actions may have sabotaged the whole program. All his hard work was now in the hands of his mortal cyber enemy.

"Where is the location of the lab?" Jamie asked.

"Don't even think about it!" Brad exploded. "I've already got one missing agent. I'm not going to have another."

"Let me go to South Korea at least," Jamie retorted. "I'll snoop around and see what I can find out."

"Out of the question!" Brad countered. "You're as bad as Alex with your lone ranger, shoot from the hip, charge up the hill, and take no prisoners attitude."

Jamie forced a smile on her face. "I think that's a record for the most metaphors in a sentence."

"I'm serious," Brad said. "We've warned both of you that going off mission was going to backfire someday. Well now it has. Big time."

Jamie could see his emotions coming out. Brad seemed genuinely concerned for Alex but would also be ticked beyond measure that Alex got himself in this predicament without authorization. And he was powerless to do anything about it. They were always warned that the CIA would deny even knowing them if they fell into harm's way.

"Alex wouldn't have taken that big a risk if it wasn't important," Jamie said. "He found out something. I want to find out what that something is."

"Go home, Jamie. I'll let you know when I hear something."

She opened her mouth to protest, but Brad shut her down with a stare and his hand in the air, palm out to her face. His head was down like he didn't want to hear anything more.

She took the cue and stormed out the door, closing it loud enough to let Brad know she wasn't happy.

***

Jamie walked out of the building, got into her car, and drove forty-five minutes to a storage locker in Maryland she shared with Alex. She made several counter-surveillance moves to make sure she wasn't being followed. Her cell phone was turned off so it wouldn't ping her location to any of the cell towers.

When she arrived at her destination, she entered the gate code and drove to the back of the complex where their locker was located. The back building, in the farthest corner, was chosen because it was the most private. The facility allowed them to rent the locker with no ID and pay cash, which they did every six months in advance.

Inside was a large safe. Jamie opened it with the memorized combination. One envelope had her name on it, and one had Alex's. Instinctively, she looked around to make sure she was alone before opening her envelope. Inside were fake IDs and passports under different aliases. She scrolled through them like she would a deck of cards until she found the one she wanted.

The passport was guaranteed to withstand scrutiny from any airport security including the United States. She couldn't tell it from the real thing. One of Alex's contacts in Istanbul was the master forger who created the documents.

Deeper inside the safe were cash and credit cards. A black American Express card with a sixty-thousand-dollar limit was in the same name as the one on the passport. Jamie put the card, passport, and two thousand dollars in cash in her purse.

All kinds of various weapons were stashed in the storage locker, and she wished she could take one with her, but that wasn't an option. She'd have to find a weapon in South Korea.

The next thing she retrieved was a black case with a laptop inside. Alex designed the system and apps for them to use in unsanctioned operations. Alex had taken it apart and rebuilt it to his specifications. State-of-the-art, the computer was as powerful as any the CIA issued.

Jamie plugged it into the electrical outlet in the unit and powered it on. A few strokes on the keyboard took her to an email account only she and Alex knew about. In a time of emergency, this was their way of communicating without anyone else knowing about it.

All email correspondence was captured by the NSA. As a precaution, they communicated through the draft section of the email account. One or the other could type an email, save it to draft, and the other could log in and read the draft email and delete it. No one would ever know it existed.

Disappointment came over her when she saw that Alex had not left her a message. She opened up a new draft and typed in *R U Okay*? She hit save, careful not to hit send. If Alex logged in, he could open it and communicate back to her.

Jamie powered the laptop down and stored the computer back in the case. In a box in the corner were a dozen or so burner phones. She turned one on and dialed a number she knew by heart.

A woman answered on the second ring.

"Hi. It's me." The woman didn't know Jamie's name and Jamie didn't know hers.

"Hello. Haven't heard from you in a while. How are you doing?"

"Fine."

"What can I do for you?" the woman asked.

"I need a ticket on the next flight to Seoul, South Korea."

27

Somewhere in the Southern Mountains of North Korea

"I'm hungry," I said to Bae.

She retorted, "Alex! You just ate."

"That was two hours ago." I had eaten some of our snacks back at the hotel before we left.

We were driving through the southern mountains of North Korea in the police cruiser, in a region that could only be described as dreary. Even depressing. The scenery matched the weather. The weather was overcast and gloomy. We hadn't seen a house for miles that I thought was habitable. Yet, someone was living in every one of them. Even the most dilapidated shanty had signs of life.

Bae smiled and said, "It's against the law to have more than two meals a day."

"Really?" I said. "I didn't know that." I shifted the position in my seat.

Every day I learned something new about North Korea that made me hate the country and its regime even more if that was possible. I'd been to some horrible third-world countries. The conditions in North Korea were the worst I'd seen.

"Do you want me to get out some of our snacks?" Bae asked, undoing her seat belt, and turning toward the backseat where we had our grocery sacks.

"No. I want a real breakfast. Ham. Eggs. Pancakes. Bacon. Biscuits. Maple syrup."

"I don't know if we can find all that," Bae said with a frown. "But we can probably find you some eggs."

We rounded a curve and started a descent down the mountain into a valley. A stream ran next to the road the whole way and emptied into a beautiful lake. The first pretty thing I'd seen all day.

The town, and I used the term loosely, had the same worn-out structures in various stages of disrepair, just had more of them. Standing out among them all was one building in better shape than the rest. Outside was a sign that read *Momma-son Diner*.

"Let's stop there," I said. I could already taste the eggs. They might not have pancakes and maple syrup, but they'd have something to sate the raging hunger I felt inside. When on a mission, I never seemed to get enough to eat. The adrenaline sucked up every carb I inhaled.

"Don't park in front," Bae warned.

I asked, "Why not?"

"That will run off the customers. No one will go there with a police car in front of it. Everyone's afraid of the police. The police will arrest you if you look at them wrong."

That made sense, so we parked a block away out of sight of the road and walked over. I had my gun inside the front of my pants just in case we needed it. A weapon was like my security blanket. I felt safe when I had one.

Bae wore the satchel on her back. It seemed that she felt the same way about the bag as I did about the gun. Both were always within arms-reach of us.

At some point, we were going to have to address the nuclear codes in the bag. Up to now, Bae was protecting it almost as well as I could. I had several opportunities to go through it when she was in the shower or sleeping, but I didn't want to break the trust I built up with her by going through it behind her back. We'd talk about it after breakfast because we were about to come to the entrance of the diner.

The front of the building had a new porch and new steps leading up to it. They weren't painted, but they also weren't rotting away like most we'd seen. On the porch were metal chairs and a swing. Several patrons, all men, were sitting in the chairs, shooting the breeze like something you'd see in any small town in America.

I braced for a reaction that never came. I thought the sight of an American would create scowls or words of disgust. At least suspicion. All we received were warm smiles. In fact, the men stood and bowed and welcomed us. I bowed as low as I could without looking foolish, considering I towered over them.

Inside. I was treated even better. Like a rock star. An older teenage girl, eighteen or nineteen by my best estimate, tried to seat us but everyone in the diner felt obligated to stand and greet us with a traditional bow and warm and friendly smile.

When the pleasantries were over, I told the hostess which table I wanted. The diner was about half full and she wanted to give us what seemed like the best seat in the house. I wanted to sit at a table where my back was against the wall.

"Why did you make such a big deal about where we sit?" Bae asked after we sat down.

"Always sit facing the room and the entrance," I explained, using every opportunity I could to teach Bae something about spying. "That way, no one can sneak up on you."

Bae chuckled. "No one's going to sneak up on you in this place."

"Doesn't matter. I take that precaution even back home. A good spy tries not to vary his routine. You want the things you learn to become second nature."

Before Bae could respond, an older lady came out of what looked to be the kitchen and made a beeline to our table. Wiry and thin, her hair was beyond gray. A frosty white. If she weighed eighty pounds, it was with weights in her shoes. She was at least ten years older than her weight. As if that didn't cause her to stand out, her manner did even more. She didn't take one lazy step.

"*Annyeong haseyo*," she said while bowing, giving me the formal greeting of respect.

"Ye, Annyeong haseyo," I replied. "I'm fine. How are you?" was what I asked.

"Every day I wake up is a good day," she said with a huge smile on her face. "When you get to be my age, you enjoy them all. You don't know how many you have left." She touched my arm as she said the last sentence. An extremely affable gesture. I immediately liked her.

"You look pretty good to me," I said, and she bowed a second time, thanking me for the compliment. And she did look good. Watching her flit around the diner, I'm sure she did twice the amount of work that the young girls were doing as they struggled to match her pace.

She was back in a flash with a cup of coffee. The aroma hit me like a wave in the ocean.

I took a sip and let out a squeal of delight. I don't know if I'd ever had a cup of coffee as good as what she served me. The brew was silky smooth. The moment it reached the inside of my mouth, the caffeine bolted through me like a shot, and I felt an instant burst of energy. It was the first cup of coffee I ever remember having that didn't need to be loaded down with cream and sugar.

"You like?" she asked in English, taking me by surprise that she knew the language.

"Very much so," I replied, feeling like my words couldn't match what I felt inside. The coffee warmed my heart along with my body.

Before I could say anything else, she was gone. Back to the kitchen with seemingly boundless stamina and energy. The thought occurred to me that it could be from drinking that same coffee every day.

She returned a few minutes later to refill my cup. I thought maybe she was giving us special attention, but then I noticed her waiting on everyone in the restaurant with the same sense of urgency.

"You want to eat?" she asked.

"Do you have a menu?" I asked.

She waved her hand dismissively. "I'm Momma. I cook you up something special?" she said in broken English.

"How about you cook up something for everyone here?" I said, raising my voice so everyone could hear me. "My treat."

There was no response from the dozen or so people in the diner.

"My treat!" I said again.

"They don't know what you mean," Bae said as I forgot I was still speaking in English.

"I'm paying for everyone," I said in Korean, and a cheer went up in the room as everyone finally understood what I meant.

The other patrons crowded around our table, and we spent the next fifteen minutes, talking, laughing, and having the best time. The conversation came to a crashing halt when Momma brought out the first food.

What the food lacked in quantity was made up in quality. My plate had more food on it than the others, which made me feel a little guilty. There wasn't one overweight person in the diner. They all looked like they could use a good meal. I was almost twice as big as any of the men in the place.

The plate of food contained a bowl of rice filled with vegetables. Among them were zucchini and a delectable creamy cheese sauce. One lone egg, sunny side up, was sitting on top.

The perfectly cooked, bright-yellow yoke was staring up at me. On the side of the plate that had seen better days were three rice cakes in the shape of pancakes. They were dripping with honey and covered in powdered sugar.

I thought I had died and gone to heaven. I looked around the room that now had twice as many patrons as before as word must've gotten out that an American was in town. And that I was paying for everyone's breakfast. Didn't matter. I would gladly buy everyone breakfast.

Although, for a moment, I wondered if we had enough money left on us.

We'd cross that bridge if we came to it.

There were men and women of all ages in the diner. Their faces were bright and cheery but worn. Hardened. Oppressed. I could tell they were making the best of an exceedingly difficult existence.

A couple were Momma's age, although none were in as good a shape. I could only imagine the things they'd seen over the years. The Korean war. The takeover by the communist regime. The Yang family rose to power and immediately seized all property—from homes to businesses. These people were a step above slaves. Even the clothes on their backs technically belonged to the government.

I couldn't imagine what that was like.

Yet these people were friendly and couldn't have been kinder to us. Without guile, intent on making us feel welcome. Momma most of all. After much prompting, I finally got her to sit down and talk to us. I asked her a number of questions to get her talking.

Once she started telling her story, she didn't want to stop, as if it had been pent up in her all these years. What she told was fascinating and kept everyone's undivided attention. We needed to get on the road to South Korea, but I couldn't pry myself away. I was learning more in those few minutes than I ever could by researching online. Above all else, I was learning how good and decent some people in North Korea were.

"My momma and daddy started this diner more than eighty years ago," Momma said. "I was only eight. Momma put me to work waiting tables even though I could barely see over the bar over there." Along the wall was a counter with stools. Clean. Well maintained. The counter was painted red. The stools had black cushions and shiny metal bases. I could picture Momma on the other side, eight year's old, pouring cups of coffee to the patrons.

The only blight to the picture-perfect scene were the three frames of the Yang's on the wall behind it.

Momma said soberly. "My family was demoted to Songbun. We became the lowest class. Before then, we were one of the highest classes because we had this diner."

The Songbun was the caste system introduced by Min Yang Su when he came to power. Everyone was separated into classes. The amount of food, education, and health care a family received was based on their Songbun class.

"What happened Momma?" I asked.

Everyone was sitting on the edge of their seats. Even the locals seemed like they hadn't heard this story. It was probably against the law to even speak of it.

"Before the war, a missionary from America came to North Korea. He set up a big tent just down the road from here." Momma pointed out the window. "They called it a revival. They had loud music and singing, and people came from all around to hear the preacher. He asked if anyone wanted to live in heaven for an eternity. My momma raised her hand and went down front. He said that she had become a Christian. I wanted to be like momma, so the next night I went down, too."

I wasn't sure when my mouth flew open, but I quickly closed it as soon as I realized it.

Fascinating. Momma was a Christian. No wonder she was so joyful.

"My daddy never did go to the revival. Neither did my brothers. But momma took me and my sisters every night. My momma, sisters, and I were baptized down in the lake." That was the beautiful lake we saw when we first came into town. I could picture the scene. Everyone gathered around in the water, getting baptized.

"I was raised a Christian," I said which brought a smile to Momma's face.

"Christianity was outlawed when the divine leader came into power," Momma said. "Shortly after that. Preachers weren't allowed in Korea anymore."

Her words had a bite to it. Not resentment like I think I would have, but pity.

"My momma wouldn't stop talking about God and Jesus," she continued. "The preacher gave her a Bible, and she went around town telling everyone about what had happened to her. We were lucky they didn't throw us all in prison."

Momma shifted in her chair as tears formed in her eyes. I reached over and squeezed her hand.

A man sitting next to Momma said, "Back then, if your parents went to prison, three generations had to go as well before the debt to the government was paid." The man seemed to be about the same age as Momma. His words were labored as were his movements.

"They seized Momma's Bible. She cried for days. Then the government took our home and business. They took the diner but let us continue to run it. Momma worked here until the day she died. Then my husband and I took over."

Momma was a masterful storyteller. She was funny when she needed to be and serious when the subject matter called for it. I was so enthralled with her life story that I didn't want it to stop.

When the clock on the wall hit eleven, I knew we needed to go. But Momma was up to the Arduous March. The famine.

She was about to tell us what happened to her husband.

I had to hear what happened next.

28

Iranian Embassy
Pyongyang, North Korea

"Your two men are missing," Ambassador Hamid Ahmadi said, with some hesitancy. He then braced for the reaction he knew was coming. The knuckles of his right hand were almost white from clutching the edge of his desk with his free hand. The other hand gripped the phone with the intensity of a hyena clutching his prey.

"Missing?" Amin Sadeghi said, exploding in a barrage of expletives and accusations that went on for several long seconds.

Hamid immediately regretted his words. He should've said it differently and broke the news more subtly. A mistake he wouldn't repeat a second time.

"They didn't check in last night," Hamid mumbled, as he tried to soften the reaction from Amin, the Director of the MOIS, the Iranian Ministry of Intelligence. Amin was one of the most powerful men in Iran. Hamid was an important diplomat as well, but not like the Director. With one command, Amin could have Hamid and every member of his family imprisoned, tortured, or killed. If a mission failed, they tended to blame everyone involved, even if they weren't at fault.

That's why he put off making this call until he had no choice.

The Director had sent two men to capture and kill the girl who stole the satchel with the nuclear codes from the Iranian agent in Wonsan. Hamid picked the two men up at the airport, gave them weapons and an envelope with a picture of the girl and her home address.

That was the last time he saw or heard from them. They didn't answer their cell phones and hadn't returned to the hotel. The envelope gave them specific instructions to check in with him last night. He was up most of the night waiting for their call, hoping for word that they'd completed their mission and recovered the satchel.

When he didn't hear from them, he feared the worst. Now, he knew something bad happened, and he was tasked with telling the boss and enduring the ensuing wrath.

"Can you not do anything right?" Amin shouted into the phone.

Hamid pulled it away from his ear and could still hear Amin clearly.

"This is the third man I've lost," Amin added.

Hamid decided not to respond. He did exactly what he was instructed to do. This was a disaster, but it wasn't his fault. Hamid tried to warn the Director that sending the men wasn't a good idea but reminding him of that would only make things worse.

"What happened to them?" Amin asked sharply.

Hamid shook his head back and forth in an exaggerated motion that, of course, Amin couldn't see. He released his right hand from the death grip and threw it into the air. His voice couldn't give away his frustration, but his body language could, considering the Director was more than six thousand miles away in Tehran.

"How could I possibly know?" Hamid decided to push back some. Now, he nervously tapped the desk with the fingers of his right hand. He tried to make them stop but they wouldn't. He could feel his blood pressure rise which the doctor had warned him about several times.

He changed positions in his chair and went from his fingers tapping to his feet rapidly tapping the floor with the nervousness of an expectant father. Actually, more like a man on a death row.

"It's like they've disappeared off the face of the earth.," Hamid said. "There's no sign of them or their car."

"Where's the girl and the satchel? Is she dead at least?" Amin said roughly.

"I don't think so. I went by her house," Hamid answered quickly. "The lights were on. The windows were open. There was a motorcycle sitting in the driveway. I didn't see any people, but everything looked normal."

He wanted the Director to know he did everything he could.

The family lived in a remote location. He drove up the mountain and parked down the hill and hiked up, afraid of being seen. He could see no sign that Amin's men had even been there. No blood. No sign of a struggle. He considered knocking on the door but thought better of it. Being associated with this operation put him in danger with the North Koreans if they found out about it. The last thing he wanted was for the family to end up dead and someone seeing him leave the scene.

"I anticipated your failure," Amin said. "I have two more men on a plane headed to North Korea as we speak. They left Iran with a stopover in Frankfurt, Germany, and then Seoul. They'll board a plane to Wonsan later tonight. Pick them up from the airport."

Hamid wanted to voice further objections but knew it would fall on deaf ears. He'd gone to a lot of trouble to get the other three men in. At some point, the influx of Iranian operatives was going to raise red flags among the North Korean authorities. Especially since he went outside of diplomatic channels to get the rental cars and permission for the men to travel around freely without a government guide.

He decided to change the subject. "I called the Investigator in Wonsan and talked to him," he said. "He asked me an unusual question."

"What was that?" Amin asked, with little to no interest in his voice.

"He wanted to know if I've heard anything about an American spy operating in North Korea."

"An American?" Amin said in the form of a question, suddenly concerned. "They don't operate on the ground in North Korea. As far as I know."

"Apparently his name is Alex. Big guy they said. The way he asked was very strange. Like he was fishing for information. The question was out of the blue and meant to take me by surprise. Of course, I know nothing about it."

"I'll tell my men about that. It could be important," Amin said. Hamid could hear papers rustling in the background and then heard the Director type something on a keyboard. Probably an email.

"I think they're still trying to make us believe the Americans are behind the death of our men," Hamid said.

"Who said they are dead? You just said they were missing," Amin shouted into the phone.

Hamid winced and slapped his forehead. He kept saying the wrong thing. "What else are we to think?" he said reluctantly. "We should've heard from them by now."

"Maybe the American spy is helping the girl. If the infidel killed my men, I want him hunted down and shot like a dog."

Hamid decided not to comment. As a diplomat, he liked to deal with facts and then use them to defuse the situation. At this point, there was nothing he could say or do that would calm the Director. No amount of diplomacy could solve this problem until they got that satchel back and the girl was dead.

***

Momma-son Diner

"My husband's name was Lin," Momma said. "He died during the Arduous March. The Great Famine."

Her tone had changed. Before Momma was full of life and energy and spoke every word with a sense of urgency. Now, her tone was somber but earnest. Her face was melancholy, and her eyes sagged, and her shoulders drooped as she recounted the painful memories of the past.

"We'd been demoted to commoners," Momma said slowly. "Before, we were elite. With many privileges. Thankfully, we were not labeled anti-party."

Her voice trailed off until she regained the composure to continue.

"What would've happened to you if you were classified as anti-party?" I asked.

"We would've been thrown into prison camps. All of us. Instead, they let us keep working the diner. They actually put us in charge of distributing the rations in the valley during the famine."

"How did your husband die?" Bae asked.

"From starvation. At the end he didn't weigh much more than I did."

"If you were in charge of the rations, why didn't he take his share?" Bae asked.

My mind was elsewhere. As riveting as the story was, a sense of unease had come upon me. An intuition I got on missions, a feeling when I perceived imminent doom or danger. I searched my mind to find the source of the angst.

"He refused to eat the government rations," Momma continued. "The stubborn fool. I tried to get him to, but he gave his rations away."

What a noble thing to do.

It's been sixteen hours.

My mind was conflicted. Going back and forth between Momma's story and doing calculations. Sixteen hours ago, I knocked the policeman in Wonsan unconscious and stole his police cruiser.

"The rations weren't much anyway," Momma continued with her story. "We got the cobs from corn after they had been eaten by the elite. We got the leftover apple cores after the apples had been eaten. Bags of sugar were part of the rations. That was it."

Two to four hours. That's how long the policeman would be unconscious.

I didn't hurt him that badly. He'd still be able to remember the American spy and the girl. Would they discover him last night or this morning? That would make a difference. This morning, we still had time.

If last night...

"We grew our own rice," Momma said, "but the regime took eighty percent of what we produced and gave it to the military and the elites. We were left with twenty percent. All of the rice we grow in the valley is barely enough to feed everyone, much less trying to do so on a fifth of the supply."

I could hear the anger in Momma's voice.

"When we were left with only twenty percent, there just wasn't enough. They said it was our sacrifice for the fatherland."

The countryside was filled with billboards espousing that exact philosophy. The regime called it patriotism to work hard, and labor on behalf of the leaders who were gods and the military and others who served them. After all, the elites deserved to benefit from the labors of the commoners.

The secret police. The talk of the anti-party and police state brought clarity to my thoughts. Those same powers would be after me if they weren't already.

The SSD. The State Security Department. They were the enforcers. When the policeman regained consciousness, a call would be made to them immediately. The local police couldn't do anything about an American spy loose in the countryside. Out in the outer regions, there were no phone lines or methods to communicate. In the United States, an APB could be put out on a fugitive and every law enforcement agency in the country would be on the lookout.

North Korean communications outside of the big cities were in the dark ages. Police cruisers weren't equipped with radios. Most local police stations didn't have phones or the internet.

The SSD did have the equipment to track an American spy. They answered directly to the Divine Leader and were given the resources to do their jobs. They ran the concentration camps and arrested people for crimes against the state such as treason. This situation fell within their jurisdiction, and they would no doubt make finding me their number one priority.

Momma interrupted my thoughts.

"My husband, Lin, went to the lake and caught beetles and insects," she said. "That's what he ate."

"Are there fish in the lake?" I asked Momma, not wanting her to think I wasn't listening.

"There are. That's the only way we survived. My husband set up nets and fish traps and at first, we caught a lot of fish. We hid them from the regime, or they would've taken them. Eventually, there weren't many fish left. My husband fished until he didn't have the strength anymore."

Several people were crying now, including Momma who fought back the tears. Most of the people in the room had lived through it. Many of them may have even lost someone. They understood firsthand the horrors of living in a totalitarian state. I needed to remember that I was deep in enemy territory.

The SSD would start looking for me this morning.

That's the soonest they would act, I decided. The communication would go to headquarters in Pyongyang. They would mobilize a search after it went to the highest levels. Agents of the SSD would be dispersed throughout North Korea in every direction in search of Bae and me.

We were two hours from Pyongyang. Two cars would be sent on each road. They'd have to stop in each village and question the locals. That would take time.

The Diner.

This was where they would stop in this village. We were putting the people in the room in danger by being there.

The SSD would be arriving about now.

I abruptly stood to my feet. "Momma, how much do I owe you for the meals? We've got to get going."

Momma wiped the tears from her eyes and stood slowly. Talking about the famine had taken some of the strength out of her. She walked back to the kitchen and returned with a pencil and a piece of paper.

I saw them first. Momma, shortly after me.

Two unmarked cars drove by the front of the diner. They were clearly government issued cars.

SSD.

I reached for the gun in the belt of my pants. Momma grabbed my hand to stop me as if she knew what I intended to do.

"Come with me," Momma said.

She led us through the kitchen to a room off the back of the building. One lone light bulb illuminated the dark room filled with stored food for the diner. Momma started tugging on a shelf in the far corner. It wedged open. Behind it was a hidden room.

"Get in there," Momma said. "You'll be safe."

I had to duck my head to get into the crawl space. Bae followed. Momma shut the door behind us. The room was totally dark. I couldn't see my hand in front of my face. I reached out and felt around until I found Bae's hand which was shaking in fear. I put my hand over her mouth to keep her from making any noise.

I immediately regretted having gone in the room. We were trapped. I'd rather take my chances on the outside in a gunfight rather than be trapped like a mouse in that dark room. I put my shoulder against the door but was unable to get it to budge. I didn't dare struggle harder or it would make enough noise to attract the attention of the secret police.

Then the reality hit me. Momma locked it on the outside.

I could hear the voices of the Secret Police barking orders to the patrons through the thin walls. A bolt of panic went through my body as I feared the worst.

Momma would turn us in.

Why wouldn't she? Being responsible for the capture of an American spy would be the ultimate reward for a commoner. It would prove her loyalty to the state. Momma would immediately be restored to an elite status. There would be money. She'd be given a better house. The designation would affect her future generations. It would mean no more suffering for her and her family. The diner would be given more supplies which would mean more food for the valley.

How could I have been so stupid?

We could've run out the back and into the woods. A shootout would be better than this fate.

I still have my gun.

I took it out and prepared for whatever would happen next.

We won't go down without a fight.

29

Frankfurt International Airport
Frankfurt, Germany

Jamie slept the entire seven-hour flight from Dulles Airport, Washington, D.C., to her stopover in Frankfurt, Germany. After a long five-hour layover, she'd be on her way again to Seoul, South Korea. A ten-hour flight made tolerable only by the business class seat that reclined into a bed on the luxurious Korean Air A380.

The double deck airliner was billed as the hotel-in-the-sky. On her last flight, Jamie read about the Celestial bar and lounge on board and the audiovisual on-demand (AOVD) entertainment system available throughout the brand-new aircraft. She'd try to remember to thank her contact who made the travel arrangements. If she had to make a ten-hour flight, this was the way to do it.

Jamie hadn't allowed herself to think about what she was going to do in South Korea until now. *Sleep and eat when you can*, her CIA trainer, Curly, always said. *You never know when you'll get your next chance*. She took his advice and gave herself time to unwind and recharge her engines before what she knew would be a very emotionally charged mission.

Upon arriving in Frankfurt, she'd gone for a brisk one hour-walk through the terminal. After that, she sat down for a meal consisting of a shredded beef burrito with beans and rice. She skipped the chips, knowing she'd be well fed on the flight. When she finished eating, she found her gate, sat down in one of the not-so-comfortable chairs, and finally allowed herself to start developing a plan.

Three hours later, she realized she had no plan that didn't result in anything more than a suicide mission. The more she thought about it, the angrier she got at Alex and Brad for causing this predicament. The facts were sketchy, but she drew some conclusions from what she did know.

Alex went to South Korea to find the North Korean cyber warfare lab. He found it and then obviously went to it because he accessed Kryptonite from the North Korean server. She tried to get into Alex's mind and think like he was thinking, as dumb as it was.

When he found the server, Alex would be overly excited. Like she was when she found the head of a sex-trafficking ring. Missions had an ebb and flow to them. Highs and lows. Alex would be on a high when he discovered the lab. He should've passed on the location to Brad and come home with an attaboy for a job well done. Except, he knew the bureaucracy wouldn't act on that information, and the North Koreans would continue for months, if not years, wreaking havoc throughout the world.

She'd experienced that frustration many times herself. After risking her life to discover a sex-trafficking ring, more often than not, the higher ups sat on the information and refused to act. Sometimes, she wondered why she went to all the effort. Lately, when she got the information, she simply acted on her own, not waiting for them to journey through the red tape of bureaucracy that had become the United States Intelligence service. Made even more complicated since there were now four agencies, the CIA, NSA, FBI, and Homeland Security, all wanting their two cents considered before any actions were taken.

Knowing the location of the lab, Alex decided to act on his own. He probably thought he could go there and destroy it. When he arrived, he found a fortress with armed guards and an impenetrable building. Jamie could picture the facility in her head and the armed guards out front. At least this was the scenario playing out in her mind. She had no idea if this was what had happened, but it seemed the most plausible thing she could think of.

At that point, Alex should've gone back to South Korea. But he didn't give up easily. He got an even dumber idea—to go up to the door and offer them his services. An incredibly reckless and stupid thing to do. A smile came to Jamie's face as she thought of how much courage it took to do such a foolish thing. It's one of the things she loved about him. This was exactly the type of thing she'd do to infiltrate a sex-trafficking ring. Get as close to the head of the snake as you could without getting bit.

This time Alex got bit.

Still, he somehow managed to get inside and activate Kryptonite. He probably had to show them some results to gain their trust. Make some kind of payment through Kryptonite into their bank account. Probably a million dollars or more.

This was where it got complicated in her mind. Brad probably denied the request. That must've been why she saw the guilt written all over his face when he was going against his own rules and telling her about it. It might not have even been his decision. The Director of the CIA probably nixed the idea and left Alex to be sifted like wheat.

When Alex couldn't deliver the goods, the North Koreans arrested him. That was the only thing that made sense. Why else would Brad say Alex was in danger? Why would he think the North Koreans captured him? Brad felt guilty. He was complicit in some way. Not complicit in the sense that it was his fault, but he could've prevented it. Or at least the Agency could've.

Panic must've come over Alex when he got the word that they weren't going to pay the money. Maybe he tried to fight his way out and was gunned down before he could get to the exit. He probably took out several guards along the way. Jamie almost hoped that was the case. It would be a better ending than being captured, beaten, and tortured for decades.

That's why she was so angry. Alex was an idiot for going there in the first place. Brad was a bigger idiot for not having his back. And now they were forcing Jamie to do something even dumber to try and save their hides. She should take the advice she would've given Alex and just get on the next flight back to the United States. Her MSO, Mission Success Odds were zero. Not one percent. Not half of one percent, but zero. There was no way she could rescue Alex out of North Korean custody. She didn't even know if he was still alive.

He has to be. That's the only way I can picture him.

Jamie fought back the tears. If he was alive, Alex probably wasn't in a prison camp. They would take him to Pyongyang for interrogation. Probably the secret police headquarters. He'd be there for a long time going through unspeakable torture until they decided what to do to him.

How could she get to him?

The capital city of Pyongyang was totally locked down. There were checkpoints at every road leading in or out. Foreigners weren't allowed in without government permission and extensive scrutiny and couldn't travel alone without a monitor. If she somehow made it into the city proper, she wouldn't last a day before she got caught on the streets.

Even if she did somehow manage to stay in the shadows, what could she do for Alex? The secret police building was an invariable fortress. Hundreds, if not thousands, of armed guards would surround it with barricades. If she somehow infiltrated the outer perimeter, the building was acres of real estate. Tens of thousands of square feet of offices and interrogation rooms. She'd end up in one of them quicker than Alex had.

A suicide mission.

Except that death wouldn't come that quickly.

Go home.

Something she would never do. If the situation were reversed, Alex would move heaven and earth to find her.

I can't find him. There's nothing I can do.

Jamie was now sitting in a lounge chair in the boarding area for her flight to Seoul when the realization hit her like a fifty-pound sack of concrete falling on her. She put her feet up and pulled her knees close to her body and wrapped her arms around them. The thoughts were suddenly overwhelming her emotions.

She buried her head in her knees and allowed the tears to flow as the hopelessness of the situation began stabbing her in the heart like a jagged knife.

***

When Jamie regained her composure, a new plan had formed. If Alex could infiltrate the North Korean cyber lab then so could she. The problem was that she didn't know the location of the lab. She couldn't get it from the South Korean cyber lab that Alex had worked out of because no one knew she was there. That was a secure facility, and she'd need a pass to get in.

Then it occurred to her. Alex was meticulous in covering his tracks. The location would be somewhere in his hotel room. On his computer or written down. There would be some notes. Alex always prepared for the worst-case scenario. He wouldn't have gone to all that trouble to find the lab and then not ensure that the information could be used in the future should something happen to him.

Even something as innocuous as getting hit by a bus crossing the street. Alex would want the information protected and found. The first thing she'd do when she arrived in South Korea was go to his hotel room where the, *Do Not Disturb* sign, was no doubt still hanging on the door. He wouldn't want a maid finding the information and throwing it away. The room would be prepaid for several days. She'd have to figure out how to access it.

Once she knew the location of the lab, she'd go across the border and destroy it. Kill Pok. Exact revenge for Alex. It was the least she could do. Probably the most she could do as well. It might be a one-way suicide mission, but the MSO was in the thirty-to-forty percent range. She at least had a chance she could come out of it alive.

Success would mean she struck a devastating blow to North Korea's cyber warfare program. Her computer skills weren't as developed as Alex's, but she had the operational and military skills to rain down confusion and firepower on the facility.

But... she'd need weapons.

You're always armed, she heard Curly say in her head.

Jamie got up from her chair with renewed energy and went for another walk. She had about an hour before the flight left and a half hour before it boarded. Jamie almost ran through the terminals as resolve was built inside her. She was in such elite physical condition that it took a lot of strenuous exercise to get her heart rate up. By the time she was finished with the brisk walk, her heart rate was elevated and took several minutes to come back down.

She bought a protein and an energizer smoothie and went back to the boarding area.

What she saw sent her heart racing again.

***

Two Iranians were in line to board.

Conspicuous. Out of place. Towering above the Koreans.

Curly always said to trust her instincts. Her eyes would see something that wasn't right, and her subconscious would sound an alarm before her conscious knew what it was. The picture in front of her was causing all kinds of alarms to blare in her head.

She studied the men. They were tall. Brawny. Wearing black suits. White shirts. No ties. They were trying to look like businessmen. They were fighters. Trained killers.

Iranian Revolutionary Guard.

Jamie would recognize them anywhere. They had a certain look. The battlefields of Iraq and Syria left a certain indelible mark on a man. It was on their faces. Something impossible to describe. Like the identifiable hands of an auto mechanic that have grease permanently stained on them and black grime accumulated under his fingernails. Or the face of a construction worker who spent too many hours in the sun. Or the face of a woman who'd been in the sex trade for years. It was in their eyes. Their demeanor. Their body language. They all had a particular look, and Jamie knew the look of an Iranian Revolutionary Guardsman when she saw one.

In this case, two.

What were they doing?

They were constantly surveilling the area. Their shoulders were tense and their faces in a permanent scowl. Their feeble attempt to look like traveling businessmen only raised Jamie's suspicion further. She wasn't falling for the ruse. These men were on a mission.

Men like this weren't well trained in avoiding detection. A good agent altered his appearance to blend into the crowd. The key was to look unremarkable. That was hard for these men to do because they were in line with a bunch of Koreans who weren't as tall.

It was hard for Jamie to do as well. At nearly six feet tall and with blonde hair, she drew attention just from her looks. That's why she was wearing baggy clothes, no makeup, and her hair was pulled back in a ponytail covered by a Chicago Cubs baseball cap. The hat was to also hide her face from the security cameras. Just in case Brad was applying some facial recognition software to passengers to see if she was going to South Korea against his orders.

These men are up to no good.

All of Jamie's senses were now engaged. She skulked to the back of the boarding line to get out of the line of sight of the men who were nearing the gate attendant to have their tickets scanned. The only thing Jamie was carrying was a backpack. Curly taught them to travel light and never check a bag. In her bag was a set of headphones. She opened the backpack, pulled them out, put them over her ears, and began nodding her head up and down and back and forth like she was listening to music, making herself even less noticeable.

Let them go. It's none of your business.

Jamie should let them go and forget she ever saw them, but she couldn't make herself do it. Something was drawing her to the men.

I'm just doing surveillance.

If nothing else, it would get her prepared for North Korea and put her in mission mode.

The men's tickets were scanned, and they entered the jetway. One of them looked back and scanned the gate area. For a moment, their eyes met. Rather than look away suspiciously, Jamie tilted her head upward slightly and started mouthing the words of a song even though there was no music playing in her ears. Unlike the men, Jamie was highly trained in avoiding detection.

She waited to board so she'd be the last person on. Rather than going to the business class section, she turned right and started down the aisle of the coach seats, scanning the cabin for the two men. They weren't hard to spot. The cabin had three sets of seats. Three on each side of the aisles and four in the middle.

Their seats were on the other side of the aircraft. That was good. It gave her a chance to come up from behind them.

She went all the way to the back and circled to the other aisle. That's why she boarded last. Taking someone's seat would cause a scene and draw attention to herself. The flight was a little more than half full, so she had plenty of seats to choose from.

The row behind them was completely empty, but that was too close. Jamie took the aisle two rows back. Another passenger was in the window seat. She slipped her backpack under the seat in front of her.

The men were speaking in Farsi. Another sign they were on a mission. Iranian agents spoke the native language, feeling comfortable that no one on board would know it. Farsi was a language she was taught in CIA training school. While Jamie wasn't proficient, she knew enough to make out most of the words.

"We got an email from the Director," one of the men said in a heavy Farsi accent.

The Director. That was probably the Director of the MOIS. Another clue they were working for the Iranian Intelligence Agency.

"Read it," the other one said. His deep bass voice carried back to her seat as he made no attempt to whisper or muffle the words.

"There is an American spy on the loose in North Korea," the man began reading from the email. "He may have killed three of our men. Find him and find the satchel."

"What are we supposed to do when we find him?" the other man asked.

"Kill him."

"Do we have a description or name?"

"Big guy. His name is Alex. He shouldn't be hard to find."

Jamie's mouth flew open so fast it would have plunged to the floor had it not been attached to her face.

30

The Korean Airliner pulled back from the gate. Jamie was sitting two rows back from the two Iranians, trying to listen to their conversation and determine what they were up to. They'd just dropped the bombshell that they were searching for Alex in North Korea. She leaned forward in her seat so she could hear them better. They didn't say anything for several minutes, but eventually started up the conversation again.

"The Director wants both of them dead," Jamie heard the Iranian say to the other.

Both of them? What did he mean?

"The American is with the girl," the other Iranian said.

What girl?

The Captain came on the intercom to welcome the passengers. Jamie leaned even further forward in her seat and strained to hear what the man was saying. Something about a girl.

"The girl is the one who stole the satchel," the man continued. "The satchel contained the Pakistani codes." They were still speaking in Farsi, and Jamie was already having a hard time understanding them because of the thick accent. It was made worse by the Captain's crackling voice reverberating through the cabin.

"We're expecting a smooth flight all the way to our final destination. Which is Seoul, South Korea. If you're not going to Seoul, then I don't know what to tell you," the Captain said drawing a chuckle from the passengers.

The Iranians weren't paying attention to the Captain either as they continued their conversation. "What does the American have to do with it?" one of them said.

"He's protecting the girl. The Director said he killed three of our men."

Jamie's heart suddenly grew cold. The elation of learning that Alex was alive was now being overwhelmed by confusion and anger.

Alex did all this for a girl?

"The American and the girl are traveling together. We find one, we find the other..."

Traveling together?

The rest of what he said was drowned out by the Captain droning on about how long a flight it was and the cruising altitude.

Who cares?

Jamie wanted to tap the Iranian on the shoulder and say, *Excuse me. Could you repeat that? What about the girl? Who is she? Tell me everything you know about her.*

"We've been cleared for takeoff," the Captain said as the engines revved, creating even more noise. She couldn't hear any more of the discussion. The plane took off, and the roar of the engines and the vibrations of the aircraft drowned out anything the men were saying.

When the plane finally reached cruising altitude they were no longer talking about Alex or the girl. The Iranians were settled in and had reclined their chairs to sleep.

Jamie sat back in her seat. She considered staying in coach to see if she could overhear more conversation. More than likely, they were done. That was probably all they knew anyway. Staying in the back would create a greater risk of her being "made" by the Iranians. Besides, she wasn't going to spend the next ten hours in coach, when she could be in the luxurious business class. Especially knowing what she knew now about Alex and the girl. Which wasn't much. Just enough to make her mad.

Alex caused this whole big scene over a girl!

What a cad!

The thought caused every muscle in Jamie's body to tense in anger. She was traveling halfway around the world, risking her job by disobeying her boss's order, and putting herself in harm's way for him. Only to find out that he'd been carousing around North Korea with some girl.

Half of her wanted to catch the first plane back to the states the minute she arrived in South Korea. The other half wanted to see the look on Alex's face when she confronted him and made him explain what he was doing.

A woman's curiosity would win the day. Jamie knew there was no turning back. Now she had to find Alex. She had to know who this girl was.

Was she an agent? The Iranian said she was Korean. How did he meet her, and why was he protecting her? Was she pretty? The questions erupted in her head faster than she could process them and create a counter argument with a reasonable explanation.

The conflicting thoughts and emotions were warring inside of her. Maybe Alex had a girl in every port or "station" as they were called in the CIA. She tried to beat the jealousy back with a proverbial emotional stick.

Alex wouldn't cheat on me.

There must be some other explanation. They were talking about getting married. While they weren't officially engaged and no date was set, they were definitely dating each other exclusively... although they had been dating for two years, and she was the one slow walking the relationship.

Even after all that time, they hadn't had sex. She insisted they wait until marriage which Alex seemed okay with. Was that fair?

She wasn't ready to make a lifelong commitment but was making him wait to have sex until she was.

I'm not sitting back here in coach while I try to figure it out.

When the Captain turned off the seat belt sign, Jamie slipped out of the seat, walked around the back of the aircraft out of the sight of the Iranians, and then down the aisle to the business class section where she found her assigned seat.

It felt more like a suite on a private jet than a seat, but she couldn't allow herself to enjoy it. In the time it had taken her to walk from the back of the plane to the front, anger had returned with a fury.

You'd better hope the Iranians find you before I do, Alex Halee!

Whoever the girl is, I hope she's worth it.

***

Momma-son Diner

At that moment, I didn't remember being in a worse situation. Bae and I were in a crawl space in a hidden safe room off of the kitchen of the diner. The room was pitch black and the ceiling not tall enough to stand up, so we were crouched on the dirt floor along with no telling how many bugs and critters. The thought made me shudder.

Outside the door were four North Korean secret police agents. We could hear them shouting at Momma and the other patrons in the diner. In a couple more minutes, I expected the door to open and the secret police to drag Bae and me out of our dungeon and haul us away to what would be a brutal interrogation.

I could do little to protect us. Normally, I tried to put myself in the position where I had the option of either fight or flight. In this instance, fight was the only option. I had a gun with twelve bullets. It was firmly in my hand even though I couldn't see it with my eyes on account of the darkness.

The problem was that when the door opened, it would take time for my eyes to adjust to the light, and the police would have every tactical advantage. They had the high ground, so to speak. I would get shots off at them, but all they had to do was fire their weapons into the darkness, and we'd be as helpless as a raccoon in a trap.

The other problem was I couldn't start firing immediately. If Momma didn't turn us in, I didn't want to hit her or one of the other customers in the diner. I would have to hesitate. Wait and see who was on the other side of the door. Every part of my being said I made a mistake getting into that room.

Bae must have sensed my concern because she clutched me tighter. I tried to calm her by whispering that things were going to be okay even though I wasn't sure of it myself.

The shouting on the other side of the door got louder. I heard Momma cry out. It seemed like she wasn't giving us up which was hard for me to believe. She had every reason to. If they found that she was hiding us, she'd lose the diner and her freedom. Momma and her entire family would be arrested for treason. I shouldn't have put her in this position. We should've eaten breakfast and left when we had the chance.

For several long minutes, all we could do was wait. The only thing that calmed my fears was that the longer we were confined, the more likely it was that Momma wasn't turning us in. If she was, she'd do so immediately, and the police would come and guard the door. Maybe wait us out. I didn't know how long I could take suffering in the darkness.

Eventually, the shouting stopped, and I heard footsteps in the kitchen coming toward the door. I was holding my breath and didn't realize it until my lungs forced me to inhale and take a big whiff of the moldy air.

Bae was panting in terror. Her breaths were coming in rapid succession almost as fast as a heartbeat.

My heart raced to the point it would be impossible to tell which one of our hearts was beating the fastest.

I had the presence of mind to relax my arm and hand that held the gun. Many errant shots had been fired accidently from a tense trigger finger. Once satisfied that I had control of the gun and my emotions, I raised the weapon and pointed it the direction of the entrance.

The big heavy door began to creak and moan as it started to open.

"Don't shoot me," I heard Momma say.

I decided to lower my weapon. Even if Momma turned us in, I didn't want to risk hitting her with a bullet. I couldn't muster the slightest bit of anger toward her even if that was her decision. I understood why she would do it.

A powerful light suddenly flooded the room, blinding me momentarily to the point that I couldn't see who was in the entryway.

"You can come out now," I heard Momma's reassuring voice say. "It's safe."

Was it a trap? Did the police force her to do it this way? That made sense. The police may have deduced that it was better for them to entice us out of the trap rather than go into it and try to extract us from it. That's what I would do if I were them.

Momma took Bae's hand and helped her out first. She reached for me next, but I was too big for her, so I just got in a squat position like a duck and waddled out the door. Once out, I immediately raised my gun, and prepared for the worst.

"They're gone," Momma said.

I blinked my eyes fast several times to try and adjust to the light.

Momma had blood trickling from the side of her mouth. It was already swelling up and turning black and blue. The policeman had obviously struck her.

"Were the police looking for us?" I asked.

Momma nodded yes. She took my hand and led us out of the room into the front of the diner. The patrons had all left. The only ones still in the diner were her employees. I went to the area where she kept ice for drinks, wrapped a towel around some, and brought it back and put it on her lip. She winced in pain as I pressed the ice pack against her swollen lip.

"Why didn't you turn us in?" I asked.

"I like you," Momma said.

"They would've paid you a lot of won for me. You would be restored to elite."

"God provides for me. Besides, I'm an old woman. I have to sleep at night knowing I did the right thing."

The sadness in her eyes was spilling out more than if it had been in the form of tears. Momma probably did have a lot of regrets in life. She didn't want another one. I think I understood. There were good people, even in communist countries, who didn't agree with the violence and oppression and wouldn't be a part of it even for personal gain. Like her husband, who gave up his rations and ultimately his life so others could live.

I had a deep admiration for that kind of faith. A verse in the Bible suddenly came to mind. *Greater love has no man than to lay down his life for a friend.* Those words of Jesus never had more meaning to me than at that moment.

"You are a remarkable woman, Momma," I said.

Momma waved her hand in a half dismissive and a half appreciative gesture.

I asked, "How will I ever repay you?"

Momma sat in a chair now. The confrontation and the blow had obviously taken something out of her. "You can start by paying your bill," Momma said with a lisp, forcing a smile through her swollen lips. I saw her eye starting to turn red and swell as well. "Remember, you were going to do that before we were interrupted."

"The police took all of the won out of her register," one of her female employees said.

"How much did they get, Momma?" I asked.

"Only a couple of dollars. I'm glad you waited to pay me until after they left, or they would've gotten all of it."

"How much do I owe you?"

The amount came to about eight American dollars. It was amazing to me that all those people could eat breakfast for less than one meal at a breakfast place in the United States.

"How much won do we have left?" I asked Bae.

She knew immediately, which impressed me. "Thirty-six dollars," she said.

"Give me thirty," I said.

Bae opened the satchel and pulled out the equivalent of thirty American dollars. I took it from her and handed it to Momma. I'd just given her what amounted to two years wages for a commoner.

A tear escaped from Momma's eye and ran down her cheek. I bent down, put my arms around her, and hugged her tightly. I'd just broken another law in North Korea for the umpteenth time. Public displays of affection between the opposite sex were forbidden in a public place. I didn't care and she didn't seem to either as she returned the embrace.

"I'll never forget you, Momma-son," I said somberly as I stood to leave.

Momma sat the ice pack down on the table and went in the kitchen and came out with a pencil and a piece of paper. She sat back down and started drawing something on the page.

"There will be roadblocks set up," Momma said. "Here. Here. And Here." She put an X at various places on what was clearly a makeshift map of the area.

She drew more lines on the map which appeared to be roads. "Take these roads," she said. "The police won't patrol them."

Momma stood from the chair, handed me the map, and then put both hands on my cheeks and kissed them.

"May the Lord bless you," she said, "and keep you. May his face shine on you and be gracious to you. Let the Lord turn his face upon you and give you peace." Her hands were still on my cheeks.

"Numbers chapter six," I said.

Momma released her hands, put them together in front of her like a prayer, and bowed toward me.

I returned the bow.

"My Mother prayed that prayer over me every night," she said. "Blessings upon you. I hope you stay safe."

"I'll never forget you," I said again, knowing I would never see Momma after we left. Then I voiced that thought. "I guess I'll never see you again," I said as we started walking toward the door

"You'll see me in heaven," she shouted after me. "Although I'll get there way before you."

"I'm not so sure about that," I said aloud as Bae and I walked out the door, and I turned my focus on the mission and the hundreds of secret police who were trying to find me so they could kill me.

31

"We need to do two things today," I said to Bae once we were in the car. We had just left Momma-son's diner and were following her map in the police cruiser to the border of South Korea. We'd have to ditch the cruiser a couple miles before the DMZ and hike across the border, then catch transportation to Seoul.

"What are the two things?" Bae asked, not looking at me, instead, just staring out the passenger side window at the barren nothingness that was this region of North Korea.

I noticed before that Bae sometimes went through long periods of withdrawing when she didn't say anything. Typical teenager, I assumed, although I didn't have much experience with girls her age. Who could blame her, considering what she'd been through over the last couple days, including the trauma at the diner which still had me shaken up.

"Don't get shot and don't get arrested!" I said with emphasis.

Bae let out a chuckle that was barely more than a groan. She knew our precarious situation as much as I did. After that, neither of us said anything for a good ten minutes, which was fine by me. I needed the time to think through a plan.

At some point, the silence became awkward and I decided to break the ice. "I'm hungry," I said with a wide grin.

Bae frowned. Then she gave me a "I know you're kidding" look, as her mouth contorted into a smirk.

"I'm surprised Momma didn't turn us in," I said, trying to start a conversation.

"I'm not surprised," Bae retorted. She stared out her window. We were out of the mountains now and in the flatlands. The only thing to really see were rows and rows of flooded rice paddies.

"I thought we were goners," I said.

I still couldn't make myself relax. My heartbeat was elevated, and my senses were on full alert. I probably wouldn't fully relax until we got across the border of South Korea, still a couple hours away. A lot could happen in those two hours.

"You need to have more faith in your fellow man," Bae said in a voice and a manner befitting someone much older. "Momma was never going to turn us into the police."

"Why were you so sure?"

"Because that's how people are in the southern mountains. They aren't snitches. Some people are... I guess. But most people in North Korea just want to live their lives without being bothered. There's a lot more opposition to the regime than you would think. Most people have had a bad experience with the police and try to avoid them."

"I get that. Most people in America are that way too. Work hard, play hard, and stay out of trouble."

"What *is* America like?" Bae asked, perking up some as her eyes had a sudden twinkle and her lips flip flopped from a frown into a smile.

"Different, but the same."

"That doesn't make any sense."

"I know. It's hard to describe. People are the same everywhere, in a way. Every country has different beliefs and customs, but most people are decent, hard-working people, deep down. But in America, we have a lot more freedom than anywhere else in the world.

And a lot more wealth. Everyone has a cell phone and computer. We can travel anywhere we want. We don't have to worry about the police bothering us as long as we aren't doing something illegal."

"I can't even imagine what that's like," Bae said, as her smile disappeared. "Here everybody is forced into conformity. We're like robots of the regime. Everything is illegal."

I tried to lighten the mood. I didn't want her to withdraw again. "There's a diner like Momma's in almost every town in America. People go there to be with each other and eat a good home-cooked meal. They're good people. Like we just met at Mommas. Sometimes I forget that America doesn't corner the market on values in the world. We think everybody in a communist country supports the ideology. That's obviously not true or Momma would've turned us in."

"I wonder if I'll ever see America," Bae said, almost in the form of a question.

"I don't see why not."

"Where *are* we going?" Bae asked, as I realized I hadn't told her.

"To South Korea," I answered.

If Bae was surprised, she didn't let it show on her face. "What are we going to do there?"

I hadn't told Bae that I was going to turn her over to the US Embassy in Seoul. I'd speak to Brad on her behalf. Bae had been really helpful to me and to US interests in the region. Brad would see that she got refugee status. She'd probably be placed in a good family in South Korea. It would be a lot better than her future in North Korea. Brad might even help her get to America.

Rather than explaining all of that I just said, "I'm not sure."

I lied. Seemed like the best thing at the time. The last thing I needed was a confrontation with Bae.

"I haven't thought that far ahead," I added.

That was sort of a true statement. I really didn't know what would happen to Bae. All I knew was that I was going to get us across the border safely, hand her off to the embassy, and then go back to my hotel and get my computer. After that, I'd have to sneak back into North Korea and find my way to the cyber lab. Hopefully, I wouldn't be too late before Pok had done too much damage with Kryptonite.

A few moments passed.

The road was rough, and I had both hands on the wheel, trying to avoid the potholes and ruts. I prayed we wouldn't get another flat tire. Then we'd be on foot since we didn't have another spare. Momma's map had been helpful. We hadn't seen any secret police or roadblocks. However, the roads were in much worse shape. Nevertheless, I preferred the bad roads to getting shot at or a police pursuit.

"Maybe I could come to America with you," Bae blurted out.

I tried to control the startled look on my face. "What would you do in America?"

"Go to school. Become a spy like you. Like your girlfriend."

"We'll have to see what happens," I said, thinking ambiguity was the best option. "The first thing we have to do is get across the border in one piece. Then I'm going to my hotel and get my computer."

"I have a computer," Bae said almost nonchalantly.

This time I didn't even try to hide my look of surprise as my mouth gaped.

I asked her, "At your house?"

"No. Here with me. In the satchel."

I jerked the wheel to the right and slammed the brakes as I pulled to the side of the road. Both of us lunged forward and then abruptly back.

"You have a computer in this car?" I asked sternly with my jaw clenched.

"Yes."

"Why didn't you say so?"

"You never asked!"

I turned my body and reached behind us and grabbed the satchel off the back seat.

"Hey! That's mine," Bae said, as she tried to snatch it from my hand.

I held the satchel just out of her reach. If the seat belt hadn't restrained her, she would've been able to reach it. I held my hand up to stop her. "Relax! I'm not going to hurt anything. I just want to see your computer."

"It's mine!" she said, her lower lip trembled, tears welled up in her eyes.

"I'm just going to look at it. I'm not going to take it from you. I just want to see if it works."

I zipped the satchel open and pulled out the laptop, immediately surprised that it looked brand new.

"Please be charged up," I said mostly to myself as I turned on the power button.

"It should be charged," Bae said. "I haven't used it for several days. Do you want me to show you how it works?"

"I'm good," I said, a little smirk formed on my lips that I hoped wasn't too noticeable. Sometimes Bae's brashness and confidence amazed me.

The computer screen roared to life quicker than I expected. As soon as it opened, my fingers went to work with a flurry of keystrokes. It had been a couple of days since I'd been on a computer, and I attacked the keyboard like an addict getting a fix for the first time in days.

I quickly accessed its capabilities. The operating system was the Red Start 3 which was similar to the Apple mac OS. Slow but functional. I was familiar with it having traversed around it to find the cyber lab.

The computer had a surprising number of apps. An email client. A file management system similar to Finder which was developed by Apple. A web browser called Naenara. Not surprising since it was the main one used in North Korea. Naenara was nothing more than a modified version of Firefox.

That was a pet peeve of mine and something I found all around the world. Generally, other countries let America develop the latest technology, then they stole it and modified it for their own uses. Sometimes they didn't even pretend to modify it. Case in point. On Bae's computer was a bootlegged copy of Candy Crush.

The laptop had a fourteen-inch color screen and was surprisingly fast. Not what I needed exactly, but better than nothing. I could make it work.

Bae tensed like a bear protecting her cubs. She watched my every move. I made a few modifications that would immediately improve the performance. Once I had access to the internet, I'd make a few more that would get the laptop to do what I needed it to.

I stopped typing and looked at Bae and said, "What did you find in the satchel?" It was time to have that discussion.

She hesitated then looked down.

"Bae this is important," I said firmly. "I need to know."

"There were some papers with numbers on them."

I started rummaging through the satchel.

"The papers aren't there. I threw them away."

I threw my hands in the air in disgust. Those papers had the codes. I needed them. That's why I went to all that trouble to get the satchel. Now I learned they were in the trash somewhere. The only good thing was at least they weren't in the hands of the Iranians.

"Why would you throw them away?" I asked, even though I knew the answer. What would a thirteen-year-old girl want with those papers? She just wanted the satchel.

"I didn't know what they were," she said defensively, almost reading my mind.

I asked, "Was there anything else in there?"

Bae reached over to take the satchel from me.

I pulled it away.

"I'm going to get it for you," she said roughly, adding a strong glare to the words. If her eyes were a laser beam, they would've burned a hole in my chest.

I let her have it.

Bae rifled through the satchel. A few seconds later, she pulled her hand out. In it was a flash drive. My heart skipped a beat. This was even better than the papers.

"This was in there," she said.

I reached for it. Bae pulled her arm back.

That flash drive contained the nuclear codes and passwords. I was sure of it. If I had to overpower Bae and take it from her I would.

"Bae, I need to look at that," I said firmly. "It's important. I need to know what's on there."

She handed it to me reluctantly.

"Bae you have to trust me. Do you know what this is?"

She shook her head no. I suddenly remembered that the best approach with Bae was to include her. Mentor her. I went back into teaching mode.

"This is called a USB flash drive," I explained. "It stores data. These have been around forever."

"I thought it was called a thumb drive," Bae said.

"You can call it that. Or a flash drive."

Bae's eyes immediately beamed as her body language changed entirely.

I pointed to the end of the flash drive. "Do you see that?"

She nodded yes.

"That goes right in here," I said, as I inserted the drive into the laptop. I turned the computer so it faced her, and she could see what I was doing. The drive contained sensitive information, but I figured it wouldn't hurt for her to see it. She'd have no idea what it meant.

I did some more typing. The screen barely kept up.

"You type fast," Bae said.

"I'm looking for the files on the flash drive. Right here." I pointed to the screen, focused totally on the task at hand. "That's the drive. Now, I'm going to open it." Before I did, I made sure it didn't have any viruses or any self-destruction mechanisms built in.

I could sense the excitement in Bae as the computer began spinning to open the drive. She was almost as excited as I was. If this contained the nuclear codes, then this was valuable information. It had better be. I risked my life to get it.

Immediately, hundreds of files began appearing on the screen. I started typing with a flurry.

"What are you doing?" Bae asked.

I ignored her, so I could concentrate fully. When I confirmed that the files did indeed contain the codes, I reached out with my hand and held it high. "High five," I said when Bae didn't immediately respond.

She hit my hand with hers and a loud smack reverberated in the car.

"What are we high fiving about?" Bae asked.

"You have no idea how important this information is. You did good, Bae. Really good."

Her eyes told me she had no idea what I was talking about, but the rest of her face beamed with pride.

"So, what does this mean?" Bae asked.

"It means we don't have to go to South Korea. Not yet, anyway." This would save me valuable time. We could go straight to the cyber lab. I could hack into Pok's phone from this computer if I could get close enough to intercept his wireless signal.

"Where are we going?" Bae asked.

"To pay a visit to someone I know."

"Who?"

"Someone who is going to be very surprised to see me."

32

Korean Airbus A380
Somewhere Over the Baltic Sea

The first thing Jamie did once she found her seat in business class was go into the restroom to change clothes. In her bag were three sets of outfits that gave her three different looks. She chose business professional.

When she arrived in Seoul, Korea, she intended to follow the Iranians. The problem was that they had seen her in Frankfurt. Even though she was certain they hadn't marked her as anything more than an American tourist traveling to Korea, they did see her enough for her appearance to register in their minds if they saw her again. When operatives see the "same person, different place," it sends an immediate red flag that they may be under surveillance.

Especially when the person was out of place. Jamie suspected that the two Iranians would catch a connection to North Korea. The American tourist they had seen in the boarding area in Frankfurt would not be making a connection to North Korea. She didn't intend for them to see her surveilling them, but if they did, she didn't want them to recognize her as the same person they saw in Frankfurt. That would raise all kinds of alarms and force a confrontation she wasn't yet ready to have.

She removed the Cubs hat along with the band holding her ponytail in place. Her sandy blonde hair was long, well below her shoulders, and she ran her fingers through it and shook it out to smooth some of the tangles.

The baggy cargo pants were comfortable, but she slipped them off and put on a pair of faux-leather moto dressy black leggings that stopped slightly above her ankles. For these purposes, the leggings were better. They were comfortable for traveling, gave her the look of a business professional, and were also easy to run in, if necessary. They also allowed for enough flexibility to execute leg kicks, which Jamie assumed would be necessary if there was a confrontation with the Iranians.

Something she was determined to avoid. The last thing she needed was to create an international incident in the Korean airport when she was supposed to be back home in D.C.

Jamie slipped the white tee shirt over her head and donned a blue inverted-pleated V neck silk blouse that hung loosely just below her waist. In surveillance, she avoided bright colors. Blue, white, and black were the preferred choices for blending into the environment and not being noticed.

While also dressy, the shirt allowed freedom of movement in her upper body, and the silk made it difficult for an assailant to get a grip on her. Alex played football in college and said that they soaked their jerseys in water before a game to make them slippery for the defenders. They also applied double tape to the shoulder pads which acted like glue, making the jersey nearly impossible to latch on to.

Same principle. That gave her the idea to wear leggings and satiny shirts whenever faced with a possible confrontation. It probably didn't make that much difference, but even the slightest advantage could mean the difference between life or death.

The thought of Alex temporarily sent a warm feeling through her heart.

The sneakers were put away in her backpack for sleek, black, heeled leather boots with an empowering platform sole that rose to just above her ankle. These weren't as good for either fleeing or chasing but were a lethal weapon when a properly executed leg kick hit a vulnerable part of a man's body. The heel loop and elasticated gusset made for easy on and off access, so she could discard them if she had to run away.

Jamie applied a minimum amount of makeup and fixed her hair. She accessorized the look with a cross necklace but skipped the matching earrings. In a struggle, an assailant could do significant damage by grabbing hold of them and jerking them off her ears. Her hair covered them anyway, so they didn't add anything to the look.

One final examination in the mirror, and Jamie was satisfied that she wouldn't be recognized. She also looked more like a person traveling in business class. Jamie returned to her seat where she began to analyze the situation and think through a plan.

Analysis wasn't Jamie's strong suit. In fact, it was her worst skill as a CIA officer. Alex was great at it. That came from his computer-like, analytical mind, perfectly suited for processing information and data. Jamie preferred to fly by the seat of her pants and trust her instincts. In the fog of the moment, when bullets were flying, Jamie was as good as there was at reacting and making split-second decisions. When it came to plotting a strategy and breaking down information, Jamie hated it with a passion and only did it when necessary.

Like now. It was necessary. She had to figure out what was going on with Alex and what she was walking into, which the Iranians made more complicated. The only thing that worked for her was to break the information down to its simplest form.

So, to keep from giving herself a headache, Jamie simply sat in her seat, closed her eyes, and replayed the Iranian's conversation in her head.

There's an American spy on the loose in North Korea, the Iranian had said. She remembered that he read an email from his director. Probably MOIS.

That had to be Alex. Who else could it be?

Curly always said there were no coincidences in life. *Don't overthink it.* Just go with the obvious. That was an advantage of not being a good analyst. Jamie wasn't capable of overthinking it. Alex, on the other hand, drove her crazy. He couldn't even buy a car without researching every make and model on the planet.

Big guy. His name is Alex. He shouldn't be hard to find. The Iranian had been specific.

"It's Alex. He's in North Korea. Move on," Jamie whispered under her breath. The Iranian just confirmed what she already knew.

He killed three of our men.

Good for him.

That sounded like something Alex was capable of doing. Not very many people in the world had the skill to kill three Iranian National Guardsmen. More confirmation.

What are we supposed to do when we find him? One of the Iranians asked the other that question.

Kill him.

Jamie shuddered. Alex was in danger. She wanted to eliminate the threat herself. That didn't make sense for her to do, though. Alex killed the other three and could handle these two as well.

The American is with the girl. She stole the satchel.

That's when the analysis came to a screeching halt in her mind. She couldn't process what that meant. Jamie tried to put the emotions and the jealousy aside, but it was hard to do. Just thinking about it caused her breath to quicken and droplets of sweat to form on her forehead.

She tried to calm her fears.

Love always trusts.

The Bible verse kept coming to mind, trying to bring peace to her soul. She needed to give Alex the benefit of the doubt until she knew differently. Breaking the analysis down to its simplest form,

Alex had never given her any reason to doubt his faithfulness. He was as strong a Christian as she was. Stronger in some ways.

Not that Alex was perfect. And he was good looking, tall, and muscular, and they were apart for months at a time. What man wasn't capable of falling into temptation? The emotions played tricks on Jamie's mind and were causing confusion, so she decided to get out of her seat and stretch her legs.

The Airbus 380 was the largest passenger jet in the world she had read, so she decided to explore it and give her mind a break from the analysis. She'd read that there was a gift shop on board and a Celestial bar which everyone raved about. Jamie opted for the bar which was on the upper deck.

It felt weird to walk up a staircase on an airplane. It took a second to get her balance. At the top of the stairs, she realized it wasn't so much a bar but a small lounge. Her expectations had far outpaced what she found. For some reason, she had pictured a nightclub with strobe lights and mirrors on the wall and music blaring.

Instead, what she found was one small table with seating for two, a lounge chair for one, and a teal cushioned bench along the wall that would hold three people, but not comfortably. The bar itself was L-shaped and actually only about three feet long and about four feet high, with a countertop about fourteen inches wide. A shelf had about a dozen opened and unopened liquor bottles.

They were obviously going for a "Jetson's" type look, with yellow lights on the wall, track lighting on the ceiling, and a futuristic shape and design. Luxurious for sure. Unlike anything she'd ever seen before on a plane. Jamie probably would've been in awe of the room had her expectations not been so high.

A lone, male flight attendant was standing behind the bar. He was approximately thirty years old, Korean, wearing a brown standard-issue Korean Air pants, short sleeved matching collared shirt, and red tie. He seemed bored until Jamie walked into the room, and his whole demeanor changed. A smile erupted on his face like he'd just been told he had won the lottery.

Jamie glanced over at the mirror. She did look rather good. Even then, his reaction was overstated, so she decided that was his job. He was probably that way with all the customers.

"What can I get you to drink?" he asked in an American accent.

"What do you have?" Jamie asked, walking over to the bar.

He placed a piece of paper in front of her that had a list of drink options.

Jamie studied the list of wines, cocktails, and hard drinks. The lounge was sponsored by Absolut Vodka, so they had more vodka drinks than anything else.

"I'll have mineral water," Jamie finally said.

"Whoa!" he said, putting both hands in the air. "Don't you think it's a little early for the hard stuff?" he said jokingly.

"I don't drink," she said, willing to give him a slight grin. That wasn't entirely true. She did drink occasionally. On this occasion, Jamie actually considered ordering a glass of wine. It might calm her and settle her emotions. It would also make her sleepy. She had too much work to do before landing. Even though the flight was ten hours, she didn't want to be on the ground without a plan.

"Let me make you my special drink," he said. "It's famous on five continents."

Jamie hesitated before finally agreeing. The attendant turned his back to her and started mixing a drink. Jamie saw at least three different shots go into the glass. She needed to be careful. The last thing she wanted was to get a buzz that impaired her ability to think clearly.

The bartender poured his concoction into a metal shaker and turned back toward her with a huge smile on his face. He raised the shaker in the air and moved his arms back and forth assertively, shaking the mixture so hard she could hear the liquid clanging against the sides. The muscles in his arms bulged into perfect definition as he did it.

He set a glass in front of her and poured the lime-green mixture with a tint of orange color into it. After putting a thin, red straw into it, he propped his elbows on the bar and leaned in, waiting for her to try it.

Jamie took one sip and then let out an affirming moan. An explosion of flavor burst into her mouth as the ice-cold liquid soothed what she hadn't realized was her parched throat.

"Mmm... That's good," Jamie said, as her upper body shuddered, immediately feeling the effects of the alcohol.

"I call it the Ricky. That's my name," he said, raising back up and leaning on the back counter with his arms folded in obvious satisfaction at his handiwork.

Jamie had never heard of a Korean named Ricky.

Her face must've given her away because he said, "Ricky is actually a common name in Korea. Most of the time it's spelled R-I-K-K-Y. Mine is spelled the American way. My mom loved the show I Love Lucy. She named me Ricky after the boy. She called me Little Ricky all the time. Still does."

Jamie noticed that when Ricky smiled, he had cute dimples. She took another drink. She needed to slow down and nurse the drink and get her attention off the man.

An awkward silence pursued as she kept her head down and stared at the drink, not wanting to make eye contact with him. He was good looking and charming. She didn't have time for that, even though his tone and manner were flattering.

"Boyfriend troubles?" Ricky asked.

Jamie sat straight up on the stool, not sure what to make of such an inappropriate question. After thinking about it for a couple seconds, she decided not to be offended. She did have boyfriend troubles.

"Is it that obvious?" she said, tilting her head to the side in a disarming manner.

"Hey. I'm a glorified bartender. I see a lot of women come in here crying in their drink, because of some jerk back home."

"I'm not... I'm not crying in my drink," Jamie said as a flash of anger went through her.

Ricky held out his hands in a pose of surrender. "All I'm saying is that a pretty girl like you either has boyfriend problems, job problems, or daddy issues."

That made her laugh out loud. She had just taken a drink and had to put her hand to her mouth to keep from spewing liquid in his face. Even then some escaped, and she had to get a napkin to wipe it off.

"Turns out, I have all three," Jamie said. "My boyfriend and I work together so... the job and boyfriend issues go together. The daddy issues would take ten years of therapy to get over, so I just ignore them."

That caused Ricky to laugh. He leaned in again and reclined his elbow on the bar and rested his head on his left hand.

Jamie's dad was an astronaut on a one-way trip to the far reaches of the universe. A few years before, she had connected with him for the first time. A story much too complicated to get into with a stranger.

"What's your name?" he asked, holding out his right hand.

"Jae," she replied, shaking it firmly. Curly always said to use an alias as close to the real name as possible. She was traveling under the name Jae Chan.

"What do you do?" he asked, obviously good at keeping a conversation moving and also not allowing a pause where the woman could get away. Jamie realized the guy was a player and probably made these same moves on a woman every flight. Didn't matter. Her guard was already well fortified and in place. A drink and a few slick words wouldn't fool her. That didn't mean she wasn't enjoying the conversation and the attention.

"I'm a chemical supply salesperson," Jamie said. "For Dupont. Out of Delaware."

"Very cool."

Jamie got the impression that if she asked him to recall what she did and who she worked for he couldn't do it. He had one thing on his mind. Jamie just wondered when he would get around to it.

For nearly two hours, they laughed and joked around. Ricky was funny. Charismatic. He ordered some finger foods that Jamie nibbled on. Interruptions were few. Occasionally, someone came in and ordered a drink. For the most part, the conversation and the drink eased the tension in Jamie.

"How long are you in Korea?" Ricky asked.

Here we go.

"Just a few days."

"Do you want to have dinner with me?"

"I'd better not," Jamie said, having already rehearsed the answer in her mind. "I have a boyfriend."

"I don't see a ring on your finger," he retorted.

"You don't seem like the kind of guy who would care if I did," Jamie said. That was mean but she wanted him to get the hint.

"Ouch!"

"No offense intended. Like I said, I have a boyfriend." Even if she didn't have a boyfriend, she wouldn't fall for his charm. She'd never be someone's one-night stand or another notch in his belt.

Her lunch arrived anyway, just in time. Or maybe it was breakfast. She left home fourteen hours ago, and with the time change, she wasn't really sure what time it really was. She had ordered it from Ricky at the bar. The Bibimbap meal helped confuse the issue. The rice bowl was filled with all sorts of seasoned sautéed vegetables, marinated beef, and a fried egg sunny side up on the top right in the center.

The sauce tasted like it was made up of sprinkles of sesame and a generous heaping of a sweet and spicy bibimbap sauce. Jamie had only had the dish twice, and they were both about the same in quality and taste. She washed it down with a Sprite, served to her by Ricky who was no longer paying much attention to her since she was clearly a waste of his time.

When she finished, she dabbed the sauce off of the side of her lips and downed the rest of her drink. She took out her phone and tried to access the internet with it. She threw her hands in the air when she was unable to.

Ricky must've seen her because he said, "There's a passcode to access the internet."

"What did you *just* say?" Jamie said as a thought suddenly circled her mind like a race car speeding around an oval.

Ricky hesitated. "I said you need a passcode to access the internet."

The word passcode triggered a memory. The Iranian had used the word "code" in his conversation. What was it he said? Jamie strained to remember.

The girl stole the satchel. The satchel contained the Pakistani codes. That's what the Iranian had said.

Codes could only mean nuclear. It finally made sense. The girl stole the satchel. The satchel contained Pakistani nuclear codes. Alex went after the girl to get them. The Iranians must've bought them from the North Koreans. That's why the Iranians were hunting Alex. This wasn't about a girl; it was about keeping nuclear codes out of the hands of the Iranians.

That changed everything.

As soon as we arrive in Seoul, I have to take out the two Iranians.

33

North Korea Cyber Lab

The drive to the lab took less than an hour. We would've gotten there sooner, but I got lost on the back roads trying to find it from memory and coming from a different direction. Avoiding the police was an added challenge. Fortunately, we only saw one, and he was traveling away from us. Once we got closer to the lab, things became more familiar, and I remembered a side road that was a perfect place to hide the police cruiser.

"I don't guess I can convince you to stay here and watch the police car," I said to Bae.

"Nope!"

"It might be dangerous," I added, realizing I wasn't making the best argument. Bae seemed to thrive on the danger. I understood. I was somewhat of an adrenaline junkie. Most people like me get their kicks from bungee jumping or parachuting out of an airplane. I came alive when facing an adversary. Mano a mano. 'May the best man win' brought the best out of me.

"You might need me," Bae argued, much to my amusement.

I choked back the laugh that had formed in my throat because Bae was easily offended, I had learned that the hard way. Like my girlfriend Jamie. If I left Bae in the car, she'd just wait a few minutes and follow me anyway. I was better off keeping her in my sights at all times. Putting her in harm's way wasn't smart, but she'd be in greater danger and so would I if she was out wandering around alone trying to avoid detection with no experience.

After a short hike through the woods, Bae and I found a good hiding place among some bushes on the backside of the facility. I left her there and circled around the perimeter to surveille the number of guards. There were still a dozen or so in the front entrance. The only difference was that one guard was outside walking around the building. That meant I had to be further away from the building than I would've liked.

"Shoot!" I said under my breath, staring at the computer that was open in my lap in front of me. I tried to connect to the lab's wireless internet so I could take back control of Kryptonite.

"Alex. What's wrong?" Bae whispered.

"I can't get a signal from here," I answered, looking up and scanning the facility to see what other options I had.

"What about that building?" Bae asked, pointing to the building where I was beaten and interrogated when I first arrived at the facility. That seemed like eons ago, even though it had only been two days.

"That building doesn't have adequate power," I said. "And the battery on the laptop is getting low. We still have some juice left, but it'll run out before I finish what I need to do."

"I guess we're just going to have to find a way inside the lab," Bae said with her hand on her chin like she was thinking. Why did that annoy me? Jamie did that to me all the time when we were on a mission together. Before I had a chance to analyze the situation, Jamie would try and find the best solution. Now Bae was trying to do the same thing, much to my frustration.

"I don't guess I can convince you to stay here in the woods and be my lookout?" I asked.

"Nope!"

"Now you're just getting on my nerves," I said.

Bae's brow furrowed and tilted her head. "I don't understand what you mean, Alex."

"Never mind. I have another idea," I said as a new plan formed in my mind.

"What are we going to do now, boss?" Bae asked, bouncing up and down with excitement. She was too naive to really understand how much danger we were in.

"See that right over there," I said, pointing to the main building. "It has a fire escape right there in the corner. I'm going to sneak over and climb up on the roof. There's a heating unit up there. That means there's also a power outlet. I'm going to plug the computer into it. I should be able to pick up the cell phone signal from the rooftop and charge the laptop at the same time."

"Sounds good. Let's go," she said, clapping her hands together in a way that was muffled so no one could hear us, but so she could still express her enthusiasm.

"No way! You're not going," I said. "It's too risky. You stay here."

Bae's nose crinkled as she let out an exasperated sigh.

"See that guard, he's got a machine gun," I said as the guard came around the corner of the building. We both instinctively ducked below the bushes even though we were far enough away that he couldn't see us. "There's a dozen more around the front. If they discover us, we're in big trouble."

I watched him carefully. He was in our sight for eight minutes. It took him another eight minutes to cross the front of the building back to our side. That's how long it would take to get to the fire escape undetected.

"What about those people in the windows?" Bae asked. "They'll see us." Several offices were facing our direction. A couple of them had people in it, including Pok who I could see sitting at his desk in his office. The hairs on my arms raised as I bristled from seeing him.

I let out a frustrated sigh. The sun wouldn't be setting for another hour. I also noticed that Bae said *us* and not *you*. That meant there was no way I was going alone. Probably better anyway. Bae was so impetuous she wouldn't sit in the woods for the two to three hours it would take me to do everything I needed to do. At least on the roof, she'd be near me, and I could control her.

Somewhat.

I leaned back against a tree and closed my eyes.

"What are you doing?" Bae asked.

"We're going to have to wait until dark. There's a rule to spying you need to know. Sleep when you can. You never know when you'll get another chance. Sit back and relax. It's going to be awhile."

"You sleep. I'll take the first watch," Bae said, as she crouched down so she was looking through the bushes at the cyber lab like a watchman would.

I smiled as I felt an overwhelming urge to encourage her. "You do that, Bae. Wake me if you see someone coming."

I must've slept really hard because the next time I opened my eyes, everything was completely dark except for the lights inside the cyber lab shining through the windows.

***

Bae and I got to the fire escape and up onto the roof of the cyber lab with no problem. Once there, the problems began.

The roof did have a power outlet, but it was the wrong voltage for the computer. A simple voltage converter that cost twenty bucks in the United States was all I needed but was something I obviously didn't have with me. Technology always amazed me in that way. The largest and most sophisticated supercomputer in the world that costs millions of dollars to manufacture wouldn't run on that power outlet without a twenty-dollar adapter.

The battery level on the laptop was just above thirty percent, so I wouldn't be able to do everything I wanted. I had to choose. What I really wanted to do was email the Pakistani nuclear codes to Brad. I would feel much better knowing someone in our government besides me had that information and could do something about it. If something happened to me, that flash drive could still fall into the wrong hands.

It was also my ticket out of a court martial, should I somehow make it out of this mess alive. Coming to North Korea and letting Pok commandeer Kryptonite had been a huge operational failure and a threat to our national security. The justification that I had prevented nuclear codes from falling into the hands of the Iranians would cover a multitude of my sins.

The problem was that I couldn't do both—mail the codes and salvage Kryptonite and keep Pok from hacking into the CIA server. Since the codes were safely in my possession, I decided to use what little battery power I had left to hack back into Kryptonite and set up a booby trap for Pok that would devastate his operations. Admittedly, some competitive personal revenge might have been behind the decision.

Nevertheless, I made the decision and set out to access Kryptonite from Pok's cell phone. The problem was that he wasn't on the phone. I had to wait until he logged into the cyber lab server to access his internet.

Bae could sense my frustration. "What's wrong, Alex?" she whispered. We still had to be concerned that the guard circling the building didn't hear us.

"His cell phone isn't connected to the server. I can't hack into it until it is."

"How does that work?"

"The cyber lab accesses the internet through underground T-1 lines. There's obviously no way for me to hack into them from here."

I pointed to an antenna on the top of the roof.

"That's a portable cell tower. It provides cell phone service to the lab. There's a bigger tower somewhere around here. Probably a mile or two away. When someone in the lab turns on his cell phone, I can intercept the signal and piggyback off of it."

I showed Bae where I had picked up the wireless signal on the computer. Her eyes were glazed over as I got too detailed in my explanations. I suspected that she had no idea what I was talking about, even though she nodded dutifully. Another trait of hers that warmed my heart along with the joy of teaching her. This trip had been eye opening to me. I discovered a skill I didn't know I had. Someday I might want to do what Curly did and train operatives.

"The man running this lab is a very bad man," I said to Bae. "He steals from people all over the world by using his computer. I'm going to stop him. He's being careless by using the wireless connection. He probably thinks he's safe here in North Korea. We just need for him to hurry. Our battery is down to twenty-four percent."

We waited more than half an hour before Pok finally logged on. I quickly sprang into action and began typing furiously. I didn't know how long he would stay on.

"We're in business," I said to Bae. I gave her a running play by play of what I was doing. "I'm making my computer mirror his so the cell phone tower thinks they are one in the same."

"How are you..." Bae started to say.

"No questions," I said roughly. "I need to give this my undivided attention. Don't say anything for the next hour. Just listen. I'll explain later." I hated to be rude, but her questions were distracting and would slow me down. I was down to under twenty percent battery. I'd be cutting it close as it was. Every second counted.

"We're in."

Bae took in a breath like she was about to say something but then caught herself.

"I have a back way into Kryptonite no one knows about but me," I said excitedly. It actually helped me to talk out loud. Something I usually did when I was alone working in my home or in the CIA lab.

I let out a gleeful laugh. "Pok's not going to know what hits him!"

"Who's Pok?" Bae asked.

I shouldn't have said his name out loud in front of Bae, but it was too late. There was no time to think through the ramifications if there were any. Hopefully, she'd forget she ever heard the name.

"The man running the lab," I answered. "The bad guy. I almost have control of Kryptonite... There. I have control now. This will let Brad go back in."

"Who's Brad?" Bae asked.

I looked up from the computer long enough to glare at her.

"Sorry," she said, shrugging her shoulders. She then made a gesture like she was zipping her lip and throwing away the key. I'd seen Jamie do the same thing, although it never lasted long with her. Amazing how things like that go viral around the world.

"I'm putting in another firewall so Pok can't go back in," I explained. The effort was quickly sapping the energy out of the battery of the computer.

"Just hold on a little longer, baby," I pleaded with the computer. I felt sweat form on my brow and then run down my face. I wiped one side off with the sleeve of my shirt and changed positions so I could type even faster.

Five percent power.

The computer went into power-saving mode as the screen darkened.

"Don't do that!" I wanted to shout but whispered instead.

I didn't have time to change the settings. I typed with the intensity of a skier trying to save someone from an avalanche.

The screen went dead.

Did I do enough? I think so.

I closed the lid on the laptop and handed it to Bae. "Here. You can carry this back to the car."

My mind was processing as fast as a computer as I tried to figure out how much I had accomplished. I gave control of Kryptonite back to the CIA. That I was sure of. Could the CIA access a North Korea server undetected now with Kryptonite? That I wasn't so sure of. I gave them access, but I didn't have time to close all the vulnerabilities. Maybe I did enough. I'd find out when I got back to the hotel in South Korea.

At the very least, we were back to the status quo of how things were before I came to North Korea. No harm, no foul. Brad wouldn't see it that way, but I had the nuclear codes as my trump card. In the CIA world, nuclear was the biggest priority. Nothing was more important than stopping possible nuclear attacks. All the rules went out the window when it came down to preventing them.

Overall, I felt good that the mission was justified and a success. Brad could argue that I almost caused a catastrophe, but I would argue that I prevented a bigger one. Brad was a former field agent. He'd understand the risks involved in missions. Sometimes, things didn't go as planned. If they turned out alright in the end, then we'd live to fight another day.

That's assuming Bae and I got back to South Korea with the flash drive. Still a big assumption.

"Bae, you go down the fire escape first," I said. "I'll follow you. As soon as you hit the ground, you take off running for the woods. I'll cover you."

The problem was that from the roof, we didn't know where the guard was in his patrol around the building. The front of the building and the top of the roof was better lit, so I didn't want to risk looking over the edge and being seen. The backside was darker, so I leaned over the side and looked both ways. The guard wasn't there. That meant he was around in front somewhere. Where, though? Did he just start around the front or was he about to come to the back?

We could wait for him to pass, but I wanted to get out of there quickly before Pok realized what I'd done. As soon as he did, the dozen soldiers would be out looking for us. I wanted to put several miles between them and us before that happened.

I motioned for Bae to go. She traversed the ladder easily, even carrying the computer. I waited for her to clear the stairs in case the guard came around. From my vantage point, I could shoot him, and be down the stairs before the other guards heard the commotion.

Bae reached the bottom. Instead of running, she just stood there looking up at me. I couldn't yell at her to run without the risk of being heard. So, I started down the stairs at a quickened pace.

Out of the corner of my eye I saw movement. In the darkness.

The guard.

I stopped and drew the weapon, but I couldn't see him clearly in the dark.

Bae let out a muted scream.

I continued down, even faster. When I reached the bottom, I turned to see what I was facing. I had the weapon raised in front of me.

The guard had one arm wrapped around Bae's waist. His gun was in his other hand pointed directly at me about eight feet away. Too far for me to disarm him and close enough to where he wouldn't miss if he got a shot off.

"Drop your weapon," the guard shouted.

Not knowing what else to do, I raised my right hand in the air in a surrender pose, I slowly lowered the gun in my left hand and sat it on the ground.

Bae wasn't struggling. She just stood there, frozen in fear.

34

The guard and I exchanged a cold, icy stare, creating a momentary stalemate. It's not really a stalemate when one person has an assault rifle and the other was unarmed, but we were on even footing at least to the extent that neither of us knew what to do. I could see the indecision on his face as he shook his head back and forth and up and down.

He had one arm wrapped around Bae's waist and one clutched the weapon. I knew from experience that firing an assault weapon with one arm was difficult, if not next to impossible to do. It took hours of dry-fire practice for me to learn the skill. The man wasn't in the right position to do so. He'd need to tuck the buttstock under his arm to steady it. Even then, it took a tremendous amount of strength to hold it once the power of the weapon was released.

My preferred way was to hold it against my shoulder and steady it with my cheek, but that would be impossible for him to do and still maintain his grasp on Bae. The rifle rested against his hip and his hand was on the trigger. That wouldn't work. As soon as he started firing, he'd lose control of the weapon, and the bullets would spray erratically.

I was only eight feet away from him, so the chances were that I wouldn't get hit. The odds were just as great that he might shoot his own foot. Still, there was always the possibility of a random shot hitting me.

Or Bae.

Bae had a look of sheer panic on her face. Her mouth was open and frozen in the shape of a gasp. Her eyes were wide, her eyebrows furrowed, and the brashness she'd displayed toward me since I met her was gone. She clutched the laptop in front of her with a death grip. Her knuckles were white from holding it so tightly.

Curly trained that out of us. In a situation such as this, adrenaline spiked to incredibly high levels. That caused one of two reactions. Either your senses were heightened, and you suddenly had supernatural abilities beyond your normal capabilities, or you froze. Cognitive paralysis was the technical term. Curly called it the "pansy pose." He also used the term "death pose" interchangeably. He said your death pose would be the last thing your assailant saw before he killed you.

Bae definitely had the look and would be no good to me if she didn't snap out of it. Although, at the moment, it was the best thing. At least she wasn't thrashing around or crying or adding more uncertainty to the situation. The best thing for both of us was for her to do nothing until I made a move. When I did, he'd be forced to let go of her or I would overpower him.

The guard had a radio on his belt, but no free hand to use it. I glanced around to see if anyone else was coming but didn't expect it since we hadn't created much of a commotion. He looked around as well. His eyes flitted left and right, nervously and with uncertainty. The adrenaline was causing him to freeze as well. A pansy pose. If I still had my gun, I'd make it his final death pose. The gun was on the ground a couple of feet in front of me. I had laid it down in the optimum position to retrieve it, if that was the option I chose.

All I had to do was fall flat to the ground, grab the gun, aim, and fire. I'd practiced the move a thousand times but never used it in real life. I wanted to avoid that scenario. The way the guard held the rifle, the bullets would likely go into the ground. Right where I'd be lying if I tried to execute that move.

It didn't matter.

For some reason, the guard started circling to his left, my right. I matched his steps and kept the circle in place until we essentially changed positions. A mistake on his part. Before this, my back had been to the wall, and I was trapped. Now I felt fairly confident that I could run away and get to the woods without getting shot. He was now trapped against the wall if I were to make a sudden move toward him. The only downside was that my gun on the ground was now closer to him and out of my reach.

At that point, I had a dilemma. Did I flee and ensure that I got the nuclear codes back to the CIA or did I stay and try to save Bae, risking my own life and possibly allowing the nuclear codes to get into the hands of the Iranians? The CIA standard operating procedure would be to protect the codes at all cost. Even over the lives of innocent civilians. Even if it meant abandoning your partner or fellow officers.

That made common sense. The codes could result in the loss of millions of lives if it fell into the wrong hands. That was more important than the life of a thirteen-year-old North Korean girl I just met. Curly, on the other hand, drilled in us, "no man left behind." He always said that you should never abandon your partner unless there were no other options. If it didn't make sense in the field or he didn't agree with the principle, Curly wasn't one for following standard operational procedures or the CIA training handbook,

Was Bae my partner?

She felt like it. She was in this position because of me. Even then, I'd already saved her life a couple of times. How many times was I expected to save her before enough was enough and I needed to look out for myself? I also told her to wait at the police cruiser. She wouldn't listen to me. In a way, this was her own fault.

Still, I wasn't ready to abandon her yet. She was my protégé. Sort of. If nothing else, I had a warm affection for her and would have a hard time living with myself if I abandoned her. The thought of her being interrogated by the secret police was almost too much for me to contemplate.

When faced with a difficult decision, I liked to rub my face. Roughly. Somehow it always seemed to knock the decision loose in my head. I couldn't this time because if I made any sudden moves with my hand, the guard might react and start shooting erratically.

I shifted my weight. Something needed to happen soon. My experience was that long bouts of indecision created uncertain outcomes. Decisive action usually ruled the day. Even if it was the wrong action, it still forced the issue and put pressure on the enemy combatant. Usually people panicked when suddenly pressed into deciding. Mike Tyson, the great boxer who struck fear in the hearts of his opponents, famously said, "Everybody has a plan until they get punched in the mouth."

Curly used that quote over and over again, and it gave me strength in times like this. The problem was I didn't have a good plan. I didn't want to act until I was sure what I was going to do, and it made sense.

I didn't need to do anything.

Bae's eyes suddenly lost their glossy glaze and her demeanor changed. As did her body language and position. She moved her feet, so they were more firmly set in the ground. Probably not even noticeable to the guard. I noticed. Our eyes met. I nodded slightly. I could see the confidence return to her face as her jaws clenched and her eyes narrowed into a resolute look.

As lightning fast as a cat, Bae lifted her left leg off the ground.

A look of surprise came over the guard's face as his mouth flew open at the sudden movement.

With tremendous force, Bae brought her left heel down on the man's foot with perfect timing and precision hitting him right on the arch.

The guard let out a loud "Ooof," as if he had been hit in the solar plexus.

I don't know if it was sheer luck or Bae had really been listening when I taught her the move. Upon impact, the angle of her foot continued down from the arch toward the ground until it made maximum impact with the man's toes. His boots were worn and thin.

I could hear the familiar sound of bones cracking.

The man let out the howl almost like the yelp of an injured wolf whose foot was caught in a trap. He dropped the gun, grabbed his left foot, and started hopping up and down.

I started to yell for Bae to run but didn't get the chance.

When her left foot was back on the ground, she pivoted quickly so she was facing the man.

He released his foot and let it fall to the ground. Bae brought her right foot up in a pendulum arc right between the man's legs and connected with his groin. The impact was so severe it made me wince.

The guard fell to his knees. Bae took the computer that was still in her hands and reared back. She hit the guard in the head with such force that the impact of the metal against his skull created a sickening sound unlike any I'd ever heard before. Metal on bone.

Somehow Bae had the strength to hold on to the laptop. The man let out a groan and then fell face first into the ground, unconscious, maybe even dead. His head hit the gravelly earth with a thud.

Bae stood over him like a prize fighter standing over a beaten foe. She was on the balls of her feet bouncing up and down, ready to strike him again if he made so much as a move.

"Dangsin-I depleoun jasig-eul gaiigo!" Bae said to the man.

I think she said, "Take that, you dirty bastard."

I immediately grabbed the man's rifle off the ground and retrieved my own gun. Then I grabbed Bae's hand. Her focus hadn't left the man.

"Bae, let's go!" I said, in an attempt to bring her back to reality. I knew the feeling. Adrenaline was pulsing through her like the sprays of a drive-through car wash. Hard to bring them under control. Curly worked with us for hours teaching how to get our minds to think clearly in the fog of war.

With a strong tug of her hand, Bae finally started moving. We sprinted to the edge of the woods. I looked back at the tree line to make sure no one followed us. We ran the rest of the way back to the police cruiser. By the time we arrived, we were both out of breath.

Bae took one look at the computer still in her hands and threw it to the ground. It had a huge dent in the back casing, probably no longer functional.

She paced around the area with her hands on her hips, taking short shallow breaths muttering under her breath.

"You okay," I asked.

She stopped pacing.

I walked over to her.

She held her hand up in the air. "High five," she said.

I knew she was going to be okay as I slapped her hand.

35

Seoul Incheon International Airport
Seoul, South Korea

Jamie was the first one off the plane. As soon as the Fasten Seat Belt sign was turned off, she rushed out of her seat to the cabin door so she would be first. Getting into position before the Iranians deboarded was vital to surveilling them. They were in the back, so it would take them several minutes to deplane.

As soon as the cabin door opened, she bolted down the jetway and into the concourse area where she found the flight arrival and departure information screens. A flight to North Korea left in a little over an hour. That had to be the Iranians' connecting flight. Jamie would've preferred a longer window of opportunity to take down the Iranians, but Curly always said to not fret about things you can't control. Concentrate on the things you can.

When the Iranians got off the plane, she would follow them at a distance. If they went left out of the gate and went to the baggage claim area and exited the airport, then she'd cut them loose. No way was she going to follow them all over South Korea. She would just go straight to Alex's hotel and see what she could find there.

If the Iranians turned right and went toward the gate with the flight to North Korea, then she'd have all the confirmation she needed. Then she'd look for an opportunity to take them out. An airport was not an ideal place to do so because of the security cameras, but she had a plan. Curly taught her that in an airport setting, the restroom was the best place to act. There were no cameras and the men would have their hands occupied.

The thought made Jamie chuckle. Curly used more colorful and vulgar words to describe why the men were at a disadvantage in a bathroom setting, but she tried to block those out of her mind years ago.

Jamie took up a position where the men wouldn't see her when they came off the plane, but she could see them. When they exited the plane, they turned right, just as she suspected. They didn't even go to the screen to look up the connecting gate information. Maybe they got it from the flight attendant or looked it up on their phones. At any rate, the direction they were headed had to be to the North Korean flight.

Her pulse quickened and her senses heightened. She hoped the men hadn't used the restroom on the plane. That's why she'd wanted a longer layover. If they didn't have to go now, they would if the layover were several hours.

Play the cards you are dealt. Curly's words were resonating in her head.

The men were keeping a steady pace. They made some effort to see if they were being followed, but it was half-hearted. They had no reason to believe anyone knew who they were or the nature of their mission. Jamie wouldn't have known their true motives except that she just happened to be on their same connecting flight.

Some might call that blind luck. Curly said there was no such thing as luck. Luck was when opportunity met ability. While it was fortuitous that they were on the same flight as her, it was Jamie's skill that identified them as operatives. Then her ability to assess the situation and take the appropriate surveillance steps uncovered the actionable information. Made possible by the hours she toiled learning Farsi. Every time she complained about it, which was often, Curly would say it would come in handy someday. He was right.

The men exited the concourse and entered a long walkway that took them to the commuter gates, according to the signs which were in Korean and English. Jamie was glad they didn't have to ride a train, or she would've had to let the men go and catch up with them at the gate. Since they were walking, she could keep a safe distance behind and avoid detection.

A quick scan of the area revealed that there were no security cameras in the commuter concourse. That probably had to do with an agreement with North Korea. They wouldn't want their government officials caught on camera boarding or unloading from a flight. The early morning hour also meant there were no people milling around. She suspected the flight would only have a few passengers anyway. The two Iranians might even be the only ones.

Jamie lagged back so the men couldn't use any evasive tactics to spot her. What she would've done if she were them, would be find a hiding place at the end of the long tunnel and watch to see if anyone suspiciously exited it. Curly drilled those kinds of precautions into them. Most of the time it was unnecessary. He said over and over again that there might be one time when it would save her life. Since she only had one life to live, it was worth the effort all the other times.

The men were going into a confined area with only one way out so there was no chance she'd lose them. After a reasonable time passed, she quickened her pace and was down the tunnel and ramp in almost no time. She could see the men at a distance still walking. They hadn't taken any precautions to look for a tail.

She saw a sign for a restroom. One of the men broke stride with the other and headed toward it. The other continued walking toward the gate which wasn't much further down. Jamie breathed a sigh of relief and let out a rush of nervous energy all at the same time. The timing was perfect. She'd arrive at the restroom just after the man had settled into whatever he was going to do.

The Iranian stood, facing the wall and the urinal. Jamie took a wide angle so he wouldn't see her out of his peripheral vision. There was no mirror on the wall, so he couldn't see what was behind him. An unwritten rule in men's restrooms was that they didn't look around. Curly taught her that, and Alex confirmed it. Sort of a men's code of honor. Keep your eyes straight ahead on the wall in front of you. That was to her advantage as the Iranian was following the rule dutifully.

Jamie was in a perfect position and had two options. She could deliver a blow to the temple or a chop to the neck. Either executed properly would disable the man. Jamie had the ability to kill him with either blow. Since the man had said his mission was to kill Alex, she decided to go for maximum damage. That would be a strike to his neck and carotid artery.

It was also the most practical. It took less force, and she could attack him from behind rather than the side giving him little to no time to react. Also, there wouldn't be any blood. All the injuries would be internal.

The Iranian let out a pleasurable sigh. Jamie had no idea what that was about although she had heard Alex do the same thing.

Men are disgusting.

She tried to put out of her mind that she was in one of their bathrooms.

Since there was no mirror, Jamie had time to execute an even more devastating blow that would produce more power. Slightly past the man, she let her backpack slip off her shoulder to the floor then did a complete three-hundred and sixty-degree swivel, like she was going to execute a roundhouse kick. Instead, she brought the side of her right hand into the man's neck, like a karate chop.

He had no time to react. It was a direct and devastating blow. She could actually feel the artery sever and could hear the explosion of gases from the muscles, tissues, and vertebrae all creating a cascade of sound in the form of popping noises. Like when a chiropractor does an adjustment on your neck. The blow was so powerful it may have even broken some vertebrae and severed the man's spinal cord, although Jamie doubted it.

The Iranian let out a muted groan and collapsed to the floor. That was the reason she preferred he be in a stall. Now she would have to move him. First, she removed his wallet, ID, passport, and cell phone and stuck them in her backpack. She emptied his pockets of anything that might identify him. From behind, she put her arms under his and dragged him over to the nearest stall, kicking the door open while still maintaining her grip on the man.

He weighed at least two hundred, thirty pounds she estimated. Maybe more. When he was in position, she stepped over him, so she was facing him with her back to the restroom. That gave her a slight pause in that she was vulnerable should the other Iranian show up. She had to hurry.

After much effort, she was able to lift him up onto the stool and lean him back, so his head was against the wall. She checked for a pulse and didn't find one. With some staging of his legs, she made it look like the man was sitting on the toilet in a normal position if someone were to look under the stall door, which she hoped his partner would do soon. The stall door was closed but not locked.

She just had to wait. Eventually, the man's partner would come looking for him. When he did, she'd be ready. The bathroom had no place to hide so she got in the stall next to the dead man and waited. Trying not to breath any more than necessary. Being in the men's bathroom was grossing her out. Her hands were tucked under her armpits so she wouldn't touch anything. The women's bathrooms weren't any cleaner or smelled any better, she decided, it was just the thought of it that turned her stomach.

If she did marry Alex, they'd have to have separate bathrooms. She wasn't sure she could share one with a man. That made her think of the real mission at hand. Finding Alex and the girl. Saving their lives and then getting answers would soon become her priority. Then getting them both back home safely.

Although... Depending on what is happening with the girl, there might not even be a wedding.

***

Jamie had to wait longer than she expected which surprised her. The Iranian must not have been concerned that his partner was taking a long time in the bathroom. Maybe that was normal for men. Women tried to get in and out of there as fast as possible. Some women's bathrooms had sofas in them, although Jamie had never seen one being used. Who would want to spend any more time in a bathroom than they had to?

Apparently, men. Alex had a crossword puzzle book next to his toilet in his condo. Jamie couldn't fathom the reason why.

She was getting antsy. The other man had better come soon, or she might lose her mind. Now she was glad they had a short layover. The flight would be boarding soon, so he'd have to come check on his friend anytime now.

She thought about the blow that killed the Iranian. She chose it partly because she had never executed it in real life. It was one of the most difficult blows to strike because she had to hit him at the precise spot where it would hit the brachial nerve. A proper blow would "sheath" the artery and cause the pressure points that regulated blood pressure to overreact. The body would instinctively cause a massive drop in blood pressure which would cause the man to faint.

If the blow were strong and precise enough, it would sever the artery and cut off the vital flow of blood. The brain would short circuit and create extreme pain and then death within seconds. That must've happened to the man, because he had dropped to the floor like a bowling ball.

Jamie's thoughts were interrupted by heavy footsteps. She tensed. It had to be the Iranian. She heard him call out his partner's name in Farsi which confirmed it. His voice had only a slight level of concern, although he seemed to be moving slowly. Cautiously. When he didn't get a response, he started to look in each stall, starting with the first one. Jamie was glad she chose one past where the man was. She lifted her feet off the ground and balanced on the stool, careful to not even breathe or make a sound.

The Iranian bent down and looked under the stall next to hers. He pushed it open slowly. The door creaked. He gasped and then asked his friend what was wrong.

That meant he was confused. It didn't seem like it had registered to him that his partner was attacked. He probably thought he'd suffered a heart attack or stroke. Jamie put her feet on the ground and slipped out of her stall, careful not to make a noise.

The Iranian had made a mistake. He was in the stall and was lifting up his partner's head, not even aware that she was there. If she were him, she would've cleared the room first to make sure there were no threats before she checked on the man's condition.

Now the Iranian was in a vulnerable position, trapped in the stall. Jamie blocked his exit. He was in the perfect position for her to hit him with a kidney punch. She raised her elbow high in the air and was prepared to bring it down on his kidney with extreme force and violence.

Just as she was about to, he turned his head and looked back at her, twisting his back slightly so the blow would only be glancing, so she held off and lowered her elbow.

Instead, she said something in Farsi to create confusion in his mind. It worked. He hesitated. His wide-eyed look of surprise turned to bewilderment as his eyes narrowed almost to a squint and his brow furrowed. He clearly couldn't believe what he was seeing. His dead partner. An American girl. In the men's bathroom. She spoke to him in Farsi. For a moment, he probably thought his mind was playing tricks on him.

When he finally did realize the threat, he made another mistake. His move toward Jamie was to his left instead of to his right. The swinging door to the stall was in his way and prevented him from throwing a right-handed punch. Instead, he waved his left hand out in the form of a jab but there was no power behind it.

It also left his vital organs on the left side of his body exposed. Jamie reacted in a split second to the opening. She balled her fist and put her thumb in the perfect position below the knuckles at the tip of her fingers. Not inside the hand.

With lightning speed, Jamie twisted her body to the back and right and shifted her weight to her back foot. She then brought her weight forward and her fist cut through the air like a sword.

Her aim was for the man's liver. When he raised his hand in the air to swat his fist at her, it left his heart and liver wide open for a shot. Jamie had never executed this move before in person. In less than a second, her fist made contact. She dipped her hand slightly so her knuckles would take the brunt of the blow and their sharpness would do the most damage.

Her fist penetrated into the man's fatty area on the side of his chest, and she could feel the impact as his liver exploded inside of him. The man cried out in extreme pain. Jamie knew his death would be slower and more painful than his partner's.

He collapsed onto the man on the stool. Jamie caught him so she wouldn't have to lift him up off the floor. He moaned in agony. Barely conscious. So out of it, he had no power to resist.

Jamie lifted what was now dead weight onto his partner and positioned his legs so only one pair was visible. She removed the man's passport, ID, and cell phone and emptied his pockets. When the men were discovered, it would take time to identify them. She checked for a pulse. It was faint and weak. In a matter of time, he'd be dead.

Jamie stood at the entrance of the stall and admired her handiwork. Four hundred and fifty combined pounds, maybe five hundred, to her one-forty-five. Two blows were all it took. Her hand wasn't even sore. That had to be a record. She couldn't wait to tell Curly. He'd be impressed, although he'd never admit it. He'd find something wrong with what she did, but she knew he'd be proud, nonetheless.

Curly said that she should never lose a two-against-one fight. It didn't matter how big they were or how many weapons they had. She was one of the best trained fighters in the world. If she couldn't beat two men in a fight, then he hadn't done his job. At first, she was terrified at the thought. Today would give her even more confidence. She had flawlessly executed two new moves that she had practiced thousands of times in the gym.

More importantly, she had eliminated the threat for Alex. Now, she had to go find him.

The only question was—which one of the two moves was she going to use on Alex when she found him.

36

Signiel Seoul Hotel
Lotte World Tower
Seoul, South Korea

Jamie arrived at the Signiel Hotel more than three hours after her confrontation with the Iranians. The travel time from the airport to the hotel only took an hour of it. The rest was spent going through customs and being overly cautious at the airport.

The cleaning sheet on the wall of the men's bathroom where she left the Iranians indicated that the room was only cleaned once a day at ten o'clock at night. That meant it would be a good twenty-four hours before the bodies were discovered. The only thing that could link her to the killings were the security cameras. Since there were no security cameras in the commuter area, she only had to be concerned about those in the main concourse and customs area.

Before Jamie left the commuter area, she went into the women's restroom and changed back into her original outfit. The baggy pants, tee shirt, sneakers, and Cubs baseball cap would be a perfect disguise for going through customs. She put her hair back into a ponytail. Her backpack was reversible by design and so she emptied it on the counter, turned the bag inside out so it was a different color, and repacked her belongings.

A pain to do, but making the effort meant that anyone who looked at the security camera at the entrance of the commuter area would never connect her to the woman in the professional business suit who entered an hour before. That person didn't look like a killer, so they would assume she got on a commuter flight.

The next concern was custom's officials. The Iranians passports and cell phones she collected from the men were problematic. She had to get them through customs so she could get them to Brad. They contained all kinds of important information to the CIA. Those also linked her directly to the killings, and she would never get through customs with their two passports. Fortunately, the backpack had a secret compartment for that purpose. Jamie slipped the two passports into it and sealed the compartment. It couldn't be found without taking the whole thing apart.

So, the only concern would be the two cell phones which wouldn't fit in the secret compartment. Americans traveling to South Korea usually didn't get much scrutiny, but the phones did raise questions.

"Why do you have three cell phones?" the uniformed agent asked in a non-threatening manner.

"Two of them are for work and one is my personal phone," Jamie replied calmly.

The only problem with her ruse would be if he asked her to turn them on. At that point, she'd have to admit her status with the CIA and get Brad involved. That was something she didn't want to do. Brad would put her on the first flight home. She still had to find Alex and the girl.

The customs agent examined the phones carefully but fortunately put them back in her bag without turning them on and sent her on her way.

Jamie hailed a taxi at the airport and had him take her to the nearest twenty-four-hour, FedEx office. The cab waited while she placed the two phones and passports into a FedEx box, sealed it, and sent it two day express to Brad from an anonymous sender. She was relieved when they were finally out of her hands.

While at the FedEx, she used their women's restroom to change into a third outfit. A tight-fitting black dress with stiletto heels and pearls that gave her more of a dressy look. She let her hair down and put on more makeup and hairspray. The appearance change was necessary because she had to talk the front desk person at Alex's hotel into giving her a key to his room. She would be much more likely to give a key to a woman sharply dressed, than a young girl traveling with baggy pants and wearing a baseball cap.

She knew Alex was in room 637. He had texted her the hotel information and the room number when he arrived. That was a precaution they always used on a mission. It gave the other a starting point to investigate if either disappeared for some reason. The problem was that Jamie didn't know what name Alex traveled under. On a mission, they used an assumed name with a passport and credit card provided by the CIA. Alex forgot to tell her in the text what it was. Or maybe he did it on purpose because he was meeting the girl.

That thought caused the anger to rise inside her all over again. The adrenaline had just come down from the confrontation with the Iranians, and she could feel it rise again for the clash that would come when she saw Alex.

Jamie's plan for the front desk was to pretend to be his wife. That was the only possible scenario she could think of that might get her a room key. There were two problems with that plan. Her last name was different, and what wife didn't know her own husband's name? She could explain the different last name. This was the twenty-first century, and a lot of women didn't take their husband's name anymore. She had no credible explanation as to why she didn't know his name.

She thought about pretending to be a prostitute, and that might explain it, but there was no way the hotel would give her a key under those circumstances. The Signiel Hotel was a five star and one of the most luxurious in all of Seoul. Jamie assumed their security measures were tighter than most.

The CIA had a special device that would open the door with a key card, but, of course, she didn't have one of those with her. If the front desk wouldn't give her a key, she'd have to wait for a maid to provide cleaning service. That almost always worked. Except for the fact that it was six in the morning, and maid service wouldn't begin for several more hours.

She'd just have to talk her way in.

Jamie got into character—a snobby, southern bell, with a heavy southern accent, used to getting her way. She strutted up to the counter. Across from her was a petite, young, Korean girl with a trainee tag pinned on her lapel.

Perfect.

"Darling, I need to check into my room," Jamie said in the thickest drawl she could muster without sounding like a cartoon character.

"What's the name on the reservation?" the girl said in a meek, squeaky voice.

"My husband has already checked in. We're in room 637." Jamie put her passport, driver's license, and credit card on the counter. The girl took them in her hands and sat them beside her keyboard and began typing. She then picked up the passport and looked at it.

"Welcome to the Signiel Hotel," the squeaky girl said politely. "What brings you to Seoul?"

"My husband is here on business," Jamie said. She had her elbow on the counter and waved her hand in exaggerated gestures as she spoke. "I'm going to see the sights and do some shopping. This was a last-minute thing. He was already here. And he called me and said, 'Honey, you should come over. It's the nicest hotel. We'll make a vacation out of it.' I said to myself, 'Self. You deserve a vacation.' And here I am." Jamie let out a laugh.

She might have overdone it, but she couldn't help herself.

"Do you have a spa?" Jamie asked.

"Yes, Ma'am," the girl replied.

"Could you book me a time this morning?" Jamie stretched her arms out. "I'm exhausted from the flight. Those first-class seats aren't as comfortable as they used to be. Do you know what I mean?"

The girl looked up at her like she didn't know what she meant. She'd probably never even been on a flight and would likely never fly first class in her entire life. But she did smile dutifully. They probably got a lot of rich high-society types here at the hotel, and the first thing they probably learned in training was to be overly nice to the rich clientele.

"Ma'am, your husband didn't put your name on the reservation," the girl said as she looked up at Jamie.

"He probably forgot," she said, as her hand formed a dismissive wave.

"I'm not supposed to give out a key if the name is not on the reservation."

Jamie leaned across the counter. "Young lady, how would I know the room number if my husband hadn't told it to me?"

The girl paused before answering. Her eyes shifted to where she looked up and to the right, like she was thinking. "Your name doesn't match the name on the reservation," she finally said.

"I didn't take my husband's last name. You know, women's lib and all. Have you heard of that in South Korea? No. I guess you haven't." Jamie said rudely. Maybe she'd be able to bully the girl into giving her a key.

It got the opposite response as the girl asked, "What's your husband's name?"

Jamie swallowed hard and said, "Adam."

The girl looked at the screen. "This says Joe Hardy."

Now she knew the name.

"Joseph Adam Hardy," Jamie retorted. "Most people call him Joe.

I've always called him Adam. How long is this going to take?" Jamie said, her voice raised to try and make a scene. "I'm really tired."

A door behind the girl opened and a man walked over. His name tag said Manager. Jamie didn't know if that was good or bad.

"Is there a problem here?" he asked. He must've watched from the security camera.

Before squeaky girl could reply, Jamie said roughly, "I'm trying to get a key to my room, and this girl won't give it to me. I'm starting to get upset. I just got off of a twenty-hour flight from the United States, and I'd like to get my room. All I need is a key. Room 637."

The manager seemed confused as he narrowed his eyes and raised one of his eyebrows.

Jamie had never seen an eyebrow go that high up before.

"What's the problem?" he asked the girl.

"She's not on the reservation. She claims to be his wife."

Jamie let out a sound of disgust. "Claims?"

She tried to make it sound like she was exasperated. "I *am* his wife. You've got my passport, driver's license, and credit card. His name is Joe Hardy. Room 637. He's expecting me."

Jamie suddenly realized that she wasn't wearing a wedding ring. She took her left hand off of the counter and put it to her side.

"Mr. Hardy is in his room," the manager said. "You don't need a key. I'm sure he'll let you in if you're his wife and he's expecting you."

Jamie stood straight up.

"He's here? In the room?" That was the last thing she expected to hear. At least Alex was alive, and she didn't have to go into North Korea to look for him.

"I saw him in the lobby a couple hours ago," the manager continued. "In fact, I asked him why he didn't want his room cleaned. We haven't provided maid service for three days. Can you describe your husband?"

"Big guy. Really tall. Muscular. Brown hair."

"That's him," the manager said.

"That's perfect. I'll just go up to the room," Jamie said. "Can I have my things back?"

The girl handed them to her.

"Was Mr. Hardy alone or was someone with him?" Jamie asked.

"He was with a young lady," the manager said. Then he paused and his lips contorted like he was suddenly confused or maybe a light bulb had gone off like he may have just made a big mistake.

"Perhaps I should call him and let him know you are on your way," the manager said as he picked up the phone.

Jamie held out her hand to stop him.

"Don't do that. Let it be a surprise."

"As you wish." The manager turned and walked back through the door he had come from.

Jamie walked to the elevators.

Alex is going to be really surprised!

37

Bae and I had a complicated relationship. She was a pain in the neck sometimes, and it jeopardized my mission having to watch out for her. Nonetheless, she had become like a little sister to me. That's why I couldn't turn her into the US Embassy once we crossed the DMZ safely. What I was going to do with her, I hadn't a clue, which was why I brought her back to the hotel with me until I could sort things out.

The only thing Bae had to her name were the clothes on her back and the satchel, so we stopped at the gift shop downstairs and bought her a couple of tee shirts and shorts. When we got back to the room I said, "I'm starving."

"Why am I not surprised?" she retorted with a wide grin. "You're always hungry."

The hotel had four restaurants. Bae could hardly believe there were so many food options. Her family mostly ate rice twice a day with various mixtures of vegetables and sauces. Twice a year they had meat. For her to see a menu with all types of gourmet dishes was culture shock.

Not all the restaurants were open at that hour, and the main restaurant served fancy French cuisine which I didn't think would appeal to Bae. So, we ordered eggs and assorted pastries from the lounge. The food arrived about forty-five minutes later which gave me a chance to take a shower and change clothes.

We ate our breakfast on the round table in the corner of the room. Her plate was only half eaten, so I finished mine and hers.

I wasn't sure if she just didn't eat much or was feeling the same sense of uncertainty I was. She must certainly be wondering what was going to happen to her, even though she hadn't asked. Probably afraid to. The one thing we both knew was that going back to North Korea wasn't an option. There was a couple back in the states who wanted to adopt an Asian child. They preferred a girl three years old or less. Perhaps I could convince them to adopt a teenager.

The one thing I knew for sure was that I intended to spend the next couple days spoiling her. She already thought she'd died and gone to heaven just being in the hotel—the most luxurious thing she'd ever experienced. My room was a large suite, with a sitting area, desk, and big screen TV. When we first arrived, she plopped on the massive king-sized bed with plush gold, burgundy, and wine comforter and let out a huge "Ahh" ... clearly impressed.

I took her into the bathroom and showed her the opulent jacuzzi tub and the separate walk-in shower. Both were finished with marble tiles on the floor, in the shower, and on the bathroom counter that had two sinks and a large mirror. She described her house and it didn't sound much bigger than my entire suite.

After we had eaten, Bae said, "I'm going to take a shower."

"You should. You stink," I joked.

In typical Bae fashion, she stuck her tongue out at me. There were two sides to Bae. The warrior who smashed the head of the soldier who carried an assault rifle, essentially saving our skin, and the young girl who was still a kid just about to cross over the line into puberty and then start her journey to womanhood. I was fond of both of those girls.

I heard a squeal come from the bathroom. The shower had four different jet settings. I could hear them pulsating. The door to the bathroom was still open, so I went in to show Bae how to use them. I found her stroking the towels like a girl would pet a long-haired cat. Her mouth was agape and her eyes wide as a tea-cup saucer.

I let out a satisfied chuckle and said, "Enjoy!" and closed the door behind me.

My computer was open on the desk, and this was a good opportunity for me to do some CIA business outside Bae's nosy presence. I still needed to do several things. When we first arrived back at the hotel, I downloaded the nuclear codes and emailed them to Brad through the CIA secured system. Once Kryptonite was back on-line, Brad obviously knew that I was alive and back in the action as well. He'd be extremely surprised to see the codes, and the whole mission might come into focus for him.

Even so, I needed to call and explain things... and soon. But I wasn't ready yet. The conversation still hadn't formulated in my mind.

Another call I needed to make was to Jamie. I pulled up the email that Jamie and I shared, and in the draft box was a message from her.

R U Okay?

That caused me to wince. Jamie obviously knew I had encountered some trouble. When I went missing, Brad probably called her and told her as much. He wouldn't have given her the details since she wasn't authorized to know about the mission. Brad was a stickler for operational security. Plus, he didn't have many details to tell her, anyway.

Jamie was probably worried sick about me. I answered her draft to ease her mind.

I'm fine. Tough mission. But safe now. Miss you. Can't wait to see you. Love.

I saved the draft and closed the email.

I did miss Jamie. On this trip, I'd had a lot of time to think about her. About us. The thoughts always led to one conclusion—I wanted to spend the rest of my life with her. My dad always said not to marry the woman you love. Marry the woman you can't live without. *Feelings come and go*, he said. A woman who you must have in your life was the kind of woman you can make a real and lasting commitment to. The feeling of wanting to always have her around, would likely never go away. *That's real love*, he advised.

That's how I felt about Jamie. She was the first thing I thought of when I woke up in the morning and the last thing I thought about when I went to bed at night. When I got back home, I would ask her to marry me. The certainty of the decision had crystallized in my mind. My heart warmed as I thought about it. A sudden yearning to see her came over me. My phone was right next to the computer. I picked it up and considered calling her. It would be late at night back home, so I hesitated.

Before I could decide, something stopped me.

A noise. Faint. Almost imperceptible. Unusual.

As an operative, I was trained to tell the difference between normal footsteps and stealth shuffling of feet.

Who was it?

My mind started racing along with my heart.

I listened carefully, and barely let out a breath. My gun was on the other side of the room. That was careless of me. A mistake I didn't normally make. It never occurred to me that there might be any threats at the hotel.

When I didn't hear anything else, I decided that I had imagined it. Bae's shower was still running, and maybe that's what I heard. She probably made a noise in the shower.

Then I heard it again. Right in front of the door.

A loud knock pierced the silence and startled me. I jumped out of my seat and lunged for the gun. My heart beat wildly. My mind couldn't perceive a threat. Why would someone knock on my door at six thirty in the morning?

We'd already had our room service. It was too early for maid service.

The Iranians?

Could they have tracked me to the hotel? Did North Korea have this far a reach? I was kicking myself for not taking more precautions. I hadn't even checked to see if we were being surveilled. I assumed we weren't.

The gun had a round chambered. I crept over to the door, careful not to make my own sound. That was a risky move on my part. If someone was there to kill me, they could hear a sound and shoot a bullet through the door, chest high, and end my life. That was a move I used once at a hotel in Turkey. Killed a terrorist before he knew what hit him.

Of course, I could shoot a bullet through the door as well. If there was an assailant on the other side of the door, I could take him out before he could even react. But I couldn't do that without a visual. It could be someone who was at the wrong room.

So, I didn't do anything rash. I kept the gun by my side. This was a five-star hotel with security cameras in the hallway. More than likely, I'd overreacted. No operative in his right mind, would try something under these circumstances.

With my body turned to the side, I strained to look out the peephole.

Jamie.

What the heck is she doing here?

She didn't look happy. Her forehead was furrowed into a serious look. Confirmation came when she banged on the door a second time. It was early in the morning, and she didn't seem at all worried about waking up the guests in the adjacent rooms. When she talked to Brad, she must've gotten concerned and flew to South Korea.

That's so nice of her. But... she should've called first.

"Open up, Alex," she said in a loud and harsh voice. "I know you're in there."

What's wrong with her? She sounded mad.

The security latch was in place, which was a habit as second nature as breathing. At least I had taken that precaution. I unlocked it. I tucked the gun in the back of my pants and opened the door slowly.

Jamie burst through it. I reached out to hug her, but she shouldered me away roughly and walked directly into the bedroom of the suite. She looked under the bed and opened the closet doors.

I wasn't sure what to say, so I didn't say anything. I just closed the door, latched it, and then followed her.

"Where is the girl?" Jamie asked roughly. Her jaw was tense, every muscle in her body taut. Her eyes were firm and resolute. Cold. But on fire like burning coals, which was a contradiction, but I had seen eyes like that before. In crazy people.

"Who are you talking about?" I asked

"Don't play coy with me, Alex Halee! You know who I'm talking about."

I actually didn't. There was no way Jamie could know about Bae. I had no idea what had set her off like this.

"The woman," she said. Tears welled up in her eyes.

"Honey. I have no idea what you're talking about. What woman?"

My heart was beating faster than at any time on this mission. Which was saying a lot considering everything I'd been through and the threats I'd confronted.

"I know you have a girl in here," she said. "Do I hear the shower running?"

It suddenly occurred to me that maybe she was talking about Bae. "Yes, I do have a girl in the room," I said casually. "She's taking a shower."

I suddenly realized how that sounded. Jamie started at me with her fists raised like she was going to hit me, but she didn't. Instead, her head just fell into my chest.

"How could you, Alex?" she said. "I thought we had a good thing going. I thought you loved me."

The whole thing suddenly seemed funny to me, and I wanted to laugh, but that would be the wrong thing to do when Jamie was this mad.

"I do love you," I said with as much sweetness as I could muster.

Jamie kicked me in the shin. Not as hard as she could have, but enough that it stung.

"No, you don't. If you loved me, you wouldn't cheat on me!"

That made me mad. The kick hurt. Now she was accusing me of something I didn't do without even asking me about it. She'd owe me a big apology when she learned that the girl was thirteen-years old. Jamie headed for the door to leave and got as far as to unlatch and open it.

"Have you lost your mind?" I said, as I slammed it shut, anger rose in me to the point where it matched her intensity.

My shin throbbed from the kick.

"What's all the racket out here?" Bae said as the door to the bathroom burst opened and she emerged, wearing only a towel wrapped around her body. Her hair was still dripping wet. I could see soap on the side of her face.

A sour expression came over Jamie as her lips pursed.

"How old are you?" Jamie said sharply.

"I'm thirteen. But I'll be fourteen tomorrow," Bae said with just as much attitude.

That caused me to smile. Watching the two of them go at it would be fun. Then something Bae said hit me. I didn't know that tomorrow was her birthday. A thought came to me out of the blue. I knew exactly what I was going to get her for a present.

"You're disgusting, Alex," Jamie said, obviously getting the wrong impression. "I risk my life saving girls like her." Jamie was a CIA operative specializing in rescuing girls from the sex trade. She clearly thought Bae was one of those girls. For whatever reason, it made me want to laugh, but I choked it back.

Jamie said to Bae in a stern motherly voice, "Get dressed. You're coming with me."

When she said that I couldn't help myself and burst out laughing.

"Is this funny to you?" Jamie said.

"What's going on?" Bae asked.

I pointed my finger at Jamie and said, "Bae, this is my girlfriend, Jamie."

Bae's expression of confusion turned to a smile as fast as it would take to flip a dime over. She walked toward Jamie with her hand outstretched and said, "Jamie... It's so nice to meet you. I've heard so much about you."

I couldn't stop laughing. By this time, I was doubled over, my hands on my knees.

Jamie stared at me with an enigmatic frown. If looks could kill, I'd be dead five times over.

I laughed so hard tears came to my eyes as the tension of the mission was finally unleashed in that one moment. Bae started laughing too, although I was sure she had no idea what she was laughing about.

Jamie forced a smile onto her face.

"Why are we laughing?" Bae asked.

"Go back and finish your shower," I said to her. "I'll explain later."

Bae turned and walked back into the bathroom, closing the door behind her.

From the look of relief on Jamie's face, it was clear that she had started to figure things out. Her cheeks blushed, and she looked down and away, embarrassed.

I took her in my arms and squeezed tightly.

I took Jamie's hand and led her over to the bed where we sat down on the edge. "Her name is Bae. She's from North Korea," I said soberly.

"What is she doing here and why did you go to North Korea?"

"That's a long story," I said as I shifted positions in the bed to face Jamie more directly. I took her hand and held it.

Jamie took her hand out of mine and crossed her arms, clearly still distressed, "Take all the time you need."

"I found Pok's cyber lab," I said, after I rolled my eyes for emphasis, so she knew I thought she was acting like a fool. Then I continued. "Pok stole Pakistan's nuclear codes and sold them to the Iranians. Bae stole a satchel that contained the codes." I pointed to Bae's satchel sitting on the couch.

Jamie nodded her head. I didn't know what she knew, but I could see by her expression that some pieces were coming together in her mind.

"I had a run in with two Iranians at the airport," Jamie said. "They were looking for you."

I was afraid to ask what happened to them. If they had a run in with Jamie, they were probably dead. That would complicate things if she killed them at the airport. More importantly, I wondered how Jamie knew they were looking for me. We'd get to that. I'd tell her my story first.

I lowered my voice to just above a whisper and leaned in closer to Jamie. "Bae's parents were killed by two Iranians. They were going to kill her, but I rescued her. I didn't know what to do, so I brought her back here. As far as I know, they may still be looking for her. Sounds like they are if there were two Iranians at the airport."

"Those two are dead," Jamie matter-of-factly like she said she did the laundry today.

"Honey, I would never cheat on you," I said sincerely. "I love you."

I held out my arms, wrapped them around her, and pulled her to my chest, and she relaxed her body language and didn't resist.

"I was worried about you," she said, pulling away and then hitting me playfully on the arm.

"I was worried about myself," I said.

The bathroom door opened, and Bae came out dressed in her new clothes which fit her perfectly. Jamie and I suddenly moved apart as though we'd done something wrong. Bae had a bounce her step. The shower must've invigorated her. Or else she enjoyed the opulent life. She plopped down on the bed right next to Jamie.

"I heard all the yelling," Bae said, talking faster than a mile a minute. "I thought I was going to have to save your life again." Bae said it looking at me with a huge grin on her face, her chin up, and her chest out in pride.

Jamie looked at me with her nose crinkled, and her eyes narrowed in more confusion. "You saved Alex's life?" Jamie asked.

"I did," Bae said.

Jamie looked at me and I shrugged my shoulders. "Like I said, it's a long story."

"This I got to hear," Jamie said, her body turned so she faced Bae. She touched Bae's hand. "Tell me everything."

Bae was a handful to deal with. Jamie could be next to impossible sometimes. I had a feeling that both of them together was going to make for an awfully long day.

38

Wonsan Kalma International Airport
North Korea

The Iranian Ambassador to North Korea, Hamid Ahmadi, stood outside the baggage claim area of the airport for several hours. The two Iranian fighters sent to North Korea to hunt down and kill the American spy and the girl who stole the satchel filled with nuclear codes, inexplicably, did not arrive on their scheduled flight from South Korea. He confirmed that the flight had landed, and the passengers deplaned a long time ago.

The two men's cell phones were turned off, and they had simply vanished in the same manner as the two men who were sent before them. At first, Hamid chose not to worry. There were several reasonable explanations. They might've missed their flight. Perhaps they arrived in North Korea and went to the wrong meeting point. Maybe they came in on a different flight.

After he talked to the airlines, he was beyond worry and had crossed over the line into full-blown panic. The men left Tehran on time. They made a connection in Frankfurt on a flight to Seoul, South Korea. The flight arrived on time. That's when things got sketchy.

"Are you sure they were on the flight from Frankfurt?" Hamid had pressed the airline employee.

"Positive. They definitely made the flight. However, they didn't get on the flight from Seoul to Wonsan."

"Is it possible they missed the connection?" Hamid asked.

"It's possible. But they had more than an hour, and the gates weren't that far apart. According to my records they never checked in for that flight."

It didn't make sense. They made it all the way to South Korea and then disappeared. There had to be an explanation, but he had no idea what it was. Complicated by the fact that there was still no sign of the first two men sent to North Korea. They hadn't answered their cell phones, and their rental car hadn't been found.

Soon, he'd have to deal with the government agency that authorized the vehicle and let them know that the men and the government-owned car were missing. There would be severe ramifications from that. He had circumvented many government rules to get the men transportation and permission to travel around the country without a monitor.

How did the men, their car, and their cell phones just vanish off the face of the earth without a trace? Where was the car? If they were killed, where were the dead bodies? If alive, who had them?

For that matter, where was the satchel with the codes? It had disappeared as well. That was the most important thing. Men were expendable. The satchel was not. The Iranian government spent billions of dollars to acquire those codes.

He took several deep breaths to try and calm himself. Then he dialed the number to his boss, Amin Sadeghi, the Director of Intelligence for Iran and the MOIS. The Director wouldn't be happy.

"Dorood," Amin answered on the first ring with the formal greeting in the Farsi language. If one wanted to sound educated, they used "dorood" instead of the traditional Arabic greeting of "salam."

"Salam," Hamid replied, using the word for peace. He desperately wished he had a way to make peace become a reality. This conversation was going to be anything but peaceful.

"Man komak niaz duram," Hamid said. "I need your help." He

tried to get right to the point with the maximum amount of urgency.

There was silence on the other line.

"Your two men never arrived from South Korea," Hamid said as he broke the silence. "There's no sign of them. They don't answer their cell phones." Hamid braced for the explosion of expletives that never came. That gave him a glimmer of hope. Maybe, Amin had been in touch with the men.

Instead Amin calmly said, "You must return to Iran at once." The hope faded as quickly as it came. Like a lightning bolt strike that suddenly appeared from the sky, struck its target, and then disappeared back to where it came from in the blink of an eye. Those words could only mean one thing–Amin believed he was behind the death of the men.

"Director, I had nothing to do with the disappearance of these men," Hamid pleaded his case. "They made their connection from Frankfurt, arrived in South Korea, and then disappeared. The lady at the airlines said they never boarded their flight. Something happened to them in South Korea. I'm in North Korea, miles away."

"I have lost five men, now," Amin said surprisingly calm. "I'm further away than you are. You and I are the only two people who knew these men were coming to North Korea. Somebody tipped off the Americans, and it wasn't me. That leaves you."

"It wasn't me either. I would never betray the motherland."

"Tell that to the interrogators," Amin said, then the line went dead.

Hamid winced. The interrogators would torture him until he confessed, even if he wasn't guilty. He had only one option.

To disappear like the others.

***

Signiel Hotel
South Korea

Jamie picked Bae up off the ground and body slammed her into the bed in Alex's hotel room. Bae scurried off the bed before Jamie could jump on her and like a cat was across the room. Jamie was almost as quick and was on her before Bae could react. She picked her up by her waist from behind as Bae turned her back to her. Bae tried to stomp on Jamie's foot, but Jamie anticipated it and had her leg just out of reach.

Bae struggled, and flailed left and right, back and forth as she tried to break the grip but couldn't. She pulled on Jamie's hands, but they were locked around her like a boa constrictor. The more Bae struggled the tighter Jamie made the vise.

Jamie picked her up to body slam her again but instead fell backward onto the floor with Bae on top of her. She wrapped her forearm around her neck and started choking her. She continued to hold the choke until Bae quit struggling, and then she released it.

Bae jumped to her feet and clutched her throat, trying to catch her breath. As soon as she did, Bae said, "Let's do it again."

"Okay. But you have to listen to me," Jamie said. "Don't flail around and struggle like that. It makes your opponent more intent on harming you."

"But what do I do? I tried to stomp on your foot but couldn't."

"I was ready for it. You can't use the same move every time. Just because one doesn't work doesn't mean there aren't more options."

Bae had told Jamie how she disabled the guard. She'd stomped on his foot, kneed him in the groin, and then crushed his head with her laptop, destroying the computer in the process. What was left of the worthless piece of dented metal lay on the floor,

Alex left the hotel a couple hours before to run some errands, and Jamie was trying to teach Bae more moves. The girl was relentless in not wanting to stop, and Jamie was happy to dish out the lessons—and the punishment as it turned out when Bae refused to go down easily.

"The reason it worked on the guard is because you were going by instinct. You weren't thinking. You just reacted."

"That makes sense," Bae said. "Everything was in slow motion. Like I could see everything clearly and knew just what to do."

"The more you gain confidence, the easier that will be," Jamie affirmed.

"Can you teach me that hold you just did, where you choked me?" Bae asked, seemingly with as much excitement as she could muster. "That was awesome. And teach me how to get out of it."

Bae grabbed Jamie's arm, turned her back to her, and put it around her neck.

Jamie smiled and held back an audible laugh. She didn't want Bae to think she was mocking her. It was obvious why Alex liked this girl. She never quit.

"Remember how I taught you to tap out," Jamie said. "We're just practicing here. If you ever feel like you want to give up, just tap on my arm, like this." Jamie showed her a tap. "Do that, and I'll release the hold immediately."

"Never! I'm going to get out of it. Show me how."

"It's called a rear naked chokehold. The key to getting out of it is to never get in it in the first place. You have to stop the choke before your opponent gets it locked in. Don't give someone your back if there's anything you can do to help it."

Bae nodded in agreement. Jamie saw it in her eyes. She wasn't listening. Bae was too excited to get to the action. Jamie had been the same way in training. She remembered how Curly broke her of it. That wouldn't work in this situation in that it would border on child abuse.

"Bae, listen," Jamie said sharply to get her attention. "Face me. Try not to ever let anyone get behind you."

Jamie positioned Bae's shoulders, and they faced off. Before Bae could even react, Jamie was behind her. Jamie didn't apply the chokehold, she just did it for effect.

"Wow! You're so fast," Bae said.

"Let's do it in slow motion," Jamie said as she stepped back in front of her "If I go behind you, the first thing you do is lower your chin and raise your shoulders. Try it."

Bae made the funniest face and Jamie laughed. Her eyes squinted to where they were almost closed, and her nose crinkled. "You don't have to make a face, silly," Jamie said. "You look like you're constipated."

That caused Bae to burst out laughing. The training stopped until they could regain their composure. The two were bonding. Jamie saw Alex's dilemma in not wanting to turn her over to the embassy to never see her again.

Jamie demonstrated how to lower her chin and raise her shoulders in a defensive position without making a weird face. "That's how it's done. See no one can get their arm under your chin,"

Bae went back and forth between raising her shoulders and lowering her chin and then returning them to the normal position. Jamie got behind Bae and tried to slide her arm under her chin. Bae got in the defensive position. Jamie could have overpowered her and forced Bae into the choke, but for training purposes, she wanted Bae to think she was successful. In her training, Jamie spent nearly a week practicing applying the choke and learning how to get out of it.

"I get it," Bae said. "Chin down, shoulders up."

"Always! Always! Always!" Jamie said. "If someone is behind you."

"What do I do if they do start choking me?"

"Anything you can to get out of it. Don't go for the arms, though. Most people reach up and try to pull the arm off. Go for the fingers. Rip them off of his hand if you have to."

"That would hurt," Bae said, her nose crinkled again.

"If someone's trying to kill you, then no mercy," Jamie said in a stern voice. "You do anything you have to do to get out of it. Gouge their eyes out. Pull on their ears or nose. Use the heels of your feet to kick them in the shins. Or ankles. Whatever you have to do, you do it!"

They kept practicing until Alex returned. Bae couldn't get enough, and Jamie was enjoying the banter. When Alex walked in, they barely acknowledged him until they saw he had three bags in his hands. Two larger and one smaller.

"What's in the bags?" Bae asked.

"It's something for you," Alex said.

That got Bae's undivided attention. "What is it?" she asked as she tried to grab the bags out of his hands. He held them high in the air to keep her from doing so.

"None of your business," Alex retorted.

"If it's for me, then it's my business," Bae retorted with a sideways grin.

"It's for your birthday. That's not until tomorrow. You can't open it until then."

"I can't wait until tomorrow. If you don't let me see it, I'm going to put you in a naked chokehold."

Jamie burst out laughing as Alex had a confused look on his face.

"That's a rear naked chokehold," Jamie corrected Bae. "You should have clothes on when you do it."

Bae's cheeks turned bright red.

Alex changed the subject and said, "I guess it won't hurt for you to open your present a day early."

Bae squealed with delight. She grabbed the bag out of his hand and pulled out a package that was wrapped.

Jamie was surprised Alex had gone to the trouble to wrap the present. She tried to remember if he'd ever done that for her. A little twinge of jealousy rose inside of her, but she tamped it down.

Gifts weren't really her thing anyway. Nevertheless, by that point, she was as curious as Bae. She had no idea what was in the package. Alex said he was going shopping for a birthday present for Bae but wouldn't tell her what it was.

Bae tore into the package like a monkey in a zoo attacked a meal. Inside the package was a box. "What is it?" Bae said with her eyes widened.

"Open it," Alex said.

Jamie suddenly thought she knew what it was.

Bae ripped the box open and pulled out a shiny, new, metallic, laptop computer. She held it carefully, like she held a newborn baby. Her eyes were affixed into a stare of amazement.

"Is it mine?" Bae looked at Jamie who nodded and then at Alex who also wore a wide grin. That was the first time Jamie had really seen Alex interacting with a kid. That brought a bigger smile to her face as she thought about the possibility of Alex being the father of her kids.

Don't go there. We're not even engaged.

Bae clutched the laptop to her chest and spun around in a circle and danced.

"Happy birthday," Jamie said.

Bae sat the computer on the desk and ran over to Jamie and threw her arms around her.

"Thank you so much," Bae said.

"Hey! What about me?" Alex shouted.

"Don't thank me," Jamie said. "Thank Alex. He's the one who bought it for you."

Bae walked over to Alex and into his arms and clutched him tightly. "Thank you so much. This is the best birthday ever."

"Let's get it set up," Alex said as he walked over to the desk, sat down in the chair, and plugged the laptop into the electric socket. For two hours, he taught Bae everything there was to know about the computer. Jamie noticed that he had spared no expense and had gotten her the top-of-the-line computer.

Alex loaded all kinds of games and apps on it. He did things to boost its performance. Bae was set up with a new email and an account to purchase music and videos. Alex purchased wireless headphones as an accessory and Bae had them on and walked around the room humming to the music.

"What's in the other bags?" Jamie asked as she walked toward them. Bae took off her headphones.

"One is a case for the computer," Alex answered. "The other is a present for you."

A sudden warmth came upon her. Gifts might not be her thing, but she still liked it when she got one. Especially since she was feeling a little left out. Alex had spent so much time with Bae, it started to bother her. She'd come all this way to save his life and wanted him to acknowledge it. The fact that he bought something for her was so unexpected and made her feel better immediately.

She opened the small bag. In it was another bag with a square box that was also wrapped and had a ribbon around it. It looked like a jewelry box.

Jamie took off the wrapping carefully as Alex stood from the desk and walked over to her. She sat down on the bed and took off each piece of tape. Bae came and sat next to her.

"Hurry up," Bae said. "I want to see what it is."

Jamie got the wrapping paper off and inside was a box. She opened it. An empty ring box.

Alex reached into his pocket and lowered to one knee.

Jamie gasped and put both hands over her mouth.

"Jamie Austen, will you marry me!" Alex said.

"Are you serious?" she asked.

"I'll take that as a yes," Alex said excitedly as he took her left hand and slid the finger on her index finger.

Jamie held out her hand to look at the ring. A large solitaire. White gold. It looked to be at least two carats. She'd never seen anything so beautiful.

Before she realized it, her arms were around his neck and her eyes were wet. She squeezed her cheek into his and then kissed him warmly.

Suddenly, Jamie felt incredibly special.

39

Jamie and I decided to give Bae a taste of what freedom was like. Our plan was to spend the day seeing the sights of Korea and lavishing her with all kinds of fun, food, and gifts. While I finished up some work on my computer, Jamie and Bae were on Bae's laptop making a list of things to do in Seoul.

A few minutes later they had a list. Much to my displeasure, only one thing was on it.

"All you want to do is shop?" I asked with exasperation.

"Yes!" Jamie and Bae said in unison.

Turns out the best shopping was right by our hotel. The Lotte World Tower and Mall boasted hundreds of stores. Bae wanted to go to the electronics store first. Then the clothing stores.

I insisted we do something fun.

"There's an ice-skating rink at the Tower." Jamie said.

"I meant like an amusement park. With rides. Roller coasters. Arcade games."

Jamie pulled up trip advisor and the list of top fifteen things to do in Seoul.

"There's the DMZ tour," Jamie said.

"No!" Bae and I said in unison. After having made two illegal border crossings, I saw all I wanted of the DMZ.

"There's the Gyeongbokgong Palace," Jamie said. struggling to pronounce the name correctly.

"What is that?" I asked.

Jamie started reading something from the computer screen. "The National Museum of Korea and the National Folk Museum are located on the grounds of this palace, built six centuries ago by the founder of the Chosun dynasty."

I looked at Bae and shook my head no, which she confirmed by wrinkling her nose.

"That sounds boring," Bae said.

Jamie kept reading.

"At the heart of Seoul lies this ancient, yet historically significant, center of the Joseon dynasty. The eternal, grand, beautiful and enchanting Gyeongbokgun Palace, the largest and grandest of the five."

Bae and I started laughing as Jamie totally butchered the pronunciation again. Jamie ignored us and kept reading.

"Here's a review. This palace thoroughly impressed me, especially the great statues of Admiral Yi Sun Shin and King Sejong the Great."

We kept laughing at her jokingly. She was ignoring us and kept reading.

Finally, I asked, "Are there any amusement parks?"

"The Tower has rides but they are mostly for little kids."

Jamie peered at the screen and typed something into the computer. "The Coex Aquarium is home to 40,000 sea creatures from over six-hundred-fifty different species. There are fourteen themed exhibits."

"That sounds good," I said.

Bae walked over to where Jamie was and looked over her shoulder and read from the screen.

"They have a mermaid show!" Bae said excitedly. "Can we go there?"

"It's not far from here," Jamie added.

"That sounds better than shopping," I said.

"We're still going shopping," Jamie said, looking at Bae and both of them nodding. "We'll go to the aquarium after we go to the Tower."

That sounded like a good compromise. I would like to go to the electronics store as well.

Our conversation was interrupted by an alert on my computer. That could only mean one thing–Brad was calling me through the CIA server. He had initiated a facetime call. I almost ignored it, but I'd been back for several hours and should probably have called him by now.

I motioned for Jamie and Bae to keep quiet. With one stroke of the keyboard, I accepted the call request, and Brad's face appeared on the screen.

"It's nice to see that you're alive," Brad said, in a dissociative, emotionless tone. The fact that he led with that statement told me that he really did care. Sometimes we wondered if the higher ups cared more about us or the mission. I still didn't know, but it was at least good to hear some expression of concern from Brad.

"It's nice to be alive," I replied.

Brad looked like he hadn't gotten much sleep. I'm sure he saw the bags under my eyes as well.

"I got Kryptonite back online," I said.

"I saw that," Brad replied. He'd always been a man of few words, so I didn't read anything into it. From experience, I could tell that he would wait for me to explain what had happened without him having to ask.

So, I obliged him. "I captured a satchel containing Pakistan's nuclear codes."

I decided to lead with that. Curly always said to talk about the most successful aspect of a mission first. Save the worst for last.

If the success was good enough, you might not even have to get to the bad stuff.

Out of the corner of my eye, I saw Bae make some kind of gesture to Jamie after I said it. I could imagine what it was. Technically, she stole the codes, not me. But I wasn't going to tell Brad about her at this point. As far as the CIA was concerned, I had secured them for us.

"Tell me about that," Brad said as he shifted positions in his chair and picked up a pen like he was going to take notes. Mostly a symbolic gesture. Brad would make me fill out an entire report. I also knew he had perfect recall. He didn't need to write anything down to relay to his boss. He'd remember anything I told him. The only thing he might want to write down was his spin on it or a reminder of what not to tell the Director.

I explained everything. How I found the lab. Snuck across the border. Let myself be captured. Got into the lab and saw Pok. Installed Kryptonite. Got arrested. Killed two Iranians. The only thing I left out was information about Bae.

"Pok hacked into the Pakistani nuclear server," I said. "He stole their passwords and codes. The North Koreans sold them to the Iranians. That's why I went after the satchel."

"At no time did it occur to you to get operational authority?" Brad asked.

I had anticipated the question and my answer.

"There wasn't time. They had already transferred the codes to the Iranians. I took them out and secured the codes."

"The Pakistanis could always change their codes," Brad said. "What difference does it make if the Iranians get them? They become worthless as soon as the codes are changed. We change our nuclear codes every day."

Another question I anticipated.

"Pok built a backdoor into the system. It's in the codes. I almost missed it myself. The Pakistanis could change the codes, but Pok would know it when they did. Think about it Brad. If Iran had those codes, they could launch missiles against us or Israel, and we'd think they came from Pakistan."

Brad nodded his head in agreement. "I get that. If they can't build their own nukes, the next best thing would be to commandeer someone else's. You did good work, Alex. We wouldn't have known about the stolen codes if it wasn't for you."

Words of affirmation were few and far between with Brad, so I locked that compliment into my memory. I looked at Jamie, and we shared a smile. While I was still looking at her, Brad said something that caused Jamie's eyes to widen and her whole body to stiffen.

"Hello, Jamie," he said.

I kept my eyes fixed on the computer screen so as not to give anything away. Did he see me looking at her? How could he know she was there?

"Why would you think Jamie's here?" I asked.

"Because I sent her there."

Jamie walked over and stood behind me and leaned over my shoulder as her image suddenly appeared on the screen.

"Hi, Brad," Jamie said. "What do you mean that you sent me here?"

"Why do you think I told you that Alex was captured in North Korea? I knew you would go and find him."

"You could've just told me and sent me after him," Jamie said roughly.

Brad shook his head no. "I have no authority to sanction a mission to North Korea. I could never get that approved."

"So, you told me that Alex was captured... Then you told me under no uncertain terms that I couldn't go find him... All the while knowing that's exactly what I would do." Jamie said the words slowly and deliberately like she was recapping the final seconds of a football game that was already over.

Brad sat there in silence while Jamie matched his stare. It reminded me of the staring game we used to play in grade school. I wasn't sure who'd blink first.

Brad finally relented. "It worked, didn't it. Clearly, you found him."

"Yeah! I'm glad I did. Look I'm engaged," Jamie flashed her ring to the camera, as she changed the subject and the tone of the conversation.

"Congratulations," Brad said. "You two deserve each other."

I laughed.

"I don't know if that was a compliment or not," Jamie said.

"It's a compliment." Brad actually forced a smile. "All I meant is that the two of you are well suited for each other. This means I'm going to have to start another pool." His smile had turned to a smug grin.

"What kind of pool?" I asked.

"Which one of you will kill the other first?" Brad said. "We have been taking bets ever since you started dating. Now we'll have to start a marriage pool."

"You should bet your house on me," Jamie said, as she pushed me out of the camera picture.

That comment made Brad laugh out loud. Even Bae snickered in the background which fortunately was drowned out as Jamie and I roared in laughter.

"On a more serious note," Jamie said.

"Here we go," Brad countered.

"Since we're on the subject of the Iranians, you have another problem," Jamie said.

He put his hands to his face, then removed them and sat forward in his chair. "What's that?"

"There are two dead Iranians in the Seoul airport. Men's bathroom. One of the stalls. Commuter terminal. If you hurry, you can get cleaners in there before they're discovered."

It made sense to tell him. Since he knew Jamie was in Seoul, and he knew the purpose of the mission was to stop the Iranians, then what Jamie did fell in line with the mission.

To that point, Brad hadn't written anything down with his pen. Now, he tapped it nervously on his desk.

"The two Iranians were on their way to North Korea to kill Alex and find the codes," Jamie explained. "I had no choice but to take them down."

I suddenly realized that Bae shouldn't listen to all of this. We should have made her put on headphones or leave the room. This was a classified CIA conversation. Rather than interrupting our conversation and saying something to her, I decided to just let it go. Really, she had risked her life as much as I had to secure the codes, so as far as I was concerned, she had a right to know everything I knew. Besides, who would she tell?

"Give me a second," Brad said as he left the screen and was no longer sitting in front of his computer.

He was gone for at least five minutes. Probably talked to the CIA office in Seoul to get over to the airport and get those two bodies out before they were discovered. More than likely, they'd send a team disguised as a cleaning crew and then take them back to the CIA office for disposal.

When Brad returned, he said, "Anything else I need to know about?"

"I'm sure there is," I said. "But I can't think of anything at the moment. With Kryptonite back online, you should have a field day inside of the North Korean cyber lab."

"We're taking it down," Brad said.

Anger exploded inside of me like a firecracker. I couldn't believe the words I was hearing.

"Why would you do that?" I asked, not hiding my vitriol. "I risked my life to get Kryptonite on their computer drive. It's there now. They can't do anything about it."

"We're going to put them out of business," Brad said defensively, clearly feeling the anger in my voice. "I have instructions to unleash the Kryptonite virus on the North Korean server."

"They'll just rebuild it," I countered. "Pok will have them up and running within three months."

"Yeah, but it will shut them down in the meantime. We can't sit back while he steals money from innocent people when we can stop it."

I understood that. I'd thought of the same thing. It was a moral dilemma. This was always the case in surveillance. The unwritten rule was to watch a suspect until you could stop a crime. In our training classes, the instructors presented several scenarios. An undercover informant in the mafia wouldn't let them kill a person in his presence even though doing so might save more lives in the future. If we could, we were to stop any crime before it happened.

With Kryptonite, we could monitor all of Pok's illegal activities longer if we did nothing. In the meantime, innocent people would have money stolen from them. The decision was made to take them down and stop what crimes we could now. It wouldn't do any good to argue the point. Their side was valid.

I made a different argument. "Then let me take Pok out," I said.

"Can't do it," Brad said, fixing his stare on me. "I'm serious, Alex. Do not go back to North Korea."

"I'll go with him," Jamie said.

The level of conversation was getting so intense that Bae stood up. I could tell she wanted to say something. I held my hand out from me to stop her from getting in the picture.

"Come on, Brad," I implored. "We know where Pok is. We've been looking for him for months. I can be in and out of North Korea in a day. Dead or alive. You tell me how you want him."

"I'm on your side, Alex," Brad said. "I agree with you. But now is not the time. Kryptonite is going to destroy the lab. Your mission, as ill-conceived as it was, was a success. I can cover your back on it. You got the codes. You found the lab. And we've shut it down. Even though it wasn't authorized, I can make an argument as to why you did it."

I started to continue making my case, but Brad cut me off.

"My neck is way out on a limb for both of you," Brad said. "I got an officer going into North Korea with no authorization, and I got two dead Iranians in a South Korean airport. There are a lot of eyes on this."

"The Iranians were going after the codes. Their mission was to kill Alex. What was I supposed to do... let them?" Jamie asked with intensity.

"That's the argument I'm going to make. The two of you found out about the codes and took matters into your own hands and went into North Korea to stop it."

That's not exactly how it went down, but I could see why Brad was spinning it that way. I couldn't think of a reason to correct him.

"I want the two of you on a plane back home today," Brad said. "There's a bird waiting for you at the airport. A private jet. I don't want you going through security and flying commercial."

"Can it wait until tomorrow?" I asked, looking at Jamie and then at Bae.

"Do you think I'm stupid?" Brad said. "You just want a day to go back into North Korea and go after Pok."

Brad didn't know we had promised to spend the day shopping with Bae. Celebrating her birthday. Going to the aquarium.

"It's not that," I said hesitantly.

"Be in front of your hotel in thirty minutes. A car will pick you up and take you to the airport."

The screen went dead before I could protest further.

"Thirty minutes? That's not enough time," I said.

What are we going to do with Bae in thirty minutes?

40

Three months later

I emerged from behind the abandoned boxcar and sprinted across a small field to a dilapidated log cabin thirty yards away. The maneuver left me exposed for more than four seconds, but I was sure I was safe. My target was on the other side of the ravine, hiding in the rocks.

Once safely behind the corner of the cabin, I raised my weapon, looked through the scope, and scanned the horizon to focus in on where I thought the target was hiding. My hands were steady and my breathing calm, even though I'd been in the throes of the search for more than two hours.

I clutched a new weapon that I'd never used before. A Tippmann US Army Project Salvo Sniper M-FDP Edition. It could be set to semi-automatic or automatic discharge. Semi-automatic was fine for these purposes. I only intended to shoot one round. The red dot scope would allow me to lock onto a target and hit my prey from as far as several hundred yards away with reasonable accuracy.

I wanted to be closer so I could see the reaction when I fired the shot. I was close. You get a sense about these things. The cat and mouse game would be over soon. Movement caught my eye in the bushes right where I suspected my prey to be. Nothing more than a twig moved but perceptible, nonetheless, for someone with my level of training. Confirmed when a light reflected off of a helmet. The target faced away from me, but I didn't have a clear shot.

I'd have to get closer.

The stream was no more than a foot deep, so I waded through it behind the cover of a fallen log. Careful not to make a sound, I skulked across the trail toward where I'd seen the bush move and the light reflect. From that angle I could see the top of a helmet. Another reflection.

Clearly my target. Facing away from me. I had the element of surprise. Now was the time to make my move. I let out a shout and sprinted to the rock, my weapon raised. Locked and loaded. Ready to fire as soon as I had a clear shot.

What I saw stopped me in my tracks. What I had seen was a helmet, but it was being held up by a stick. Just barely above the rock.

It's a trap!

Before I could react, Bae emerged from behind a tree, raised her gun and fired. Slow. Deliberate. Calculated. I could see her stone-cold eyes and the red laser coming from her weapon affixed on my chest.

The paint exploded on my coveralls.

Where the ball hit me stung but not as much as my pride.

Bae jumped up and down. Shouted. Her weapon raised above her head. She taunted me.

"I finally beat you! Fair and square!" she said mockingly.

According to the rules of engagement, I had to raise my gun above my head and shout, "I'm hit." Anything more than a nickel sized mark was considered a hit. In our game, we didn't require multiple hits.

"Say it!" Bae shouted.

I didn't want to.

"Say it!" she insisted.

"I'm hit," I said weakly. "You win!"

"Yes!" she shouted and began her victory dance again.

We came to the Boar Mountain Paintball course in Northern Virginia every week for the past three months. When we boarded the private plane from South Korea, we brought Bae back with us to America. Brad secured refugee status for her and a new identity once he learned she was the one who'd stolen the codes, and we needed to protect her.

The couple who wanted to adopt a child took Bae in without a second thought. Brad arranged all that paperwork, and the adoption had already gone through.

They were a perfect match, as if God had arranged it all. Bae was close enough for us to see her as often as we wanted, but she also settled nicely into a new life and school with her new family and friends. Apparently, Bae was a math whiz. She struggled some with English, history, and literature which was to be expected being from a foreign country, but she did well in all her other subjects, especially math.

She decided that she no longer wanted to be a spy. She wanted to be a doctor like her new mother. We assured her she had plenty of time to decide.

Now that she had beaten me in paintball, I knew I would never hear the end of it. The only thing to do was be magnanimous, which was hard, considering the amount of teasing I knew would come my way from her, Jamie, and from all my colleagues at the CIA who would certainly hear about it.

I couldn't believe I fell for such a simple trap. If Curly heard about it, he'd disown me and claim he never trained me. For now, I just let Bae bask in her triumph.

"I beat you!" Bae said over and over again.

"That wasn't fair," I protested. "You took off your helmet and tricked me. It's against the rules to take off your helmet. You should be disqualified."

"No way... You fell for it."

"Did Jamie give you that idea?" I asked.

"Maybe. Maybe not." Bae said with a wide grin. I was actually happy she won. I'd never let her win, but it was fun to see her so excited.

We got back to the main office area and took off our gear. Jamie walked through the door with a huge smile on her face. She saw it all from the observation tower.

Bae hadn't let up on the banter.

"Ms. Jamie. Did you see me?" Bae asked.

"I did. I saw the whole thing. I'm proud of you," Jamie said as she gave Bae a hug.

I still was suspicious that they had conspired against me.

Bae left and went to the girl's restroom to shower and get dressed.

"That was nice of you to let Bae win," Jamie said, as she gave me an approving kiss on the lips.

I thought about playing along.

Instead I said, "Truthfully, I didn't let her win. She won fair and square."

"Ouch!" Jamie said. "I guess the torch has passed."

"I guess you're right," I said and didn't stop the smile that had formed on my face.

"There comes a time when the teacher is surpassed by the student," I said. "I just wished it hadn't happened so soon."

GET YOUR FREE GIFT

As a thank you for finishing my book, I want to give you a free gift. Go to terrytoler.com and sign up for my mailing list and I'll give you the first three chapters of *The Launch*, a Jamie Austen novella free of charge.

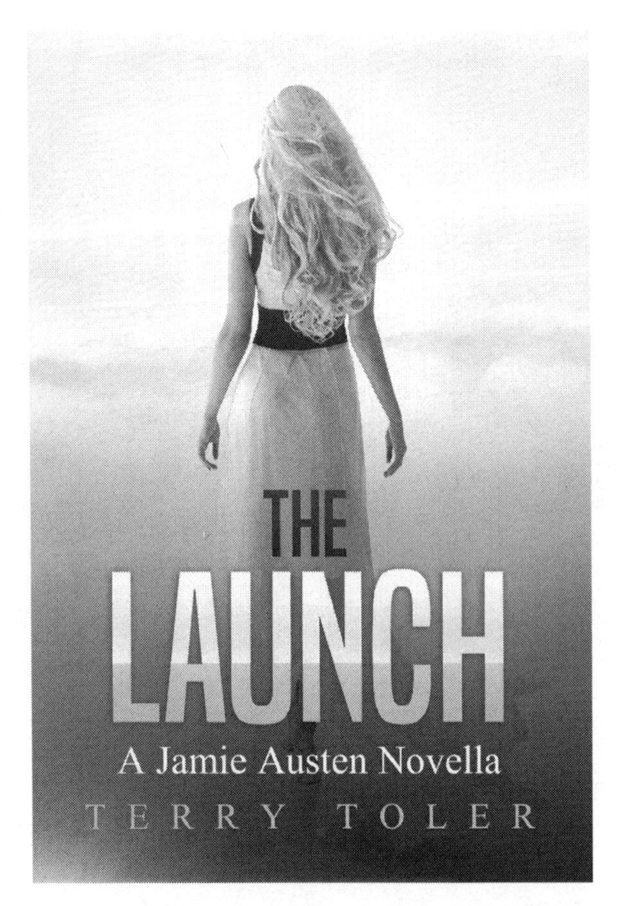

Terrytoler.com

SPY STORIES

A Jamie Austen Thriller
SAVE
THE
GIRLS
TERRY TOLER

A Jamie Austen Thriller
SAVING
SARA
TERRY TOLER

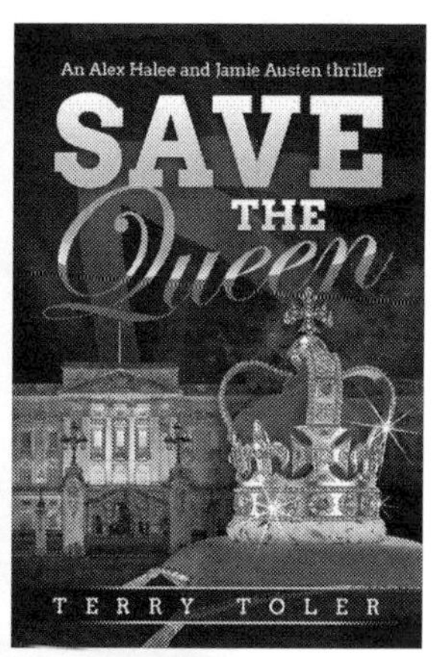
An Alex Halee and Jamie Austen thriller
SAVE
THE
Queen
TERRY TOLER

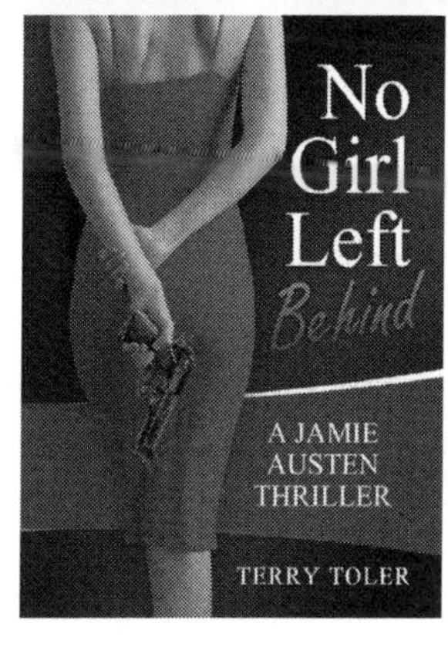
No
Girl
Left
Behind
A JAMIE
AUSTEN
THRILLER
TERRY TOLER

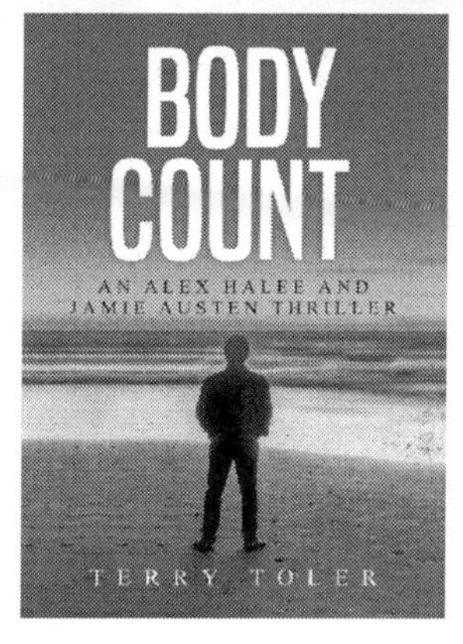
BODY
COUNT
AN ALEX HALEE AND
JAMIE AUSTEN THRILLER
TERRY TOLER

Thank you for purchasing this novel from best selling author, Terry Toler. As an additional thank you, Terry wants to give you a free gift.

Sign up for:

Updates

New Releases

Announcements

At terrytoler.com.

We'll send you the first three chapters of The Launch, a Jamie Austen novella, free of charge. The one that started the Spy Stories and Eden Stories Franchises.

About the Author

TERRY TOLER is the author of the Jamie Austen and Alex Halee book series along with *The Eden Stories*. He is a minister, public speaker, counselor, and retired entrepreneur. Impacting the lives of people worldwide through storytelling has become one of his passions in life. He can be followed at terrytoler.com.

Made in the USA
Monee, IL
01 April 2024